BIRCH AND JAY

THE KNOWLEDGE SEEKERS: BOOK 1

Allister Thompson

46

Library and Archives Canada Cataloguing in Publication

Title: Birch and Jay / by Allister Thompson.

Names: Thompson, Allister, author

Description: Series statement: The knowledge seekers ; book 1

Identifiers: Canadiana (print) 20240529642 | Canadiana (ebook) 20240530985 | ISBN 9781988989921 (softcover) | ISBN 9781988989938 (EPUB)

Subjects: LCGFT: Novels.

Classification: LCC PS8639.H623 B57 2025 | DDC C813/.6—dc23

Printed and bound in Canada on 100% recycled paper.

Cover Design: Laura Boyle

Author Photo: Greg Janveau

Editor: Randall Perry

Published by:

Latitude 46 Publishing

info@latitude46publishing.com

Latitude46publishing.com

We acknowledge the support of the Ontario Arts Council, the Government of Canada and the Ontario Media Development Corporation for their generous support.

Dedicated to the youth of today who are fighting for their future and for the future of every living thing on Earth

"...and there was fire, and storms, and a mighty chaos [...] surely it was proper to think that the end had come. Yet was it, in truth, but the beginning of hope of a new Eternity of Life; so that out of the End came the Beginning, and Life out of Death, and Good out of that which did seem a dire matter. And so it is always."

—William Hope Hodgson, *The Night Land*

"All agreed that the amenities of the past couldn't be restored at once; destruction is an easier, speedier process than reconstruction."

— Albert Camus, *The Plague*

"Only now do I begin to perceive how many paths lead us to knowledge, that study is not our only way to do it, and perhaps not the best to follow. Certainly it is mine, and I must keep to it."

— Hermann Hesse, *Narziss and Goldmund*

BIRCH AND JAY

THE KNOWLEDGE SEEKERS: BOOK 1

I.

NOW

JAY

All right, everyone. Gather around and take your seats, please. I know you're eager to get out of this dim, musty room, away from this old windbag, and into the sunshine, and you'll have that opportunity soon enough.

This is a very significant time for all of you, and for me as well, your instructor and guide of so many years. In exactly one week, you will graduate and go forth into the world to take up our mission. We believe it's one of the most important callings a person can have. And I guess you believe that too, since you've endured all the lectures and training for several years now.

The future will be yours to mold, and our people will be relying on you to provide knowledge and wisdom. My time to do so will soon be ending, and yours is beginning. And that's how it should be.

I want you to know I'm proud of the dedication all of you have shown to that calling, which of course is the collection, preservation, and dissemination of all the useful knowledge our species has ever gained and lost and providing guidance to all on how to use it. What seem to have been our glory days as a species may be behind us, but now, we who remain have the greatest opportunity in human history: to build something beautiful out of the ashes, something far better than anything that came before, and to live in accordance with our natural place and proper role on this planet.

But to do that, we need to complete the picture of what has happened and why: the good, the bad, and the very ugly. We need to figure out where we went astray and what can be safely salvaged of technologies and philosophies. Our labours are undertaken for the good of our entire species, and for all other life forms as well. In the last few decades, I'm happy to say our message has caught on, and we are able to provide leadership for as many communities as will listen.

But really… You know all this already. You've heard this old man repeating it, forgetting what he already said, repeating it again. You've been patient students, and I'm grateful. Hopefully, I've armed you well enough with the knowledge and skills to fulfill your mission.

Before I turn you loose, however, I have one more gift for you — a gift and a warning. Some of you have very curious and penetrating minds and have plied me with questions about my own long career out on the roads; what dangers I faced, who I met, what I achieved, how I failed. And I admit I've been a little tight-lipped about it. I didn't want to influence the choice you made to join this guild, either for or against.

Those of you who wish to go out and enjoy what's left of this gloriously sunny and temperate week, please feel free to leave now. I won't be offended. This part of the week's lessons isn't mandatory. But for those of you who wish to stay, I have a story to tell. It's a long one: the story of my first journey. And a special guest will be coming by, too, to help me tell that tale; most of you know her well, so you can probably guess who she is.

But she knows this story already. She doesn't need to be here for the beginning. She's not as energetic as she once was, either, though she's probably in better shape than me.

So grab a cool drink from over on the side table there and retake your seats, please. I'll indulge my old bones by sitting down for once, and I'll regale you with the dramatic story of my first mission as a Knowledge Seeker. It's a story that will take a while to tell, but it will help those of you who have yet to venture far from our home to understand the world that's out there — its dangers and lures, as well as its history.

It's a vast, wonderful, *beautiful* world still, one we once dominated. One we manipulated and changed and ultimately ruined because of our foolishness.

But, amazingly, we persevere.

Anyway, I'm digressing again. Let me take you back fifty years to the year 2123. I was only twenty back then, as you are now … eager and ready to see what was out there.

II.

BEGIN

JAY

I was finishing breakfast at our round kitchen table when my father, Aspen, sat down across from me with a cup of tea in his favourite, truly ancient, chipped blue mug. He had that look in his eye I knew well from previous lectures: something *important* was about to be imparted to me. Dad was light-hearted by nature and a quiet, hard worker, not given to discipline and lectures. Not generally, anyway.

I put down my spoon and looked at him expectantly as the mixed smells of strawberry juice and mint tea permeated the kitchen. Sunlight had just crested the horizon and was blazing in through the east-facing windows; someone had forgotten to close the blinds again last night, which meant the house would be positively roasting by midmorning.

"So, it's time, huh?" He levelled his green eyes at me.

"Yes, Dad. The big day." I eyed him back. Considering the importance of the day, this lecture was bound to be a doozy.

Dad had turned forty-five just a few days before, but he looked a good deal older with his thick hair now mostly white and his snowy beard. He was like a wizard from a fantasy novel.

He heaved a small sigh. "Your mother is still against all this because of what happened to me in '95. And I can't blame her." He lifted his right knee to emphasize the prosthetic below. "You wouldn't believe how many I had to try on before this one fit. They salvaged them from all over the region, since of course no one can make them anymore. Not yet, anyway. It was quite the excitement; everyone came together to help. I just barely avoided having a wooden peg-leg like a pirate."

"I know all this, Dad. I've been studying and training for five years. I know the risks."

He frowned, and the deep lines that had developed on either side of his mouth in the last couple of years deepened. "Do you? Because here we live in a safe place, for the most part. The safest place we know of. But it's not always safe out there. And I obviously wasn't expecting the attack. I was going about my business, free and easy, then *wham!*"

"I'm not sure anyone expects to be attacked by a pack of wolves, Dad," I said dryly.

"Don't get sassy with me, boy." His face lightened a little, though. "But that's the spirit. *I* support you doing this. You know that. The Knowledge Seekers are the whole point of our community: its lifeblood and its spirit. Without that spirit, this town wouldn't even exist. We provide hope for our entire species, as pompous as that sounds. And it's a tradition in our family. It's who we are, and it gives us purpose. I just don't want you treating this as some sort of fun, zany adventure. It's dangerous but also important. Remember, your mission is always the first and last priority. After your personal safety, of course."

It was my turn to sigh. "I love you, Dad, and I even love your lectures, really, but I gotta go. I'll see you for the graduation lunch."

His lips finally curled up. "Okay, Jay, off you go. I'll be heading with Cedric over to Trout Lake to see if we can catch some of that lunch for the minority that eats fish."

"Where is Mom, anyway?"

"She's already over at the community garden. She'll see you later for the graduation meal too. You know, there's a really good crop of tomatoes and zucchini to harvest this time of year. If it weren't for these studies of yours, we'd have you out there, picking and jarring and helping out along with the other young people. Your brother's with her. Not sure about your promised, though. She's less reliable. And you have a gift for sleeping in — but you won't be doing that on the road, mark my words. You'll be sleeping with one eye open all the time."

I sighed loudly again but let him slap me on the back, and I dashed out the door, grabbing my worn and slightly torn bag. It wasn't half the size of the equally venerable hiking backpack I would be ceremonially presented later this very day, but it had seen plenty of use — by me and many others before, just like almost everything used and worn in the town of Norbay, the home of the guild of the Knowledge Seekers, the keepers and collectors of the knowledge and ways of the Old World, from the time when humanity reigned supreme on planet Earth, so dominant, in fact, that we almost caused our own destruction.

Yes, it was deathly serious business being a Knowledge Seeker in a fragmented, depopulated world where some were still determined to ignore and forget the lessons of the industrial and technological ages that led up to the Great Ruin. Our principles would, hopefully, lead to a renewal in which humans would assume their proper place as "proper contributing citizens of the ecosystem," as Cedar put it.

We collected and studied knowledge, though in those times it was as much collection as it was study, and the balance has shifted in recent years toward study and dissemination. With massive depopulation came utter neglect of libraries of books, DVDs, CD-ROMs, magazines, musical recordings, microfiche, and so on. As humanity risked descending into total dark ignorance, there was a greater risk that while we might indeed rise again, we would only make the same mistakes over and over, as our ancestors did, leading to the complete and utter extinction of our species and dragging down more species with us. Since the Anthropocene Extinction caused by human-made climate change had taken countless species with it, this made humanity not lord of the world, as it had arrogantly thought itself, but rather its curse and its destroyer. It was imperative that knowledge be retained and studied, and this was the rationale for the idealistic formation of the Knowledge Seekers, based in the town of Norbay, after the Ruin and the slaughter that followed.

Do I sound like I believed in all this? Well, I do now. Fully. Back then, though, mostly. Dad was a wise man, and he understood the lure of a "zany adventure." The opportunity to see what was *really* out there in the world, far beyond our town, and not just other tiny settlements nearby like Sturgeon or Great Sudbury, the sparsely populated wreckage of a once-polluted, sprawling industrial city that was the farthest I'd ever made it from Norbay for field trips, about a seven-hour bicycle ride at a good clip on broken roads. The opportunity to be independent, without chores to think about every day, surviving by my wits with limited supplies, sounded very appealing, and scary too.

Dad had been a Knowledge Seeker, sent on missions around the land to recover important books and other items like CD-ROMs, DVDs, and other such things that had been left behind, so they could be collected and analyzed at the university building up on the escarpment, until he ran into that fateful pack of wolves in '95. Now he divided his time between fishing, gardening, and helping analyze and catalogue all the items that were brought in. He was a very knowledgeable and useful man, and his were big shoes to fill.

My mother had done her time on the roads as well, but she quit earlier, after her sister was killed — and not by wolves. But that's a different story and another tragic one. When Dad was hurt that was the end of his travelling days, as well — and in a way, he was lucky, because otherwise she might have left him. He seemed to think so. Hence, Mom wasn't exactly thrilled about my choice of study and life plans and had made that quite clear. And she wasn't the only one.

I didn't need a bike to get to the school, which was close by, and I enjoyed the walk, except on days when it was already too hot by early morning. I turned off our street, Eastview, onto McKay, passing the fallen, ivy-covered walls of an old cinder-block school; there had been lots of such schools in this city, but now only a couple were still standing and in use. The hundred-plus-year-old street signs were barely readable now, rusted away. No one had bothered to repaint them or replace them with wooden ones, but they were still lovingly propped back up on new wooden posts. There's no time for niceties like new signs and other beautification when all your hours are filled with subsistence farming and learning. Still, the town was peaceful, except when the weather was dangerous. Which was often.

Ours was one of only three occupied houses on a street, a "crescent" that once had about twenty. The occupied ones were selected ages ago because they had woodstoves installed and roofs ideal in size and pitch for a few solar panels; this was before enough gear like windmills and solar panels were collected to get a rudimentary power grid up and running to power needed infrastructure. Now, solar and wind provided everything we needed, considering our electrical needs weren't great and were rationed, in any event. Most of the electricity was needed at the university to power the recovered, restored equipment, and at the healing centre.

A good, solid basement is also a must for tornado and derecho protection in the spring, summer, and fall, as you well know. We still burned a lot of wood on cool days and for cooking, something that's less common now.

It was already pretty hot out, though that wasn't surprising for late September. Apparently, the eldest in the community remembered speaking with people who could recall times when it wasn't surprising to see the first snowfall in early October, which seems a crazy notion now. I think at that age I'd seen snow maybe three or four times in my life, and I've only experienced it a few times since. When it happened, it certainly was a welcome celebratory break during the long, chilly, rainy season. Everyone stopped what they were doing to go out and play in it.

This day, it'd probably hit 30 degrees Celsius, which I shouldn't have found that hot but did. Mom said I had some "Nordic blood"; she was perfectly comfortable up to 40, she claimed, because of her "subcontinental blood," which apparently meant from India, which was once home to over a billion people and countless animal species before the equatorial and subequatorial regions became, as far as we know, uninhabitable.

Dad said that "subcontinental blood" stuff was all nonsense and the improper language of the Dark Times when people still thought of their personal characteristics in terms of antiquated concepts like race. But they never really argued seriously about it.

I cut through the pleasantly shady forest on the wide, well-trodden path for about ten minutes. I waited a minute for a red squirrel I was acquainted with to appear, chew me out, and stomp its little feet, but it was absent today. I passed no other people and stopped a few times to listen to the cacophony of birdcalls in the still-green branches and deeply breathe in the scent of pines and soil, watching the morning sun dappling the leaves and then emerging after ten minutes onto the street where Norbay's main Knowledge Seekers academy stood. It was one of the last standing ancient schools in town, reinforced and reroofed with cannibalized old metal roofing. It was an important place, so it had a bunch more solar panels and some windmills to power our studies on darker days.

It wasn't the most attractive building in a not very attractive town — I'd seen lots of photos and footage of castles, mansions, grand cathedrals, and glass towers in the main cities back in their heyday — but in a way it was the heart of our community, or at least it was the heart of what our community *meant.*

I stepped through the double glass door, cracked in a couple of places but miraculously intact after all these decades, and into the cool of the hall, lined with the carefully closed lockers of kids long dead. Places like this would seem like mausoleums and memorials to a long-lost world — if that wasn't just the daily reality we lived in.

We were surrounded by the detritus of ten billion people, which was often strange to think about. To this day, we can't avoid the reality of living with those ghosts. And those specters' lives are the basis of our culture. We inhabit this city of the dead, rarely building, always preserving, so that we can gradually rebuild in a new, different, responsible way. And all over the world, or so we were told (and it turned out to be true), small groups of people with similar ideas were working to start building a new, saner world.

But I wasn't thinking of any of that as I turned into the classroom and saw my nine classmates, all age twenty, already seated at the small chipped and scratched desks, just like the students of two hundred years ago in a one-room rural schoolhouse.

I was thinking that my own life was just about to start. *Really* start.

III.

GRADUATION DAY

JAY

Cedar stood before my classmates in front of the dusty blackboard that she hardly ever used, looking magisterial as always in the sort of plaid shirt with metal snap buttons she favoured that she called "Western shirts." No strand of hair was ever out of place from its tight white bun, which contrasted with her brown skin, and she peered over the top of her salvaged spectacles with slight amusement. Cedar was the legendary main instructor of the guild, one of the Elders of the town, and a councillor. One of her most important roles was educating us about the world beyond our town, our missions to come, and their dangers, as well as the chaotic world she had grown up in and which of its leavings we were to be tasked with collecting. Hers was probably the most respected voice in the entire guild and town. I didn't know her exact age, but she had to be in her seventies at least. It was strange to think that she was probably born before the collapse; she and the others her age were living, breathing, genuine relics — treasures, even, of a vanished world.

She gave the wind-up wristwatch she always sported an exaggerated look. "Good of you to join us, a little late as always, Jay. Even late on graduation day. Consistent to the end." Her low-pitched, authoritative voice was scolding but affectionate.

I slid into my desk. "And as always, only by a minute," I added cheekily.

"A minute can be the difference between life and death in the wilderness or the ruins." Her tone was stern now, and I assumed she was done bantering. "Lollygagging in the forest again, I'm sure. But you know, there's nothing more I can do about that. You'll have to learn the harder lessons from experience from this point on."

From across the room, I heard my friend Hawthorn's audible laughter. Hawthorn was slight of frame but tough and the star pupil of the class as well. I wouldn't say I was the dunce — I think I was considered to be quite intelligent — but it could be said I lacked some discipline. I had a zest for knowledge but could get lost in some topic for days instead of following along properly with organized lessons. Despite Hawthorn's merry sense of humour, they were always on time, always completed every task, and retained every fragment of historical detail. They were the teacher's pet.

Cedar launched into her final lecture to us. "Regardless. We don't stand on ceremony here. This is a lean world we inhabit, and we don't have the resources or patience to put together a more pompous convocation to send you off on your first mission. You already appreciate the significance of this day and how proud we are of you. But today you'll receive the tools of your trade, the few things you'll be taking with you, at the noon meal, as you celebrate along with some of your family members who have put up with you studying instead of working and being useful these last few years."

We all exchanged excited glances.

"Over the last few years I've regaled you with a few stories of my time on the roads, as have the other instructors and Elders." Cedar's voice snapped us back to attention. "And some of you have parents with yarns of their own to spin." She looked directly at me. "So, I won't bore you with any more of that.

"But let me offer some words of summary. It's easy to get lost in the minutiae of the expected task and the history we've taught you, but let's not forget the purpose we cherish to ennoble our lives and provide meaning to our journey. For we are the lucky ones." Her voice had by this point taken on a sort of ritualistic, rhythmic intensity we knew well, but today it felt even more significant.

"This is an auspicious time for me because of the year. One hundred years ago, in 2023, both of my parents were born in the great city over three hundred kilometres from here, in Great Toronto. They were born into a time and place of seemingly boundless prosperity, of overwhelming and never-ending consumption, of excess being considered a benefit, even a virtue. Those people believed our role as a species on this planet was to dominate and mold it as we wished, to use up its resources however we pleased, and to toss away our refuse in any casual way we wanted. Their society used and used and used, and their industries spewed forth flame, smoke, radiation, and chemicals. They razed forests, bleached coral reefs, contaminated the soil — but still they consumed. Great prophets, the thinkers and scientists, warned them of their impending end, of the collapse of the very climatic conditions ours and so many other species depended on, but their leaders and the people themselves wouldn't listen. And those prophets were correct."

She stopped to take a sip of water. I looked around me to find everyone attentive, eager despite having heard all this before, except for Daisy, who was an insomniac and was usually tired. She had her head propped up on one arm. Personally, I was ready to move on from all the lecturing, despite my admiration for Cedar.

She seemed to have read my mind. "Yes, yes, you know all this, but we should remind ourselves regularly of this terrible legacy, for it's this legacy we are duty-bound to remember. Remind yourself daily! Today you will swear an oath to make your life's work collecting, bringing back, and studying the knowledge of that time from the places where it was collected, so that we, the survivors of our species, will *never* make the same mistakes again. We can also learn from the scientific achievements of that era, if we choose them wisely and use only those that heal and help, not destroy and pollute. We are rebuilding. We will not always be like rodents living off the garbage heaps of a lost civilization; we are building anew, but better.

"My parents had their whole lives ahead of them in peace and comfort, or so they thought. But even before I was born, the signs of the end increased with frightening rapidity. Massive storms, floods, rising temperatures, the death of ecosystems like reefs and jungles, rising waters. Vast areas began to become uninhabitable. Then, in 2045, changes in ocean currents precipitated a final collapse, and all those terrible events increased in number and severity. Entire thickly populated areas of the planet, like the British Isles and the equatorial regions, became barely habitable, and they remain so as far as we know. Economies and infrastructures collapsed as well, leaving billions of people who had depended on the hive-like organization of civilization without any livelihood, often without homes, without safety, and at the mercy of the weather and of each other. Desperate migrations all over the globe led to mass death, massacres, and even war as nations tried keep out refugees and selfishly tried to retain the stores of food and energy they possessed. Almost all vestiges of compassion and empathy were gone.

"Factions that were born from drastic political and social polarization that started in the early 2000s, aided and abetted by the advanced communications technology to which their society was addicted, fought bitterly, first with words, then with laws, and finally, when law and order was gone, with weapons. Sometimes the fight was even race against race or gender against gender. Today, we can still see the terrible effects of this throughout our scattered and disparate communities such as those with which you have strict orders to avoid contact.

"As you've learned, in the midst of all this strife, completely disorganized humanity was left defenseless against new pandemics of the kind that started in 2020, and worse, and the death tolls were in the tens of millions each time. All of these terrible events that we brought on ourselves caused a massive depopulation after untold misery, which increasingly authoritarian governments were powerless to halt.

"And as I've always made clear — this is the most important point of all — it was not climate change that caused all this chaos, disease, violence, and repression. A unified world could have dealt with this situation, as terrible as it was, with compassion and reason. There was more than enough wealth and resources to take care of everyone. But there was no will to do that, and selfishness and fear had taken over."

She took a longer pause after that heavy bit of exposition, and a longer swig of water. Through the open window, I heard a faint snatch of someone singing in the distance.

"You may not know that I was born shortly before 2050 — I don't know the exact year — and spent my childhood in a camp during the worst time of chaos the world has ever seen. I haven't spoken to you of that. And my young life was filled with deprivation and cruelties, as was everyone's. I was very lucky to survive to my teens. And in the end, we all had to disperse and go it alone because all vestiges of a government or even an army were gone and there was no food or medicine left. My parents had both been university professors before the Ruin. The things they taught me allowed me to be amongst the first founding Knowledge Seekers, which as you know was a movement that started in discussion groups in the camps, the results of long, heartfelt dissection and analysis of what brought our world to this unhappy end. And," she gazed out at our faces, "what was the central guiding idea that would eventually create this guild?"

Hawthorn's hand shot up first, as usual, and Cedar nodded. "Until our civilizations develop into truly compassionate ones deserving of advanced technology, our duty is to learn as much as possible about the old world and guard that knowledge until the time is right to make use of it again, at which point we will use it to help all humanity."

Cedar nodded again. "Yes, and only to use the best parts of it that are beneficial to all life, not just for certain humans to benefit themselves without care for others. This was our founding principle. In the twentieth century, when scientists considered the question of why there was no detectible sign of life from other planets, evidence such as radio transmissions, some posited a civilization that acquired advanced technology was bound to misuse it and destroy itself before it could harness and control the powers of that technology. I often think we can safely assume this to be true. Unless our civilization develops ethically *before* using the technology so that it can wield it with wisdom. This is our aim and our principle.

"Guided by that principle, our mission is to collect as much knowledge of the old world as possible here in our guild town. Not just scientific knowledge, of course, but also cultural, artistic, and social knowledge. We must understand everything about the world that existed one hundred years ago to avoid repeating its mistakes. We must understand those people and what motivated them; how they essentially lied to themselves and to each other in a sort of powerful death wish.

"Hence, while you are each given a main destination for your mission, which you will receive just before our lunch banquet today, you are also charged with stopping in as many places as possible on the way to search for evidence. Carry what you can back with you or take note of the location for others to collect later. At each place, you will leave the sign of the Seekers to show others that you have been there so they don't duplicate your work. No home or any other building is unworthy of searching; there's still plenty of knowledge out there! Use this first trip as practice in all aspects.

"Now, I'm old and tired and looking forward to some time off before my next round of students start their classes. I will field a few minutes of questions, and then I'll tell you your destinations, how you will be equipped, prepare for our celebratory lunch, and then on to the next stage of your lives!"

Hawthorn's hand went up again.

• • •

Lunch was a lively affair, held outside at a collection of long wooden tables. Vegetables were roasting in the firepits, beans were boiling, and there was plenty of fresh orange juice from the grove right by the school. Dad had caught a few fish for those who weren't 100% vegetarian. It had felt sometimes that our studies would never end, and the excitement was palpable. Life was truly starting! My whole family was there, along with all the other students', and even Cedar's partner Ash, a solidly built, reserved woman of roughly the same age with surprisingly black hair for someone so elderly. There was also a stranger, a man with a brownish complexion and long salt-and-pepper hair tied back in a ponytail, wearing a Western shirt of the same kind as Cedar's, chatting and eating quietly at the same table as Cedar and Ash. I asked Mom about him, and she said he was a visiting dignitary from the prosperous Indigenous community far to the north, Moosonee.

And of course there was my own promised, Birch, nineteen years old, all nervous energy, her long, dark hair flying around with her animated conversation. She was all angles and planes: long face, long nose, sharp elbows sticking out of the sleeves of a light blue T-shirt. I loved everything about her. She and I had gotten progressively quieter with each other in the weeks leading up to my impending departure. And when we did talk, it was awkward and often led to arguments. Birch's family were not Knowledge Seekers; her parents were farmers and very valuable to the community, and while Birch wasn't exactly hostile to the aims of our guild and was certainly curious about the world — possibly even more so than me — she'd never shown any inclination to join the Seekers. In fact, she still wasn't sure what she wanted to do amongst the few occupations our community offered. Most that weren't guild work involved growing food or maintaining our infrastructure, none of them at all enticing to a fiery, active, inquisitive disposition like Birch's.

She plunked herself down next to me at the table after refilling her plate and gave me a lopsided smile. "Eat up, buddy. Your last meal before execution. Need to put some meat on you before you lose it all starving on the road."

I snorted amiably. "Thanks for the vote of confidence."

Her face softened a little, and she even put her hand on my shoulder, briefly. "I'm just grouchy because I don't want you to go. You know that. I'm only a *touch* worried about you." She lowered her head, and her hair fell over her face a bit. She rarely looked or sounded this vulnerable.

I put my hand over hers. "As long as I follow what I've been taught, everything will be fine. It's not even that long a trip. A few weeks and I'll be back, and then I'm sure it'll be a while before I go out again. I want to *see* things, Birch."

Her head snapped up and her eyes bored into mine. "Don't you think I want that too? But all this … *collecting.* All this thinking about getting ready to *maybe* start constructing some bright new future, after we study things for who knows how many years… What's stopping us from starting *now*?"

I sighed. "You know why. Yes, aside from learning to grow our own food again, we mostly just live on the scraps of a lost world. But we need to learn to be good citizens of the planet first. It's everything."

That slightly disdainful smile was back. "Right, Jay. Being a good citizen. Most important thing in the whole wide world. And the all-knowing Elders will determine when the time is right, huh?"

"Look, I didn't mean—"

I was interrupted by someone calling for quiet.

Cedar was standing at the head of the row of tables, under the awning of a wide umbrella. "Well, everyone, I think over the years you have heard enough blather from me. So I'm not much for giving long speeches at formal events, believe it or not."

There were muted, knowing chuckles all around.

"Instead, in a more interesting vein, we are occasionally lucky enough to have a dignitary amongst us, and today is one of those occasions. Waubun is an elder from Moosonee, which I'm sure you know is a prosperous town far north of here. He's here for diplomatic and trade reasons, which we won't bore you with at this time. But his presence here is lucky for you graduates."

The stranger closed his eyes for a beat and gave an almost imperceptible nod.

"I asked him if, since he's here, he'd be willing to give a short address to our graduating class, and he graciously agreed. So, please welcome our friend, Waubun."

We clapped politely as the stranger stepped up to the front, took a sip from his glass, and cleared his throat. "Thank you, Cedar. And thank you, Knowledge Seekers." Waubun's voice was low, not loud, but it carried over the assembly and held a leader's authority.

"I wanted to extend the greetings of my community and best wishes in your lifetime of important work. Let me tell you a little about my people and why we are such enthusiastic friends to this community. Before the Ruin, as some call it, the people who brought about that downfall had many faults in their nations. One of those terrible faults was their addiction to feelings of superiority, of despising the Other, of the worst form of tribalism, one based on domination and refusal to acknowledge the dignity of other lives ... the oppression of other people, animals, the Earth itself. They refused to understand their proper place, and the results were disastrous. You'll have learned all about this in your classes, not to mention we can see the signs all around us and experience nature's wrath.

"For centuries my people, the Indigenous peoples of the world, were oppressed, beaten, and killed. The lands we were honoured to live on were stolen from under us. We fought, and by the time of the Ruin we had managed to relight the flame of our cultures and claw back some of what was ours. We were making a comeback. How did we do this? We had our own long tradition of knowledge-keeping, through things like the oral tradition and wampum belts, and before that, pictographs and other methods, then later through modern technologies. Our methods were effective, and no matter what was done to us, no matter how the evil world before the Ruin tried to stamp us out, we persisted. Our memories were long.

"As everything finally collapsed and the climate changed and everything that *everyone* knew and trusted was finally gone, our leaders called to and gathered diverse groups of our people in the north. As things warmed, we adapted and worked together. We collected knowledge of our own, from elders and from sources similar to those you collect, and we integrated that knowledge back into our communities, which now, despite the same challenges all communities face — unpredictable weather, bandits — are thriving.

"For many years we kept to ourselves, not trusting the world of white men, for reasons I'm sure you understand." He paused and looked knowingly around. "When we sent out parties to investigate how things had changed in the south, maybe twenty-five years ago, our fears proved to be mostly well-founded; those that remained were reduced to brutality or were scattered survivors at best. But moving farther south, we came upon Norbay and the community the Knowledge Seekers had built here.

"And here we found our kin. We share the same goal of rebuilding a world that is fair for everyone and for all things that live on what my ancestors called Turtle Island. A life lived in harmony with all creation.

"This is a long way of saying that our best wishes go with you on your journeys, and we also wish you safety. I came all this way mostly by a very traditional method — on the water, in a canoe, and you'll be travelling by a different method. Remember, as you go, the things that grow, crawl, and fly are not your enemies. If you react with fear and with the goal of harming them, disrespecting them, you will only end up reenacting the harm inflicted by your ancestors. Go with compassion and friendship, and you'll fulfill your goals and come home safe. I know this.

"I won't bore you any longer, and I'll let you return to this delicious feast of foods grown and prepared in your own community. Thank you."

Waubun took his seat and Cedar stood again, facing us. "So, here are my final remarks to you. This is the happiest day of each year for me. When this community was founded long ago — well, not *that* long ago for us old-timers..." (A few more chuckles.) "We dreamed of establishing a place that would be a beacon to the world, a place where goodness reigned and where compassion and reason was a way of life. When I see our graduating classes ready and eager to help carry on that tradition, it fills me with joy.

"I raise my glass to you, the class of 2123. May your time on the road be safe and full of wonders."

The applause was hearty and sustained.

I turned to Birch. "So, did that change your mind?"

She rolled her eyes. "Can't wait to sign up." She got up and went in search of more food.

I caught my brother Oak's eye across the table. He shrugged sympathetically.

• • •

The celebration was intentionally held at noon and ended by two thirty because mid to late afternoon was almost always uncomfortably hot every day before the rainy, chilly season that had replaced "fall" and "winter." Three of us graduates would be leaving town at first light the next day, too... Not that I expected to have much success at sleeping.

The last half hour of the celebration was given over, as it always had been, to music and poetry.

We were a community of singers. Everyone loved singing together; songs from before the Ruin, some far older, and others more contemporary written by the particularly talented among us. Today, there were original poems and songs written especially for this occasion and also songs salvaged from the old world mixed in to add poignancy and weight to our departure. It felt as if voices from that past, so different and yet so similar to our own thoughts and concerns, were reaching to us over the gulf of time. It also reminded us that the past held good people, too, who had wanted to make things better. Artists had always tried to warn others of the impending Ruin, to no avail.

The best singer and overall musical talent in our entire community was Sparrow, who was about thirty years old that year. She was kept busy almost daily, performing, and in a way that more than earned her share from the town's storehouse. There were a few such talented artists in different disciplines, and all were cherished, though everyone was welcome to lead the singing at any given gathering.

Her voice was husky, light, but controlled. She often told us her inspiration came from compact discs from a very creative period in history, the tumultuous 1960s, and its idealistic folksingers. She also liked to wear long, flower-patterned dresses, emulating her heroes.

She played a guitar that was one of the very first pieces of special woodworking done in the community that wasn't reserved for a practical purpose like home construction; her father was our town's foremost craftsperson in wood. So, in a way, this instrument wasn't any relic — it was a symbol of rebirth as well as a thing of intrinsic beauty.

Today, as the midafternoon sun neared its zenith and we shielded ourselves under hats and umbrellas, Sparrow concluded the performances with two songs, the first a special composition of her own about life on the road under the stars — very elegant and romantic and just what we needed to buck up our spirits.

But after absorbing our applause, she grew solemn.

"I'd like to sing you something now that is meaningful for several reasons. The person who wrote and recorded it lived in our very own community one hundred years ago, during the time when humanity was finally waking up to the dangers it faced. It was too late, but there is so much evidence of good people trying to warn others to act before it was too late; some of these were famous people like Greta Thunberg, while the names of others are lost in time. But in the case of this musician, it was someone who, from what we can unearth about him, never achieved any fame or accolades. We don't know what he did for a living or if anyone appreciated what he did. Songs like this one are warnings from the past that remind us of the suffering people endured in the times of the Ruin, and since we still have access to them, they were a warning to the people of the future. The song, which I found on a compact disc in a basement just two streets from where I grew up, is titled 'The Last Ones.' It tells a tragic story. I'd like to thank Douglas and his team at the archives for allowing me to use their equipment to listen to the song over and over again while I learned it."

She started fingerpicking a delicate progression in a minor key, and her voice was almost a mournful whisper.

Here on this shore, when we were young, we could still see the sky
Watching countless stars glow above and beautiful birds still flying
I stood there with her, hand in hand, and she gave herself to me
The world was ours, no end in sight, as far as we could see

But the sky was poison, the seas were plastic, the ice melted away
And the time finally came when we knew that we just couldn't stay
A long march in search of shelter and food, we starved along the way
Some stumbled and cried and fell down and died every single day

Why did we do it?
Why wouldn't we listen to the wise ones?
Why could we not change?

Living on trash, the detritus of the damned, finding whatever we could
We cursed ourselves and our kind for not doing what we should
But still I had her to light my hope, happiness could be found
Until her strength gave out and she died and was left abandoned on the ground

Now I stand old and tired by a dead, brown, choked sea
And I wait for the mercy of death to claim what's left of me
One of the last of a ruined species that destroyed this whole earth
That raped and cut and bruised and finally killed the place of our birth

Why did we do it?
Why wouldn't we listen to the wise ones?
Why could we not change?

And we knew, as we listened in awe, that this forgotten minstrel's predictions eventually came true, that untold millions, maybe billions, had ended up suffering in just this way.

It did put a damper on the end of the party, but a dose of reality in a harsh world can be the right medicine.

IV.

TAKING LEAVE

JAY

I spent the evening with my family, and with Birch, of course. Things were a little tense, since neither Birch nor Mom could really be said to be supportive of my choice of career. I mean, they didn't speak out against it, not anymore, so they were kind enough not to ruin my last night at home. But after the positive mood of that big midday party, it was a very restrained evening of conversation that sort of circled the reality of my leaving but never settled on it. I was happy enough when it was time to turn in. I walked with Birch in the dark to her house in the evening cool, feeling our way along the road step by step under the glow of millions of tiny pinpricks, as we always did, but we didn't even touch one another before wishing each other a good sleep.

I arose in the grey of dawn when only the earliest avian risers had started their sleepy songs. I had tossed and turned and slept lightly, full of excitement but also with pangs of apprehension and outright fear. Of course, as it tends to, that led to some odd and intense dreams; in the last one before I woke, I was on a road that stretched straight and clear into the hazy distance, as though recently paved. In the distance stood a figure, the full sunlight gleaming off milk-white hair, beckoning to me with one arm. I still felt its intensity as I blinked and stretched my legs before hauling myself out of bed.

I'd barely left the safety of this community in the past. It was a place not often threatened and one generally free of perils. Now I'd chosen to go far from home and far beyond aid, all in the name of my community's exalted ideals. I imagined all sorts of horrible dangers I'd heard about: from the climate, from people reduced to murder to feed themselves, from animals. I wasn't sure if undertaking this made me a hero or a fool — the latter was what Birch preferred to imply.

But my course was chosen, and being anxious about it wasn't going to achieve anything.

I finally rolled out of bed, my mouth dry and eyes stinging. My lower back hurt a little. I would have appreciated a bit more sleep.

I pushed back the curtains and saw that the sky appeared clear, which was a good sign, but it was hard to tell, since the light was still so dim. It had to be about four thirty. Still, it was time to get up. For whatever reason, we were always to set out at dawn on these expeditions, to maximize the amount of ground we could cover before nightfall, I suppose, considering the middle of the day was often too hot to travel without the danger of dehydration and severe heat exhaustion. When travelling alone, it could progress to heat stroke, and that was likely to be fatal.

I pulled on the T-shirt I'd picked out especially for the occasion — it was a snazzy burgundy, had the faded words *North Bay* emblazoned across the front, and almost had the status of a family heirloom, since Dad had owned it before me — and a pair of only slightly ratty cargo shorts, and lumbered out of my room. I'd thought my parents would be up already, but I could still hear two sets of soft snores from their room and one from my brother's. Rubbing my hand drowsily over my close-cropped hair and sparse facial growth, I walked up by the door to the pile of stuff I'd been given the day before: the giant backpack people once used for long recreational hiking trips back when wealthier classes had all kinds of leisure time, filled with a couple of changes of clothes, herbs and other medicines, dried foods packed as tightly as possible so I'd be able to ration them, a toothbrush, a water bottle with a filter, and a few other small, helpful tools.

I also had two books. One was an ancient, tattered sheaf with a yellow cover in a ring binding: a Perly's map book of Ontario with all the roads I could potentially follow. It was bizarre to think about the millions of petroleum-guzzling vehicles that once roared down those red and black lines on the maps, spewing forth the very exhaust that would contribute to the end of their hapless civilization.

We all received this map book when we graduated. I guessed they must have collected and stockpiled a bunch of them ages ago. The cover of this one was dated 1988. I suppose that made it a real antique.

The other book was a small paperback Dad had given me. He admitted I could probably do without the extra weight, but to him it held an important meaning for our mission as a guild, so I couldn't turn it down. It was titled *The Plague,* by Albert Camus, a writer from almost two centuries ago. Dad said it was about people doing their best to be kind and decent when plunged into an inhuman situation in which people might easily lose their empathy and become brutal — much like the world we had inherited.

It didn't sound like very cheerful reading for lonely days on the road, but I packed it anyway. I could always discard it if I finished it or didn't like it.

So, I had some interesting reading material, but one thing that was missing was the very thing you'd think would be most handy: a weapon of some kind. Yes, there was a sturdy little "Swiss Army knife" to help with any prying or whittling I might need to do, along with some other small tools like a tiny axe, but, naturally, the Knowledge Seekers are pacifists, and we also don't hurt animals unless we absolutely have to. That's part of the code. Sure, some people in the community ate fish from the lake, but many were vegetarian... Both of my parents would carry troublesome insects, even earwigs, outside rather than kill them.

If you're going to completely reject everything bad about a world of war, abuse, massacres, poisonings, torture, animal testing, and other horrors, you have to walk the walk at all times.

And I would be walking unarmed into a world of dangers unknown to me.

• • •

When my watch read 6:00 — I'd have to remember to give that watch a frequent winding up, or I'd end up trying to tell the time by the sun, which wasn't my forte — we were just finishing up breakfast. I was having a double portion to generate some extra energy.

Oak, my brother, eighteen years old and usually pretty quiet and thoughtful but possessed of whip-smart sarcasm, was even quieter than usual. After all, my parents' experiences on the road hadn't exactly left them without physical and emotional scars. And now I was about to go out and do the same foolish thing. Dad had tried to keep things cheerful for days, but even he couldn't really get it going this morning.

As we finished our fruit and cornbread, Oak finally seemed to feel the need to lighten the mood in the best way brothers know how.

"Soooo, have you said goodbye to your sweet Birch yet?" Oak formed his best kissy face.

I ignored him and reached for the last piece of bread... My next decent-sized meal might not come any time soon.

"Ohhh, somebody already misses his sweetie-pie," he crooned.

"Oak, lay off, will you?" Mom said, trying to sound angry but achieving only about half. Her brown-streaked grey mane was unbrushed and standing on end. "You aren't going to see your big brother for weeks or even months, and this is how you want him to remember you?"

"It's okay, Mom," I said. "Oak is just trying to conceal the depth of his own unbearable grief at losing my guidance for any length of time."

Oak managed a gagging face. He was the one member of the family who had never shown an interest in the guild. Instead, he was an apprentice carpenter, helped out with the crops, and was also learning about medicinal plants and contemplating joining the healers; in other words, a typical teen who hadn't yet figured out his path in life. But he was going to be a model member of the community.

Dad, always knowing when to be serious, leaned over the table. "Oak, I get that you are trying to lighten things up here, but this is no laughing matter. Your brother is undertaking a mission that dozens have undertaken before, something that will benefit all of humankind and give his life meaning. And he's probably scared witless. At least lay off the jibes for one solid hour, please."

"It's okay, it's okay." I held up both hands. "I'm going to use the washroom one more time." I stood up and left the kitchen. I needed a clear head, and the family bickering, however light, was not helping.

I stared into the mirror, which, like everything in our mostly salvaged society, was a bit cloudy and cracked in a couple of places, a shadow of its former glory. My beard was still growing in patchy, but I'd trimmed it close yesterday. The brown eyes gazing at me from the mirror looked scared, but I stared back and told myself I could do this.

And yes, I was thinking of Birch, who I'd known since we were young children and who I'd loved just as long. Not that I'd expressed it to her quite that honestly. Not yet. I'd come close, though.

She'd always had a restless, nonstop energy that contrasted with my dreamer's ability, which frustrated her, to spend hours looking through long-abandoned homes and imagining the generations of lives that had slowly unfurled there. How many people had lived and died in this community over decades and decades before the Ruin? What had worried and soothed them? Which of the fragments of plastic and glass and fabric were the remains of cherished possessions? Sometimes I'd examine the photos and paintings that had fallen from the walls, imagining what the people were like, what they did, who and what they loved before their entire world came crashing down. Did they get to live out their lives in relative peace, or did they meet their end by disease or violence? The chances were good it was one of the latter.

I also loved looking at dog-eared zoology texts and things like bird-spotting guides, wondering how many of these species had been wiped out by climate change and whether I'd ever get to see them. I could become lost in examining anything historical, geographical, or zoological.

Birch had little time for that stuff, preferring to do things like climb the escarpment that almost fully ringed the part of town that wasn't a lakeshore and then run down the hill at top speed, often falling and skinning her knees; swimming as far out into Trout Lake as she could before her strength began to fail and she had to flounder back; and riding her bike on the cracked, overgrown country roads till sundown, having to find her way back in the dark. She was smart — smarter than me. But while I fit the community's spirit like a hand in a glove, serious and mostly studious, Birch almost seemed like a throwback to the restless energy of the old world that was always working, always on the move, always building, with no end in sight and none wanted, endlessly progressing toward an unknown goal. It had energy, and so did she.

Her parents and the other elders tried to channel that energy into the sorts of jobs that the community valued — construction, farming, maintenance, but still at the age of nineteen she still couldn't stick with anything for long. People were getting concerned about her, since members of the community were expected to be productive in return for the food, shelter, and safety Norbay provided.

We were as different as two people could be, and yet somehow we complemented one another; we *fit* together. I guess she lacked my Seeker ambition, but she filled me up with her fire and energy. And, somehow, there was something in me she wanted to be around, too.

How many times had we stood hand-in-hand on the escarpment, in the gap where an electrical line used to run up the slope, broken pylons leaning and fallen all around us, early on a summer morning before the brutal heat could engulf the town, looking out to the southeast, hazy for large parts of the year from forest fire smoke, wondering what lay beyond the partially obscured emerald hilltops of the Almaguin Highlands? How many times had we speculated what it was like to be out there on the roads, the things we would see, the wonders of a landscape reclaimed by nature?

Yes, we both dreamed of leaving, but for different reasons: she'd never have the discipline and seriousness to be a Seeker. She'd have to leave on her own terms. And she might already have by now if it wasn't for me.

Well, now I was the one leaving, so where did that leave Birch?

• • •

Here I was not long after sunrise, with the sun just poking above the leafy horizon, standing on the road out of town with my family and friends and the guards who manned the roads into town. Of the three Knowledge Seekers setting out today, I was the only one who would head south, into the heart of the old world. Hawthorn was heading east toward a place called Ottawa, once the capital of an entire vast nation-state that spanned from coast to coast. Another classmate, Larch, would be heading west.

I would be taking Highway 11, a mighty road that stretched all the way from Great Toronto on the shore of Lake Ontario to far, far north of Norbay, farther than anyone I knew had ever travelled, even some of the more experienced adults. I was standing in the two right-hand lanes, where I'd found the official group waiting for me; vehicle traffic used to travel down the right-hand side, so we did it to keep to some forgotten tradition.

This was the edge of the city; on the right were the crumpled remains of a petroleum station and just beyond that the caved-in, mossy metal roof of what had been called a "box store." On my left were industrial buildings and shops, equally decrepit, though the former automobile dealership, one of the last buildings before the tree line, was kept in good shape and manned twenty-four hours a day to monitor comings and goings from the town. It had been a long time since there were any serious incursions, though. The guards were amongst the very few people chosen to bear weapons. Certainly, the Elders preferred that the rest of us stay unarmed and think our way out of a crisis. In a reasonably secure town, that worked fine, but how would that play out on the road? That was one of the thoughts that nagged at me.

In front of me stretched the highway, once a busy four-lane artery that connected the sparsely populated northern parts of the province of Ontario with the crowded southern ones. Any paint that had separated the lanes was long gone, of course, and the road itself was ruptured, fissured, frequently caved-in, and there were grasses, shrubs, and even some trees thrusting upward through the holes and cracks. One certainly would have had trouble driving one of those massive vehicles from the past on this road now. Even riding a bike was tricky, and you had to keep your eyes fixed squarely on the road.

Fortunately, we still had access to that method of transportation. In a depopulated world of abandoned possessions, we had our pick of them. There were even stockpiles of repair kits, tires, and inner tubes to be found everywhere people went. Whenever Seekers came across these materials, they were brought back to Norbay for our use. We'd never run out of bicycles and parts. In fact, they could have made a bicycle the official symbol of the town. Almost since infancy, we were all taught how to keep a bicycle in good repair. This model that I'd been given especially for this trip was called a "touring bicycle" and was equipped with panniers that held a lot of extra food and some other sundries. I was leaving well-equipped.

I decided I'd have to think of a personal name for this new friend I'd been gifted, something that would help us form a bond and a friendship. I'd have plenty of time for that on the long ride.

Cedar was there with my family — Birch was wearing a black shirt, maybe as a symbol of her displeasure — as well as Raven, another representative of the Council, the elected leaders who made the big decisions about life in Norbay. Despite her name, Raven had a pile of blonde hair.

She stepped forward.

"Jay of the Graniteville neighbourhood of the town of Norbay, you are hereby starting your life in the quest to gather the knowledge of the old world armed with that knowledge so that we can build a new, just society from the ashes of the old. We thank you for the service you are about to render. And we wish you friendship with all living things you encounter on the road. You may face many dangers, but if you keep our vows in your mind at all times, you will come through them safely. Remember what we say: the only way to handle any bad situation is to be fully present in the world at all times. Not lost in the grasping of ego. That was what led to our downfall as a civilization."

With those thankfully brief ceremonial words, she stepped back and let my family cluster around me.

"Just remember what they've taught you, son. Be aware at all times. Be mindful. You'll be great at this." Mom hugged me tightly. When she pulled away, her eyes were glinting.

"I know, Mom."

Dad put a hand on my shoulder. "We're proud of you. Do your dad one better and come back in one piece."

"Yeah, don't get bitten on the ass by a feral dog."

I turned to Oak. "Thanks for the touching words, brother. You always know what to say. I'll cherish them forever."

"My pleasure," he said and moved away to give me and Birch some privacy. Everyone feigned that they saw something interesting on the horizon.

Finally, I turned to her and pulled her close. "Don't forget me, Birch."

She didn't bother to conceal the gleam of tears in her eyes and wiped angrily at them. "You know I don't like this…"

"I do know." I felt something in my throat.

"And I wish they didn't have all these stupid rules about going alone, and only with another frigging Seeker." She shot an unfriendly glance at Cedar and Raven, who were standing a respectful distance away, also pretending not to listen. "But I'm proud of you too. Come back in one piece, and please try not to get bitten in the ass."

I had to chuckle a little, appreciating the lightening of the mood. "Not sure why you're both all of a sudden so interested in my butt's integrity, but sure." I hugged her and kissed her quickly on the mouth, wishing I could hold her longer, then stepped back. The morning sun gleamed off her dark hair, and I wondered if I'd ever really noticed how beautiful she was. I did now.

I put a leg over the frame of the bike, inelegantly catching my boot toe on the pedal.

"Okay, well, that's me." I raised a hand, got settled on the seat, and moved forward with the most significant pedal stroke of my life.

I resisted the urge to look back, and no one offered any more calls of encouragement as I left what I knew of civilization behind.

V.

THE ROAD

JAY

It was already uncomfortably hot, even though it was still early in the day. At this time of year, you never knew when you were going to get a forty-five-degree scorcher, and it seemed today might become one. You'd think we'd be more used to it, but the combination of heat and humidity could kill, so we had to take it very seriously. I was happy to have a decent supply of water with me; finding ways to slake your thirst was an ongoing problem all Seekers had to deal with on the road. I had a bottle with a filter in it, but it was still best not to take water directly from half-dried-up, muddy lakes if you could avoid it. A wide area south of Norbay had once been renowned for the sheer number of beautiful lakes it held. Most of the smaller lakes were now more like scum-covered mud pits.

I'd been as far as Great Sudbury before, so I was no stranger to lonely stretches of northern highway, and there wasn't usually much variety to see. I had to keep my eyes on that pitted road or I'd take a header over a twisted piece of asphalt.

There were also occasional rusted, crumbled shells of motor vehicles, from small cars to giant "rigs," which had been the main way goods were transported from place to place. That always seemed very inefficient to me in such a populated place, putting small amounts of things on the road dragged along by pollution-spewing engines, especially considering they also had rail lines, but the ways of our ancestors are often incomprehensible to us. Look at the mess they got themselves into, after all. The long boxes attached to the rigs were collapsed and rusted almost into nothingness as well and strewn across the road, the contents long removed or rotted away.

What had happened to owners of these cars, what had made them abandon their vehicles on this lonely stretch of road, and where they had gone was lost to time.

Occasionally I'd see the remains, skeletal or otherwise, of an ungulate, stripped of its flesh by the packs of wolves and coyotes that had reclaimed much of the land in this part of what was once called "Ontario." It was reminder to keep my wits about me.

On both sides of the thin slash of highway there was nothing but lush, almost impenetrable scrubby forest and undergrowth.

About an hour or so of cycling south of Norbay, it started to get hillier around the narrow expanse of four-lane highway, and I had to do some heavier pedaling in places, while still weaving painstakingly around jagged obstacles and crevasses, usually where there'd been a culvert. It was gruelling. I had spent the last couple of years cycling religiously for at least two hours every day in preparation for this moment, and my leg muscles were well developed, as was my lung capacity, but it was still taxing work, especially with the sun beating mercilessly down. If it was as hot by noon as I suspected it would be, there wasn't much chance of making Huntsville by nightfall.

Just as I passed a place called Trout Creek, a few hours into the journey, the area around me to the left and right was suddenly bare, and the road itself was even more chewed up and washed out than elsewhere. A wide strip of vegetation had been torn away from the hills as though by a set of giant teeth, leaving a gash in the dense thickets and exposing the shield rock. I realized this was probably the result of the tornadoes of 2115 that I'd heard about in my early teens. I remembered the mega-cells passing to the north and south of the town, just barely missing us while we cowered for hours in the basements of our houses, listening to the howl of the wind. There were tornado warnings at least twice a year, but that had been the most destructive one so far in my lifetime.

Despite my desire to make good time, I had a sudden urge to look out over the landscape; the escarpment in Norbay gave a fairly impressive view but wasn't really that high. Because of the storm's devastation, I would have a panoramic view of the whole region from here. The crown of a nearby hill had been completely denuded, aside from scrubby, low thickets, by fire or storm and should provide a clear line of sight.

I hid my bike behind a huge piece of granite, took out the reasonably fresh sandwich wrapped in leaves that Dad had sent with me, and my water bottle, hopped over a soggy ditch, and headed toward the slope. It was a lot farther than it had looked, and I started to regret it halfway there, but it was too late to go back without rendering the exercise pointless, so I took a break to eat the sandwich, then kept going. About thirty minutes later, gasping, I crested the hill to find another massive chunk of rock dominating the hilltop like a sentinel or an altar. I sank down into its lee, slugged back some water, wiped my forehead with my arm, and looked out over the landscape. I surveyed an unpopulated land, an ocean of leaves marred by frequent large black and brown patches caused by the giant forest fires. In fact, far off to the east I could see one raging now, sending up a spreading plume of smoke that looked like photos of atomic mushroom clouds I'd seen in old books. Of course, this scene was part of life most of the year; today, fortunately, a strong breeze from the west kept it away, otherwise I'd have been cycling in a giant cloud of noxious dust and debris. I could still smell its distinct tang.

Not too far away, I saw birds of prey with wings spread wide coasting lazily and gracefully on the currents of overheated air.

Darker patches of green, almost bluish, in the landscape indicated lakes still covered with the summer's thick mat of algal bloom they always acquired that rendered the water undrinkable and unswimmable. We had to take our drinking water from flowing streams or collect rainwater or suffer dire physical consequences.

Nowhere did I see any signs of activity — just the tiny broken buildings of the town of Trout Creek off in the distance. Everything was peaceful, untouched. My excitement had somewhat dissipated after the sweaty ride; the breeze provided only a slight relief.

It struck me that I was completely, utterly alone for the first time in my life. I hadn't seen a soul on the road; I didn't see any signs of human life in the vast vista all around me, no matter where I turned. All my life I'd been in the vicinity of Norbay, or, if travelling, it was in the company of others. Cedar said that the fewer people there are, the more you rely on each other; only people who grow up in crowds long for solitude. It was both frightening and liberating to be so far from help. It reminded me that this trip was also a test of my mettle.

I thought of Birch again and whether I really wanted to spend my life making frequent trips away from her, while she did ... what? Took up a trade? Would she even be there waiting for me when I got back? I knew that I loved her, but sometimes I wasn't so sure whether her love for me was stronger than her dissatisfaction with everything else.

Opposites may attract, but if in a partnership one person's ambitions and traits are sacrificed for the sake of the other, that's a recipe for unhappiness, and even my callow young mind could already divine that.

We had often stood at the top of the escarpment, hand in hand, looking to the southwest, dreaming of seeing distant places and different and exotic people and animals. We knew most of the things we saw in books were long gone, but what was left to be rediscovered? If only she'd joined the guild, she would have been going on her own mission soon. But Birch followed her own star, even if she had no idea where it might lead her. I had faith, though, that she'd do something special in the end.

There was a fire inside her that Norbay couldn't contain, that much I knew.

• • •

I descended the slope, picking my way over sharp rocks and through prickly raspberry tendrils, glad it was so much easier going down. An hour of cycling later, I was nearing the ruins of two more towns, South River and Sundridge. It was strange to think of all these empty little ghost towns dotting the landscape, abandoned and almost completely consumed by nature's crawling carpet of life, the inhabitants now clustering for comfort in the few settled places left after the Ruin took away the reasons for these small communities to exist at all; no electricity, no water, no heat, no jobs, no protection from ravaging disease and destructive weather, nothing to make, nothing to do.

These places had been carved out of the wilderness to serve some industrial purpose, and now that same wilderness was relentlessly reclaiming its lost territory. Eventually, and probably not too long from now, there'd be few signs of us left. I remembered seeing photos in books of places like Angkor Wat — but that was made of stone, not the materials of industrial humanity, which weren't constructed to last and soon rotted or crumbled away.

I had just pelted a little too fast down a fairly steep decline, narrowly avoiding face-planting on a chunk of asphalt, and started up an incline, huffing and puffing, when I had a feeling something was behind me … you know, that prickly feeling you get when someone enters the room and you didn't hear anything, but you know they're there.

Turning around, I could see in the mounting glare a fast-moving group of something indeterminate far in distance but coming on fast: a big, dark blur, made hazier by the heat blasting up from the asphalt. I had no idea what this blur could be, but I also knew that most of the larger things you encountered out here should be considered dangerous.

I decided it would be very wise to get off the road, immediately. I was in the middle of a cutting where the builders of this highway had blasted the shield rock away with explosives to widen the road; this highway had once been two lanes, but the appetites of our forebears for their petroleum-guzzling vehicles and for things like "vacations" and "vacation properties" eventually dictated the need for ever-widening roads, like the ten lanes of Highway 401 in Great Toronto that I'd heard of.

I quickened my pace, and as soon as I could, I hauled myself and my bike off to the right, over the remains of a fallen wire fence, and behind the nearest thick bush to wait.

It only took a few minutes before I heard a mighty rhythmic clattering approaching, and I realized what it was: horses! But with or without riders?

Just as the clipping and clopping became loud enough that I felt the animals were about to pass by, I peeked out and was rewarded with a breathtaking sight. At least ten of them were galloping past, their shaggy, unkempt manes flying. Brown horses, black ones, spotted ones, and a couple of smaller animals that could have been foals, racing surefootedly like they were being chased by a pack of wolves. It was magnificent; I'd never seen anything like it. There were packs of feral dogs and cats around our town, sure, but I'd never seen anything but a few solitary horses; we didn't use them as beasts of burden and only rode the few domesticated ones that seemed interested in maintaining a relationship with us.

Not wanting to scare them any more, I waited until they passed by, and then a bit longer in case there were indeed pursuers.

But when I emerged, the road was still again, as though I'd never seen this wonderful sight at all.

I can't hazard a guess to this day whether something had frightened those horses or whether they were just running for the sheer joy and freedom of it on this stretch of straight asphalt.

This was already more excitement than I'd experienced in the last several years of my life put together.

• • •

It was now about 1:00 p.m. and so hot that I knew I wouldn't be able to move on until late afternoon at the earliest; my water supply was limited, and it had to be getting up to forty degrees. You could boil yourself in these conditions if you weren't careful.

Since I was passing the highway exit for South River, which my map told me was not far off the road, I decided to look for shelter. It took a lot more rigorous uphill pedaling, but I got up the ramp with sweat oozing from every pore. The pavement had mostly caved in on the bridge over the highway, but the bridge structure itself still stood. I'd already gingerly picked my way around the fallen girders and massive chunks of concrete of a couple of fallen bridges during my ride so far. I managed to haul my bike over these holes and after a few minutes hit the weedy main street of what was once the small town of South River, now completely uninhabited.

Most of the buildings had fallen inward: gas stations, a pizza shop, a place that advertised "crystals," whatever that meant — maybe one of those obscure religious cults of the twentieth century. A larger, sturdier building announced "South River Brewing" in faded letters. The building looked mostly intact, and a big loading door was open, so I steered in and flopped down right on the cool concrete floor.

After a few minutes and some gulps of water, I got up, inspected the giant vats where they'd once brewed the beer, and was ecstatic to see rainwater had fallen recently through the roof and collected in one of them. It looked fairly free of sediment or any tell-tale greenish hues, so I splashed my face, drank a bit, and filled my bottle. It tasted musty but would be safer than taking water from streams.

I explored further and went into what had once been the store that sold the beer. It was empty, of course, including the refrigerators that lined one wall, and the windows were long smashed in, but since the roof was intact, I figured it would be safe to curl up behind the counter and take a nap in the shade while I waited out the heat.

However, it was too horribly hot even to do that, so I just lay there, pondering my mission. They always made your first destination an important place so you could experience appropriate awe; the one they were sending me to was bound to have been picked over many times, but a prominent institution of learning contains so much material that you could visit year after year and still find something of small value to rescue in a dusty corner.

I was headed to a place called Kingston and something called Queen's University, apparently once one of the great seats of learning in this part of the world, to see if anything remained in its libraries and classrooms. It had been visited by Seekers many times, but I was to find out what was left, take an inventory, remove the most valuable smaller things that could be carried in my panniers, and report on where to find the rest. The more dangerous mission to collect any larger collections of value would be undertaken by more seasoned Seekers who sometimes went out in teams if something of special value was found.

Ultimately, though, I think the idea of this first trip was just to get the new Seeker's feet wet and see how they could adapt to solitary life on the road; it wasn't for everyone, after all. Some Seekers preferred to be alone, while some of the older ones liked to and were allowed to go out in pairs. I didn't know what my preference would be — though if Birch or Oak had joined the Seekers, I would already have been certain.

I was to choose my own route; the most obvious one was to follow this highway down to the giant one, the 401 that once connected southwestern Ontario to Quebec, and then turn east and head all the way to Kingston, a journey of a couple of weeks, tops.

However, smaller roads branched off from the one I was travelling on, and if I wanted to, I could instead wend my way down them. Cedar said there were two schools of thought that debated which was best; on the smaller highway you were more isolated and more likely to encounter packs of animal predators. On the larger, very wide one, the lower reaches of which met Great Toronto, you were more likely to run into potentially much more dangerous predators: other humans.

I hadn't made my mind up which of these approaches I would take, but I had plenty of time to do that; there was a day or so of hard riding ahead before I even got out of what was once called "cottage country," where — and it's hard to believe now — the rich of the old world had often kept a second country home they could escape to on the weekends in their vehicles, trying to find solace in the incredibly stressful lives they inflicted upon themselves under the tyranny of the clock and the dollar.

On a Friday nights, old newspapers told us, this highway I travelled on would have been carpeted in "stop-and-go" traffic, meaning they'd sit in their vehicles, unmoving, for hours as those same vehicles spewed out the very exhaust that would choke the world, all trying to reach their country getaway at the same time. Then, after a night or two in their vacation home, they'd turn around and reverse the long journey back to the big city.

And, of course, this honour was reserved for those who had been treated best by the capitalist economic system, those whose labour was considered to have more value and hence were rewarded better simply because of the perceived value of the work they'd ended up doing. For us, the idea that any kind of labour is worth more than another seems very peculiar, but then the old world really was a bizarre place. I honestly don't know how they put up with it all.

• • •

I did finally manage to doze off for a while, and when thirst and uncomfortable sweat woke me again, I could see the sun was a bit lower. I felt better and somewhat restless, so I put my cap on and took a walk down a nearby residential street. The glassless windows of the houses were like gaping mouths and eyes. Most of the houses were caved in and some were no more than skeletal frames; trees and shrubs had even taken root in some front rooms. In other words, it was what every former settlement in Ontario looked like, as far as I knew.

I chose the most intact home I could find and cautiously went in. The remains of carpeting were disintegrated to the point that they no longer even smelled. Turning in to a front room, I saw pieces of disintegrating furniture, peeling wallpaper, and not much more. Obviously, these houses would have been picked over by scavengers and even Seekers many times over the decades.

I went upstairs, testing each stair; several threatened to give way under my weight. I found two bedrooms and a bathroom, and half of the roof had been torn away. Late-afternoon sun glared into the room on the right, so I went left.

There was no moldy collapsed bed in this room, but there was what was left of what had once been a very big stereo system; our library had revived several of those to play the media that we scavenged, so I was familiar with them. Clearly, the owner of this house had loved music. This stereo system, though, was unsalvageable, damaged by rain and sun.

Scattered all over the floor amongst piles of leaves that had drifted in were dozens, maybe hundreds of warped, black LP records, and still more flaking, deteriorated compact discs, all unplayable. Water and drastic temperature changes in the house over the decades had made these objects worthless, which would explain why, even if Seekers had already combed through this place that was so close to Norbay, these materials had not been collected. To the right of the stereo cabinet, a framed picture had fallen down by a huge speaker, and even though the images in the photograph were badly faded, I could make out a shirtless man with a bushy moustache, jutting stomach, and a ponytail with his arm around a woman with very long hair, posing in the sunlight, maybe at some kind of "vacation resort."

I put it down and reached for an equally-faded CD cover; these were scattered all over the floor, along with rotted LP sleeves. It bore a picture of a curly-haired man with a moustache on it as well. "Gordon Lightfoot," I read aloud. *Gord's Gold*, it said underneath in smaller letters. I hadn't heard of this particular musician, but his serious gaze straight into the camera roused my curiosity.

It struck me that it would be a poignant symbolic act to take my first object from this house, and since I did love music, how about this CD cover? Too bad the disc itself was cracked in half and the silvery part had flaked away. I'd have to ask the Elders or Sparrow if they knew anything about this guy and whether he had been a very popular singer.

I tucked the CD cover into my bag and gingerly made my way back downstairs. The sun was three quarters to the horizon, making it very late afternoon, and the air felt a touch cooler, so it was time to hit the road again.

On the way out of the house, I remembered to look at the doorframe, where, sure enough, I saw carved the symbol used by the Seekers: the rudimentary shape of a pine tree. The carving itself looked very old, which made sense, considering the vicinity of the town to the highway and to Norbay. We were told to leave this symbol at any house we investigated to let other Seekers know it had been checked for items of value. For all I knew, they'd covered the entire province by now.

I made my best attempt at duplicating the symbol and added the date and my name. Then I hopped on my bike and headed down the ramp toward Huntsville, where an old friend of Dad lived — or least he had, years ago, when Dad last heard from him. If this man wasn't there anymore, I'd have to find somewhere in the town to shelter.

As I pedaled under the golden dome of the fading day, it struck me that this entire day, I had not seen a single human being.

The land of Ontario was not the dominion of humankind anymore.

VI.

GRANITE

JAY

A few hours later, the orange sun was just about to sink below the tree line, and it was getting very dim. Long, purple streaks in the clouds made for a stunning sight that I'd have loved to stop and take in if I had time. An almost deafening chorus of crickets was now the only accompaniment to the whir of my tires on the asphalt. I had seen signs for Huntsville (someone was still doing the public service of propping them up, it seemed), but if I didn't reach it soon, I'd be risking making my bed under the stars or in the unsafe shell of a roadside shack. Fortunately, it appeared it would be a fairly full moon, so in the worst case, I'd still have some illumination. Still, the thought of sleeping on the ground with bears, coyotes, and wolves sniffing around wasn't at all appealing.

Finally, I saw a mostly-tipped-over sign on which I could make out the number 60, the name of the road Granite supposedly lived on. Granite had been a Seeker himself but had moved down to Huntsville for love, I'd been told, living in almost total isolation. Granite's partner had died a few years later in one of the last pandemics, but Granite had stayed on in Huntsville, living alone on this road. Dad hadn't seen him in at least a decade, which I guess was the last time Granite visited Norbay.

The town itself was, like Norbay, partially inhabited, but in this case very sparsely. I supposed if Granite wasn't there, I could screw up my courage and see if one of the other residents would take me in for the night. People in small places like this were suspicious of strangers, and rightly so. I wondered if they also posted guards.

I figured I had about fifteen minutes more of hard riding ahead. I was exhausted and famished, but it was the day's final push.

At long last, I stopped and checked the foldout road map of northeastern Ontario I'd also been supplied, with the location of Granite's house marked roughly with an X. I could barely make out the map in the twilight. I was close. A few minutes later, having seen no guards or any other people, I spied the rusty number of the property in the failing light and turned down a long, narrow, weedy driveway. It was dark enough that with the rustling black canopy above me, I could barely see a thing and was feeling my way. But soon I saw light! Faint, but still, a light ahead meant people. I could also detect the smell of smoke.

Finally, and with some caution, I emerged into a clearer area and saw the outline of a small house against the faint glow in the sky and a small amount of light bleeding through a closed curtain. I made my way toward it.

"Stop right there," ordered a gruff voice. "I'm armed, and I can see you better than you can see me." How had this guy noticed my approach?

"Um, are you Granite?" I tried to keep the quaver out of my voice.

There was a long pause, and the crickets seemed to fill it deafeningly.

"Who wants to know?"

I heard something metallic click from the porch and swallowed hard.

"My name is Jay. I'm from Norbay. You know my father, Aspen."

The crickets filled another long, uncomfortable silence, then there was a clunk, the door opened, and light poured out, blinding me for a moment. I raised my hand to cover my eyes.

"C'mon in, son! You're welcome here. Aspen is a dear friend." The voice still sounded intimidating but was now friendlier.

I left my bike on the grass and lurched up the stairs to the porch, suddenly well beyond tired. As I entered the house, an imposing husky walked up to me and sniffed at me and my pack, which I had immediately hefted off my back and dropped just inside the door. Two more huskies were around the corner in the cosily lit room, regarding me with ears pricked up and eyes shining.

The house was small, really a cabin, with one main large room. I could see a small kitchen butted from one end, and then a hallway that led to one or two more doors. Everything was made of wood, from walls to floor to furniture, except for the stove. Oil lamps cast a soothing maple syrup glow on the pine walls, on which were hung what looked like old rugs or tapestries, maybe the work of Granite or his deceased wife. The chairs were also wooden, except for a torn armchair that looked out of place but must be where Granite spent his evenings. There were plenty of books strewn around the room.

Granite turned into the living area and then around to face me, and his three dogs parked themselves around him, staring up at me. He had a tanned complexion and frizzy grey hair pulled into a long ponytail. He was thin of body and face, had a prominent Roman nose, and wore a well-trimmed beard. Despite that, his face was youthful and unlined. His eyes were penetrating, sizing me up, but he was smiling.

"Yes, I can see it. You look like an even combination of both parents. I'm guessing you're here on your first expedition. Time really does fly. I have no idea where the last few years have gone."

"That's right, my first time out." I shifted uncomfortably where I stood, my pack leaning against an aching leg with one of the dogs sniffing at it.

Suddenly, his face lightened even more and looked almost jovial. "Well, don't just stand there. Take your boots off, come on into the kitchen, and I'll get you something hot to eat. Raspberry, get away from there!"

The dog moved away, and I sighed and let my pack keel over.

• • •

Granite might not have been a Seeker anymore, but he appeared to have maintained the vegetarian diet, or he was being sensitive to my presumed needs. Later, my belly was full after a hearty meal of greens and beans, and I was splayed out in the armchair he'd offered me. I was sleepy after the day's exertions; it was likely from the meal but also from the warm cast of the flames in the lamps and the cosiness of the atmosphere they created. The big woodstove would keep things comfortable in the chillier, damp months. Raspberry and the other dogs — I didn't inquire if they were named Blueberry and Blackberry — were strewn about the floor, looking sleepy themselves.

Granite had been a sparse conversationalist so far, so in order to engage him and revive myself a bit, I asked, "So how long have you been here on your own?"

He had been patting one of the dogs at his feet. "It's five years since Patricia passed on."

Argh. I'd forgotten that part. "I'm sorry."

He grunted. "That's okay, boy. Life and death are just two sides of the same coin. In order to appreciate what we love, we have to lose it."

I smiled. "You still sound like a Seeker."

He chuckled dryly. "I'm sure I do. I thought about going back many times, but I'm used to my own company now. I have no appetite for further study and I'm too old for those strenuous missions. And I have my friends here for company and protection." He gave the dog a little tap, and it licked his hand. "There are also a few dozen more people, including a couple of families, living around here, and we're not unfriendly and look out for one another, even if we do keep to ourselves. It's not a bad life."

I nodded and gazed around the cozy room. "I can see that. But isn't it dangerous to live alone?"

"Life is dangerous, boy. They used to say in the old world that you could get hit by a car at any time; you never knew when your number would be up. We don't have to worry about that, at least. We just worry about marauders and predators, and we have our ways of protecting ourselves. But there are fewer of the former now, and more and more of the latter. All you need is a well-oiled shotgun and some faithful dogs to protect yourself." He pointed over at his gun leaning in the corner. "That's one thing I don't agree with about the guild ... sending kids out into the world without any protection but their wits. What's that symbolic nonsense going to prove?"

I didn't have anything to offer in response to that, considering I sort of agreed with him.

There was a slightly awkward silence, then he cleared his throat. "Anyway, we don't make the rules, but you have to follow them. Tell me about your trip and maybe I can give you some pointers."

I told him about my mission to Queen's University, what I knew about the place, and the general route I was planning to take to Kingston.

Granite's eyes narrowed when I mentioned my plan to stick with Highway 11 down to the 401, then to head east. "Not sure I like the idea of that. If anyone told you to do that, their information is clearly not up to date. Not one bit. That brings you close to dangerous humans. I'd rather take my chances with the wolves on the highways that go near old Algonquin Park."

This didn't sound good. "What do you mean? I was told there are people living there, and it would be good to be wary about going near it, but not much more than that. Maybe I can even learn something there."

"I guess Seeker intel isn't what it used to be. Not surprised... Idealists sometimes only hear what they want to hear. Looks like it's good you came here, for more reasons than a roof and some grub."

Granite got up to refill our mugs with fragrant mint leaves and water heated over the embers he kept going in the fireplace, despite the persistent mugginess of an October night. A few powdery moths flapped madly around an oil lamp in the corner. The minty odour briefly covered up the persistent scents of pine and dog.

"What do you know about what would once have been called the 'political geography' of Ontario?" Granite asked.

"Well, first of all, I know there's no such thing as Ontario," I said cheekily, by now feeling completely at home with Granite.

He laughed. "Fair point. There's no such thing as Ontario, or Canada, or, as far as we know, anywhere else. There's just people, right? Just our basic humanity."

I decided not to answer that.

He continued. "Wrong. Humans tend to organize into tribes. We're a herd species. Only isolated weirdos like me choose a life completely alone. We naturally gravitate together. But it's how we do that, and the end results tend to vary."

"Yes, like political parties and systems like communism and capitalism and democracy."

"Right." Granite leaned back. "Like that. Well, in Ontario, you'll still find groupings like that. Some of them are very nice places to live, like the communities of Norbay and Moosonee, reasonably well run, founded by people of principle. And some … not so nice."

"I've heard of some strange places in south and central Ontario. Seekers know to avoid them."

"That's right, there are places founded by cults or by strongmen or the remnants of the police and military. They come and go depending on who's stronger at any given time. People band together for safety, but they don't always live well that way. They mainly scavenge, and some rob. But those groups don't tend to stay together for long. When you get down around what was once called Barrie, you still have to keep an eye out for danger, just because."

Granite leaned forward to accentuate his next point, "No … the bigger danger is farther south."

"You mean Great Toronto? Like I said, I know people do still live there."

"Yes. Once, that area held millions of tightly packed souls. Now, just a tiny fraction of that, but I don't know the numbers."

I leaned forward excitedly. Something had been bugging me for a while. "Wasn't Great Toronto once the seat of learning and culture for the whole country in the old world? Wouldn't there be libraries and libraries full of stuff there? There were several universities, and big libraries, and—"

"Yes, and we used to go there. I've been there. But not in some time. Great Toronto is now … organized and cut off. That's why I suggest you stay clear. There's now a government of a kind there."

I was shocked. I'd never heard any such thing. "A government? Like, over all the people? A really organized one?"

"Yes, and I've heard a few disturbing things about it. The people running Great Toronto are authoritarian and ambitious. They represent the other side of the coin of which our Knowledge Seekers are one face; they too want to rebuild the world. Maybe it's some complex they developed from being surrounded by the remains, the corpse of the old world at its most imposing and powerful, but they now have a desire to revive that world in its entirety, at any cost. A council of powerful people called the Six run the city, and they don't brook any dissent. They run it as a sort of oligarchy. People who go there don't come back out, either. We don't know what happens to them. People who have gone near the border see a heavy presence of guards with guns, and not just shotguns, but the worst weapons of the old world: assault weapons."

I was very surprised. "Why wasn't I told of this? Surely our leaders know?"

He shrugged. "Maybe they haven't heard everything I have, maybe they are too comfortable by this point and underestimate the possible threat, or they have too much trust in their disciples to follow instructions. But mark my words, boy, you need to stay away from there. And in the future, we may all have cause to worry. In the old world, states regularly went to war; tens of millions were killed in the twentieth century alone. Sometimes there were civil wars within a country, and citizens killed their fellow citizens. Along with everything good that civilization created, those things died with that world. But the dark side of human nature tends to revive like a zombie, time and time again. You can't stop it and you never will."

Now I knew another reason why Granite had left the Seekers; that sort of bleak cynicism was most definitely frowned upon in Norbay. In fact, they tried to drill hope into us as part of our schooling. Even in Cedar's most honest moments, she wouldn't talk quite this darkly.

I thanked him for the warning. I wasn't sure what to do now. If I believed him, I *should* take the more northerly route across — but I was now also maddeningly curious about that old city. It would be a thrill to see its crumbling skyscrapers and the sheer expanse of concrete, brick, and asphalt where millions upon millions of people had lived and died.

Conversation lapsed after that. Granite had become a bit more taciturn after making those revelations and mostly just patted his dogs and sipped his tea.

But after a little while, he abruptly suggested taking in the view of the stars before bed, so we headed to the porch, leaving the dogs inside. The crickets were chirping, the underbrush rustled, and I could smell the loamy forest scent mixed with smoke. There was no breeze.

No matter how many times you look up to see the band of the Milky Way overhead, uncountable glittering pinpricks on an obsidian backdrop, it never gets old. If I gazed long enough, I could see the occasional flash of light as a meteor died, and less occasionally a slow-moving speck that would be one of the thousands of satellites our ancestors had sent up, miraculous science used for mundane purposes like making phone calls and watching television. It was funny to think that not long ago, many people believed we'd be making journeys to the stars and colonizing them, but now the only evidence of that aspiration were these totally unused hulks of telecommunication satellites that would vanish, crashing back to Earth one by one, in the coming decades.

Granite's voice rumbled out of the darkness beside me. "To think that there was a time when people lived in places so permanently bright, they could barely even see stars at night… So, kid, you got anyone special at home?"

I hadn't expected that sudden turn in the conversation. "Um … yes, I'd say so. There's someone."

"Someone you love?"

This was something of a moment of truth for me, at least publicly. I decided to be honest.

"Yes. Her name is Birch." It felt good just saying her name. Was I missing her already? How was I going to make it out here if I was that soft?

"A lovely name. And we are still surrounded by birches where we live. Well, of course, I had someone special once, and though I lost her, it was all worth it. That's not to say those who have never known such love can't lead fulfilling lives. But when you've tasted it, you're never the same."

He fell silent for a moment.

"That's why I'm alone. After I met Patricia, I never needed anyone's company but hers. We were enough. And seeking knowledge and adventure on the roads? That paled in comparison to just being here in our glade, together, doing mundane things like keeping our garden. And now that she's gone… Well, it's too late for me to go back and learn how to be with people again. Not that it hasn't been pleasant having a visitor, of course."

We both chuckled.

"No offense taken."

"I can't say it hasn't been tough these last years. I've never been much of a deep thinker. But when Patricia was taken away like that, it was the first time I cursed our fate and questioned our principles. If it had been a hundred years ago, there'd have been vaccines, there'd have been treatments. Now, there's nothing to protect us against many diseases. Imagine that, being amongst the first generations to take such a giant step backward. Not everything that was lost was bad. I cursed them, though, and I cursed us all. I thought in my darkest moments that it would have been more than worth it to live in a time of excess and greed, if it would just have extended her life. Gradually, though, I got my balance back and was able to put it in perspective."

I was learning a lot from Granite. We learned in school about the evils of the old world, but there had been progress then, too, and it was all lost together, the good and the bad.

"All I'm trying to say is if you find that kind of relationship yourself, if you think you have that in your life — don't dismiss it because of the promise of adventure or some kind of noble ideal. If those are what you really want, wonderful, but if you'll think of her every day and feel a hole right in the middle of yourself that only she can fill, then you know what I think you should do. Something to ponder on your first journey."

Granite's wisdom was starting to cut a little too close for comfort; I decided I'd had enough of it for one evening, even if he meant well.

"Thanks for the food, the chat, and the advice, Granite. I have to get an early start, so maybe you could show me where I'll be sleeping."

"Of course, boy. And please forgive an older man his ramblings. Maybe we all need someone to talk at once in a while after all."

He showed me to a small room next to his bedroom that smelled musty from disuse, and I fell into the tiny, short bed, completely drained. One of the dogs watched me balefully from the doorway.

"Pleasant slumbers, Jay. I hope you dream about the things you love best."

Granite left the room, tamped down the fire a bit, but then headed back out the door to do some more stargazing. I'd thought I might try reading a bit of the book Dad gave me, *The Plague,* but there was no way my body would allow it. I put out the small oil lamp on a rough-hewn table beside the bed.

I don't know how long he stayed out there in the silence and the starlight, because I was asleep within moments.

VII.

ELM

JAY

When I woke, I could hear clattering from the kitchen, but one of Granite's dogs (not Raspberry — this one was a shade browner) had gotten onto the bed with me, and I woke up with my arms around it. Its fur smelled musky and comforting, and I didn't object when my face was licked. Not a bad way to welcome the next leg of the journey.

I went out back and used his washtub to clean off the previous day's grime, then went in for breakfast. Granite had become reticent again by the light of day, though he gave me a good meal of baked beans, potatoes, and berries. He told me he was sending me on my way with food and water stocks replenished.

He also offered a few more stern words of warning about how the road would get more and more dangerous the farther south I went. "The land is sparsely inhabited, which can lull you into a false sense that you're alone. But that's when bad things happen. Be aware of your surroundings at all times, especially at dusk."

I nodded firmly to show him I was really listening. "I understand." And I did. I'd spent a lot of the previous leg daydreaming, which would be a bad habit going forward.

With a final wave, I sped down his driveway toward the road. I didn't see any sign of his neighbours, not even a plume of woodstove smoke before I hit the highway again. My aim was to reach a town called Gravenhurst, which Granite believed was still uninhabited, by noon, and then Orillia, a small city that might actually be partially inhabited, by the end of the day — weather and heat permitting.

The bit of sun I could see was just poking above the treed hills to the east. The sky was obscured by a greyish-white haze of smoke, meaning the wind had changed direction and the smoke from that fire I'd seen the day before was upon me. This would keep things cooler but it would be harder to breathe. I had masks, of course, but they would make cycling unpleasant.

Just south of Huntsville, I passed a giant bog that I assumed was what was left of the lake the town used to sit on. No wonder the place wasn't too populated; the bugs here would be hell. Norbay itself is situated on a long lake, Nipissing. You can tell where the shoreline used to be by the parklands, rotting docks, and breakwaters; now you have to walk about half a kilometre past that before you hit water, though the lake is still big enough for the pescetarians among us to get decent supplies of fish from it, if you keep away from the poisonous algae.

Even though I was getting closer to supposedly more populated areas, I still didn't see anyone on the road. I did notice more signs of the former life of the area, like abandoned gas stations and the occasional dilapidated shells of flimsy old buildings they called "burger stands," where they used to sell a kind of roasted meat on bread that was supposedly the world's most popular food. I had to dodge a lot of chunks of heavily rusted, disintegrating vehicles. There were open patches on the sides of the road where fires had decimated wide areas of forest, and more bald areas flattened by storms, but overall the vegetation was so lush that I could barely even see into the tree line on either side. The only signs of animal life were clouds of biting insects and birds of prey wheeling overhead. Once or twice I saw a deer scampering away from the water-filled ditches by the sides of the road.

I'd been going for a couple of hours when it started to get overcast and the breeze picked up. That latter part was pleasant on my sweaty skin, but the former could mean trouble, judging by the darkness and size of the clouds. At least it helped with the smoke. I had no idea where to take shelter unless it was in one of these almost roofless shells of buildings, and they wouldn't provide much cover.

I determinedly kept going, with the wind starting to pound at me from the west, throwing me off-balance, until I came across an astonishing sight that stopped me in my tracks. I'd seen trees and shrubs along the way, poking up through cracks in the roadbed — but here, smack in the middle of this highway, a giant pine had gradually ripped through the pavement and now towered at least twenty metres.

Even more amazing was that I could clearly see a person sitting cross-legged under its skirt, the first human I'd seen on the road in about a hundred and fifty kilometres since leaving home.

I slowed, wondering if this person had seen me or if I should conceal myself, but then I saw the bicycle leaned up against the other side of the trunk.

Could it be? It could mean a few things, but it could also be...

Despite Granite's warnings, I decided to throw caution to the wind and approached.

The person stirred but didn't move, seemingly not at all concerned by the sight of me. A shock of white hair sat above a wizened, heavily tanned face, but the eyes were bright and stared right into mine. The figure wore a brown T-shirt and jeans with many small holes in them. A large pack, not too different from mine but much more weathered, was off to the right side.

"Well, hello there, young Seeker," said a gravelly voice of indeterminate gender.

I swallowed. "Hello, Elder."

Then the person laughed, a nice, warm, slightly guttural sound that instantly eased my tension. "Elder, huh? I guess you could call me that. Elm's the name. Help me up."

I took Elm's bony outstretched hand and steadied myself to lift. I could now tell from the shape of the form under the baggy T-shirt that this person was female, very thin and wiry, with what would have once been a boyish frame, lacking the bowed spine common in a person of her age. She was quite small, about thirty centimetres shorter than me, and I was pushing two metres. But somehow this figure radiated strength.

She peered up at me, craning her neck and narrowing her eyes to give me a good inspection. "From the fresh-faced looks of you and the fact that you're alone with that overstuffed pack, I'd say you're a newbie, correct?"

"That's right, Elder. First time out. I'm Jay."

Elm laughed again. "Please, enough with that Elder stuff; I'm no Elder. Elder–*ly*, yes. An authority figure, no. I'm happy to meet you. If you're Jay, and if I can judge by your face as well, I'd say you're Aspen and Willow's eldest."

I was shocked by this. "You know my parents?"

"Of course; it's not *that* big a community. You won't know me because I'm a bit of a rule-breaker and have rarely been home in the last twenty years or so. I just sort of … pop in once in a while. I'm supposedly too old for this life, you know. I just didn't get the message."

I took a swig of water and eyed the darkening sky, momentarily distracted by the size of the thunderheads.

"Yes, I know your parents. Both dedicated Seekers at one point. Cedar's star pupils. The road wasn't kind to your dad, as I'm sure you know, and it only led your mother's family to tragedy," Elm continued. "I was once a very dedicated and rule-following Seeker myself, but I still had too much genuine, misdirected wanderlust, of which my colleagues disapproved. But they couldn't stop me. So now I do as I please and travel around and will do that until these creaking joints finally give out on me or my heart stops." She performed an exaggerated but spry knee bend. "Like Cedar, I was born a long time ago in a very difficult place and time … and I've been everywhere I can, while she now prefers the more sedentary and academic life. And I don't really travel with the purpose of tracking down knowledge anymore, either. Mostly for the joy of moving around and new things to see."

This was news to me — I'd never heard of a rogue Seeker. Certainly, no one had ever mentioned Elm to me before.

Then she looked up at the sky too.

"Yes, I've been keeping an eye on this as well. Looks like a full-on derecho might be on the way, if I know anything … and I know a lot. I've lived through storms so scary, they'd have you wetting yourself within seconds. I suggest we take better shelter than we can find even under our hardy, bushy friend here."

"You know where we can go?" I asked.

She snorted. "Of course, boy. I've been travelling these roads since I was your age. I know every part of Old Muskoka like the back of my hand. Let's go."

Elm hopped on her bike, which was considerably older and rustier than mine but seemed otherwise well maintained, and headed off. Even though the gale was pounding and pushing at us, her course was true and straight, or as straight as you could go on these pitted, shrubby roads. A few minutes later, we exited on an even weedier side road and headed east. The wind was really starting to whip up now, but it was at our backs and propelled us along. On the way, despite having to yell a bit over the gusts, I filled Elm in on the basics of my mission and what I'd seen so far. She knew Granite well, of course.

I'd thought I'd have to slow down for her, but she was in such excellent shape that it was the opposite; my efforts to get in good enough condition for the road clearly had not been effective enough as I laboured to keep up.

By now, towering angry black clouds had congregated overhead, and I felt the sting of raindrops when Elm turned off the road onto what would once have been a dirt road or driveway — you could barely tell now, there were so many trees, saplings, shrubs, and grasses blocking the way. But as with most old roads of this kind, you could just barely detect there'd once been an opening there, like when you're taking a lightly used trail through the woods, and you can only sort of feel out where feet have trodden. But somehow you know someone has walked there before.

I hopped off my bike and plunged after her, making my way through the greenery for a minute or two before the biggest house I'd ever seen emerged through the trees. This thing was massive! I'd encountered shells of some mansions moldering away, some almost down to their foundations, up on the escarpment that loomed over Norbay, the last tangible evidence of a time when wealth bought you the best view, but none of them displayed the faded signs of decadent opulence this pile possessed. Miraculously, it was mostly still standing, too, possibly protected from high winds by the trees. It seemed to have multiple wings, countless windows, and bits of roof sticking out here and there. The surrounding trees pressed up against it, poking their boughs through the open windows. The thing was profoundly ugly. It stood on a rocky promontory overlooking what would once have been a small lake, now of course reduced to a flourishing scum-covered bog. Peeking around the side, I could see the ruins of other large houses lining the shore, though none as colossal as this: fancy boathouses, docks, and rotting boats were also scattered amongst the bulrushes.

I was so impressed that I didn't even swat at the giant cloud of mosquitoes and deer flies that had enveloped me.

Elm was wryly watching my slack-jawed expression. "Yep, that's how I felt the first time I saw this place too. Might have belonged to a business magnate or one of the movie stars who used to visit these parts. It may be an ostentatious testament to the worst excesses of olden times, but it's mostly intact, so it's my go-to when I need shelter in these parts. Even the chimney is still intact and works. Back then, money could buy you the best."

With that, she leapt up the remains of some stone steps and in through a yawning double door.

I followed her over a floor made of what felt like real stone into a giant room with a high ceiling. Amazingly, only one wall had partly caved in. A mammoth fireplace stood against the far wall, and there was even a bit of wood stacked up beside it. Other ancient piles of wood that had probably been furniture and one reasonably intact, heavy-looking table stood around the room, covered in dust and cobwebs.

She strode over. "Good, my wood is still here. I was last here weeks ago. We can cook up these mushrooms I picked today. Found a lot of them. The chimney still works fine. If you have any Norbay delicacies to share, I'll be glad to partake." This person certainly knew how to take charge.

Outside, the wind picked up even more, and I could hear branches scraping the side of the house. It felt very much like I imagined a hurricane would.

Then it got very dark, darker still, outside as well as in, and the rain started pelting down. It sounded so heavy, like bits of gravel hitting the house, that it might knock you down, let alone the power of the wind, which was now shrieking. I could already hear the nerve-wracking boom and crackle of falling boughs and trees.

"Looks like a big one. If need be, we'll have to go down to the wine cellar, though I don't care for it … too many creepy-crawlies down there."

In the dim light I could see Elm motioning to me from across the room. This woman was quite the character, but she did make me feel a little safer.

I'd been in dangerous storms before, but never while away from home; we always knew a safe place to go. I could only hope this old pile wouldn't fall on top of us.

Elm put a few dry branches in the fireplace and expertly struck a flint. Then she sat down cross-legged on the flagstones and waved me over. "Of course, water may pour down this chimney, but let's give it a go. Come on over and sit down, Jay. You're no safer standing up. And this place is built like a fort."

I was still on edge. I could see objects flying by the glassless window, and the thin shrubbery was bent over at a forty-five-degree angle in the hurricane-strength wind.

Still, she was right. It didn't matter if I died standing up or sitting down.

We had some water, ate the mushrooms and some of my dried fruit, and then we talked as it got still darker outside, this time from the gathering dusk. The storm finally appeared to have passed, and wind had died down a lot. I started to feel a bit more relaxed and thought I'd ask the question that had been on my mind. If anyone would know the answer, it would be this wanderer.

"Elm, Granite told me I should stay away from Great Toronto. Is there really something bad about the people there?"

She laughed gently. "There's something bad about people everywhere. And something good. Even in us Seekers, there's a bit of the bad left, despite our attempts to smoke it out. Or at least a bit of the intractable and dogmatic. But Granite wasn't wrong to warn you. Things have changed there in recent years. It's been resettled a lot. Twenty years ago it was a vast city of the dead, just vagabonds skulking around there and packs of feral dogs, coyotes, and cats. A dangerous place. Giant buildings falling into the streets. Wild weather — wilder than here. That part's still the same, I'm sure. But yes, there are people there again."

"What kind of people?"

She frowned. "Not sure how they were gathered. But there are thousands now, probably. Maybe all of southern Ontario went there, I don't know. But it's an old-fashioned city-state now. And it's what they would have called an oligarchy in the old world. A council rules it, called the Six. An unelected council. They have seized control. The borders of the city are closed and guarded; that's why Granite warned you. People who go in don't come back out. I have no idea whether the population there feels happy or oppressed.

"The rumour is that the Six dream of reviving the old technology and rebuilding it much like it was before. Engines. Wires. Mining. Oil. All that stuff. Not sure how much of it's true, but if so … needless to say, they might not look too kindly on Seekers and our ways. They might see us as rivals, since Norbay could be said to be influential and will only become more so. And we certainly wouldn't approve of their ways, from what I know."

I was aghast. "How could they be so stupid? Can't they see the evidence of the old world's failure all around them? What makes them think they can do better?"

She grinned wryly. "I'm sure they'd have a few choice words for us, too. But one of the most poignant phrases from the old world was 'Those who can't learn from the past are destined to repeat it,' or something to that effect. And it's true. I'm sure you've read your history books. Over and over, humans did the same things. War, exploitation, greed… They never learned very much, or if they did, it was at a glacial pace, or they arrogantly thought *they'd* be the ones to buck the trend, and in the end… Well, here we are. Regardless, even if this crew in Great Toronto is just a bunch of dreamers, if their dream is dangerous to others, it doesn't matter whether they have any hope of achieving it."

Just as she spoke those words, there was a sound like a huge tree breaking and falling very near us. I involuntarily ducked. But then the wind started to die down and the rain slowed almost to nothing. Miraculously, the small fire had sputtered but stayed lit.

"I found this house probably about fifteen years ago and have used it as a way station ever since. We're safe here. It's almost evening now. I suggest we get some sleep and head out early." Elm had pulled a thin blanket from her pack, which was as gigantic as mine, and was already lying down.

"Elm?"

She opened an eye. "Mmm-hmm?"

"Does that mean you're travelling south with me?"

"Well, I was headed that way anyway, and a little company and conversation can be invigorating — for a while. I know it's breaking the rules of your first journey, so you're welcome to send me packing, but I'd say this could be our little secret, eh?" She closed the eye.

I pulled out my own blanket and lay down too, as close to the fireplace as I could. "Yes, I'd like that," I said. There was something comfortable and solid about Elm, something I could lean on. Sometimes even I felt the Seekers had too many rules.

• • •

I woke up abruptly, with the hair on my neck standing up, and listened. All I heard was the faint crackling of the fire, which was small and red with embers but still emitting a small amount of warmth. Surrounding its weak crimson glow, everything was inky black. The air was disturbingly thick, and, working hard to hear, I could detect water dripping from the branches outside, the ever-present mosquitoes buzzing around my head, and, of course, plenty of crickets. I started to relax, figuring maybe my instincts weren't actually well developed enough yet to detect danger in my sleep.

Then I heard something else: a snuffle, then a low bark. I sat up cautiously.

Then I heard something else: a clicking, like chalk on the board in the classroom at home. Seems my subconscious really was a better listener than my conscious mind. Good to know.

I jumped as Elm spoke softly beside me. "Darn, I knew should have rigged up a door to this place when I had the time."

Then every hair on my body stood on end as I heard a growl.

"Oh, shit, Elm, what's that?" I whispered hoarsely. Looking over to the slightly less black outline of the door, I was sure I could now see a shape … or maybe two, and two points glinting in the faint light.

"Jay, get up and get close to the fire."

I was frozen.

Louder, "Jay! Do as I say."

I jumped to my feet and the growl sounded again, more intensely.

I could now make out Elm's form beside me, blocking the weak light of the embers. She leaned down toward the fire. "See how before we turned in, I left the ends of these long, very dry, bark-covered birch branches sticking out a bit? Grab one after I ignite it."

I saw her throw some highly flammable birch-bark kindling right onto the embers. The coals ignited it almost instantly into a small but very bright blaze, flooding the room with light.

Now, at *this* sight I really was ready to wet myself!

A cluster of low but powerful dog-like forms were just inside the door, three — no, four. "Elm? Wolves?" was all I could get out.

"Coyotes," said Elm. "There are thousands of them everywhere. They don't go into Norbay in packs much anymore, but I'm sure you've seen them." I had, but we had doors to hide behind at night.

"Yeah. I thought they didn't hunt in packs."

"They will when they need to."

I could see now that they were smaller than wolves. But they looked thin and hungry. And they were fanning out a bit and inching closer across the floor, growling. All of them.

I grabbed the end of the branch, as she'd told me to do, and advanced, trying to make myself as imposing as possible. "Get!" I yelled as the nearest coyote turned sideways. I thought I had it at bay, but then it turned and leapt at me. I fell backward, thrusting the branch's orange-hot tip at it. The coyote yelped as the coal made contact with its chest, and there was a sudden vile smell of burned fur.

"Jay! Get the hell back here *now*!" I'd only known Elm for a few hours, but I recognized the power of true authority when I heard it. I scrambled backward, almost on all fours, barely keeping a hold on my smoldering branch.

Now she calmly advanced, waving the flaming tip of her branch and speaking gently, so quietly that I couldn't quite make out the words. As her branch and its small flame swept slowly back and forth in front of her, the animals cowered back, still growling. The one I had burned had already backed away to the door. In that moment, Elm seemed as vast as her shadow cast on the wall by the blaze.

Soon, amazingly, the coyotes had backed up completely, then scampered away down the hall, just as the bark kindling started to die down, as quickly as it had ignited. I saw Elm's silhouette turn back and throw more bark and a dry piece of wood on the blaze.

Then she sat down. In the weak yellow flicker, I saw anger on her face.

"Boy, I'm giving you a pass on this one, since you're at the start of your journey and easy to scare. I may not be a rule-follower, but I believe in our principles. And Seekers *do not* harm life unless there's no other choice. We have our ways, and you will learn them."

I felt the hot blood rush to my cheeks. "What, I should have just let it kill one or both of us?"

"Yes!" I heard her take a deep, slow breath. "No. Of course not. But you reacted with fear. One of the things you will learn in a life on the road is danger is everywhere. It can strike at any moment. And in forms far worse than a hungry dog. And if you react with fear, you will lose. Did you not see how you put yourself forward, away from me and the fire, right into the middle of them? The others would have closed around you and attacked."

I felt both ashamed and stupid. "Yes, I see that now," I mumbled.

"If you remember only one thing about our creed, remember we do things *differently*. Even if we risk all, and even if it sounds counter to your own instincts. Our ancestors abused animals for sport, for business, for medicine. Our ancestors eradicated countless species. We are not like them. We don't react with anger or fear. We *think*. We coexist. And if you want to travel with me, you'll follow my guidance and pay attention. If we need to kill or hurt, we do it as a last resort."

"Yes, Elm." I almost said *yes, Cedar,* so similar did they seem in that moment.

She shifted to a cross-legged position. "They may or may not try again. I guess this is really my fault. I should have barricaded the doorway, an old habit I've lost now that bandits are fewer. I take responsibility for my laxness and complacency. We'll put that piece of furniture and some wood over there in front of the door, and I'll take watch and meditate. It'll be morning in no time, so you get some rest."

I didn't protest. I lay down with my head on my pack, looking into the embers, which were dying back down again. I felt lost and ashamed.

Clearly, I had a lot to learn and was lucky to have met Elm. She would be tough, but I was feeling the full weight of my naïveté.

I woke a few times in the night to see Elm had barely moved an inch, still sitting cross-legged on the stone floor like a wise Buddha statue.

VIII.

NOW

JAY

All right, everyone, welcome back. I'm glad to see you're actually all here today. Maybe it's because today's cloudier than yesterday, and I can definitely smell a whole lot of rain coming. Or maybe I'll allow myself to believe it's the quality of my storytelling that has you nailed to your seats!

I was so long-winded yesterday that we had to put off the rest of the story for another day — or two! I'm glad you found it interesting enough to come back.

An old cliché is that there are two sides to every story; the reality is there are multiple sides to every story, and always multiple possible points of view. That's something you only learn later in life.

You've heard about a bushy-tailed young Seeker and his early days on the road, those who helped him and what he saw. I promise the most interesting parts are still to come.

But I thought I might thicken the plot.

When I left here, I was alone. But by the time this story ends, I wasn't alone any more. And despite choosing a life as a Seeker, I was never alone again.

We choose a lonely life, and that impacts our loved ones as well as ourselves; I've seen this play out in my own family. But that doesn't mean you can't still have meaningful relationships, if you find understanding people. And I have been a lucky man to have Birch in my life.

I still am today.

Birch?

• • •

BIRCH

Thank you, Jay. That was very touching. Though these kids aren't here for romance stories. Are you? No, you're here for the complete story of Jay's first big trip and the trouble he got himself into. And he got himself into a significant amount of trouble.

Now, I'm no Seeker. Never was that interested. Don't get me wrong, I approve of what you do and all that. But my own decisions have taken me far and wide, too, sometimes alone, sometimes in present company.

And the first time I went a fair distance from Norbay was when my envy of Jay — okay, maybe there was something else involved, too, as you'll discover — got too great, and combined with my wanderlust, it took me out on the road as well...

IX.

RESTLESS

BIRCH

I'd told myself over and over that Jay leaving wasn't such a big deal. After all, he wasn't leaving permanently, and when I chose a Seeker from a family of Seekers as my promised, I knew what I was getting into. Or did I? I'd thought I could stay detached from the situation and from him, and if it didn't work out, so be it ... plenty of fish in the sea, as one of those weird old expressions goes. Though who knows if there really are plenty of fish left in the oceans? I've traveled far and wide but only saw the ocean once.

In harsher moments, I even told myself I could handle it if he never came back. I was only nineteen; I'd get over it.

I think I was only just starting to realize how much I genuinely loved him. That's kind of a significant statement, as much as it's ever been. In a collectivist community like this one, founded by a group with a unified set of ideals, everyone's full of noble love for their fellow citizens as point of principle, maybe a by-product of there not actually being that many people left to cherish! But true romantic devotion, well, that's the oldest story that ever existed, right? It's the focus of most of human culture, after all.

So, there was that, but it was also mixed with a giant dollop of poisonous jealousy. I had no interest in being sent on missions to poke around the detritus of a vanished civilization, looking for bits and pieces of knowledge that could supposedly help build a newer, better society, then sitting around scratching my head over it and engaging in philosophical debates about it. Wasn't there already enough trash we could use to recycle and rebuild? Was there even a point in envisioning a "better" future for humans, when we were the ones who authored our misfortune? Do we even deserve a better future? It's a valid question and one that wasn't asked enough, I thought.

Frankly, I felt that all of that noble purpose stuff was a pretext, giving the community a reason to exist and a direction, and also a way for the younger people to satisfy their wanderlust while still giving them a reason to come back. There's a monastic utopian tinge to the life of this community, based on ascribing an almost religious significance to knowledge — even though our lifestyle is so simple that more knowledge isn't even that necessary. Or at least that was my opinion at the time...

Anyway, I had that same wanderlust as any young Seeker, in a big way. Bigger, in fact.

My parents were both very settled homebodies: my fathers, satisfied with farming, something they took joy in every day, had adopted me into their home. I had no idea who my birth parents were, and I was sketchy on the details. Everyone else seemed to be too. The story was I'd been found by one of these holy Seekers not too far from Norbay, left right there on the road to Great Sudbury, and brought to the town. My dads didn't seem to know much more, and for some reason I wasn't particularly curious to learn the rest. Just another orphan plucked from the wreckage, I guess. And why should I want to know about someone who would leave me, helpless, at the side of the road to be eaten alive by a scavenger? But I suppose if can analyze myself, some of my cynicism may stem from knowing about this lowly, mysterious beginning.

Now, I was getting to be "of age" and needed to find something productive to do, or people would really start noticing my oddball status. Of course, I helped out with the various tasks around the community; everyone does, and I've never been lazy. But I needed to decide what I wanted to make my main area of focus: there were farmers, builders, engineers to maintain the solar panels and water pipes, teachers, healers, and the other jobs necessary to run a small, self-sufficient community.

And if I wanted to be a trader, I could even travel a bit — within a certain radius of Norbay, that is. Most trading with lands to the west was done through the hub of Great Sudbury. If you spent time there, you would meet all kinds of people from the north and west and hear about the lives they led there, how their communities were organized, and the most notable remains of the civilization in the places they lived. I longed to see those places; hence, that job might be the best I could find.

But I wanted more. I was a reader as well as a doer. I read all kinds of nonfiction books about the old world, this giant place once called North America and the wonders it contained. Of course, the southern parts of it were rumoured to be barely habitable now, if at all, and in my lifetime I'd never even heard a trace of a legend about any recent visitors from below the Great Lakes. We all knew the history, though: how waves of refugees poured north from South America and then the United States of America, overwhelming the borders of the country called Canada and dispersing throughout this landmass, only to be killed off by uncontrolled pandemics and civil strife. Even being in Canada, which apparently had a high opinion of itself as a safe and democratic place, had been no protection from disease and war. Many of my friends from school were descended from those climate refugees. Maybe I was too.

In any case, dangerous or not, I longed to see it all, and that desire was only growing as I neared my twentieth birthday.

• • •

About a week before the departure of Jay to the south, Hawthorn to the east, and Larch to the west, there was one of the frequent community dinners at the restaurant building on Trout Lake that had been fixed up especially to host these get-togethers. A hundred years ago, this was where you'd take your family for special occasions because the food was more expensive; in the old days, you celebrated landmarks with lavish spending.

Attendance wasn't mandatory, of course; nothing was ever really mandatory in Norbay. Fear of letting everyone else down was usually enough to keep us productive. But these dinners were nice. You could just drop in, have some food and conversation, sing a bit. I usually enjoyed them.

There was a very beautiful view of the still, deep waters, and it being a temperate night that promised a lovely many-hued sunset, we were all relaxing inside and outside the building after filling ourselves with vegetables, beans, bread, and fruit. Some people were singing in pretty rough harmony, and everyone else was joining in when they felt like it.

I found myself on the edge of the party, sitting beside that venerable Elder, Cedar. I didn't intend that; I have to admit I'd always been a little cool and wary with her, not completely trusting someone so high up in the Seekers leadership and so gung-ho for the whole thing. They were all just so damn sure of themselves that I found it irritating and intimidating.

Yet here I was, somehow in an unwanted conversation about myself with this nosey Elder. No sooner had I made a vague remark about the weather than she launched into her interrogation.

Cedar may have been known for her subtlety of mind, but not of speech; she could be very blunt. "So, Birch, how goes your search for your life's path? Getting closer?"

Life's path. Give me a break, I thought but politely said, "I'm still not really sure, Elder. But I know that I need to decide soon."

She chuckled. "Well, pressuring you isn't my intention in asking, believe me. I'm sure you're pressuring yourself enough. Don't stress yourself out. My generation had serious problems to deal with, but not that kind of choice. Our only choice was to survive … or not."

"I know there's no comparison," I said, trying not to sound annoyed at being reminded of their heroism and suffering compared with my privileged indecision.

"Wasn't suggesting you thought that. But you know, there are options available to you. I know you chafe against the quietness of our life here."

I looked at her directly for the first time. "Is it that obvious?"

She laughed again. "Sure is. But you know, you're a really smart kid. That doesn't escape notice. There are other options, as I say. If you, for example, take an interest in helping run this place, there may be options that allow you to travel farther; like, as in diplomatic ones. For example, we have a representative of Moosonee coming down here in a few days. There are settlements throughout the area and even farther away with which we have agreements for trade and mutual aid. That takes an intelligent, diplomatic mind, since each of these communities is governed in a different way, and they all have their own perceived interests."

I almost laughed myself. That did *not* sound like me. "I think you might be giving me too much credit, Elder. A diplomat?"

Now she grinned broadly. "Maybe it sounds unattractive at the moment, Birch. But it won't always. Even an impulsive nature can even out as life goes by. In fact, it can eventually make for a very decisive and effective leader."

"You know that about me, do you?"

"I can guess it."

My annoyance had rushed back, harder, at this presumption that she knew anything about me, and my need to be polite started to evaporate. "To be honest, Elder, I'm not that sure I even *want* to represent the interests of this community. I'm not sure I even *agree* with the interests of this community. *That's* part of my problem."

Her smile remained but faded considerably. She scooped up her plate. "I think I'll get seconds. And Birch, believe it or not, it's not abnormal to feel the way you do. Many have felt that way. Even I have had my doubts over the years. No citizen is ever asked to leave here. That's not our way, no matter what you may think of the rest of what we do and stand for. But that, then, is the big decision you have to make. If you can't be happy here, where *can* you be happy, and what will make you so? Because someone denied their contentment and fulfillment can have a very negative effect on those around them. Their bitterness is like a disease eating away at them, and it always causes fallout. It can waste a life. You don't want to be a person who does that."

With that, she was gone back to the big table for more of the beans that featured so heavily at every meal, in this staid town in a deathly quiet land where nothing exciting ever seemed to happen but the odd tornado, wildfire, and derecho.

I knew something had to give for me, but I had no idea what and when it would happen. But it would.

And soon, Jay, the one overwhelmingly positive factor keeping me here, would be gone into a new life and would likely forget all about me. All I could think about was all those Seekers, and there had been several that I knew of, who never came back.

Was giving in to the feeling of love even worth it?

• • •

The day after Jay left, all of my anger and boredom and longing were bubbling to the surface. I was at loose ends, full of jittery, angry energy. This was a cathartic moment, and something really *did* have to give. And that was when I ran into Oak.

Jay's younger brother was quiet too but had a lighter, more playful personality. And he didn't have much thirst for knowledge; he was always active, picking, planting, building, singing, and happy doing any of those. He was going to make a model citizen someday, very good support staff for our noble Seekers. And he was completely devoted to Jay.

A nice thing was, since I was Jay's promised, and anything Jay did or anyone he knew did was gold to Oak, it meant Oak was also devoted to me. In fact, on the surface we had a lot more in common, like a love of movement; we could dance up a storm at community events while Jay was happy to sit nearby and listen to the singing and guitars and violins. I used to race Oak and always win, until he hit puberty and his limbs became powerful from all the manual labour. Sometimes I used to wrestle him into submission; that was a thing of the past too.

Still, it was Jay that stirred me. The things we had in common were deeper — we could roam for hours and watch out for wildlife, or try to pick out constellations from a tattered astronomy book by lamplight. We could talk about anything. Jay was the one who made me complete, in the way that has always been a mystery to those who try to figure out what true love really "is."

I wondered how Oak really felt about his brother, only a year older, taking off into the wilds on one of the guild's crazy missions, which, as you know by now, I felt were based entirely on an abstract principle and not on anything that could practically benefit us or anyone else. What had they ever brought back that had actually been put to good use? Well, I supposed there had to be a few things, but in my mood, I wasn't prepared to acknowledge any of it. Maybe I should have been paying more attention.

Anyway, that day I actually met Oak about halfway up the steep, dry, rocky trail up the escarpment (it had once been something called a "gas line" cutting that supplied the town with heat). I was going up fast, watching my footing and enjoying the discomfort of the lactic acid building up from ascending too quickly, and he was going down at a pretty good clip. It was about 6:00 p.m. and the sun was sinking, so the heat wasn't too overpowering. He skidded to a halt, bracing his foot against a large projecting stone before he could topple and tumble down the incline.

"How you taking it?" he asked with barely any preamble.

"Taking what?" I knew what he meant but wasn't taking the bait.

"Lover boy leaving for a while." Oak stood facing out onto the view of green hilltops far in the hazy distance. I turned too and could see an ominous fire haze heading our way; the sun was already more orange-tinged than yellow. That could mean a smoke fog was on the way. I couldn't smell it yet, though.

"I should ask you the same. You guys are almost inseparable when he's not in that classroom."

He crouched, plucked a long blade of grass, and stuck the end between his teeth. "Yeah. Well, I can admit I miss him already, but he's doing exactly what he wants. And helping pass on the skills of the Seekers to a new generation."

Now that anger of mine started to rise again. "Great, great."

"I'm sensing some displeasure." I turned to see him grinning stupidly.

"It's not actually that funny, Oak. I'm worried about him. I'm bored. I'm directionless. I'm pissed off all the time. I'm not sure how long I can handle it, to be honest. I'm reaching a breaking point. I don't know why."

I was surprised all that came out of me; I hadn't intended it, and I'd never been that frank with him, or even with myself or Jay.

Oak perched on one of the granite boulders jutting out of the slope. "I see."

"Do you?" I glared down at him. "Because all I've gotten is a bunch of wise mumbling from Cedar and my dads, predicting how my personality will eventually 'even out' and 'mature,' and there are so many wonderful jobs I can do to serve the community, blah blah, and I don't need any more of it from you."

"No, no." He leaned back to look up at me square in the face. "I get it. I really do. I mean, I don't feel the same things, but I think I can imagine what it's like to feel unfulfilled, like you've got nowhere to spend your energy in the way you want to. I'd hate that."

I was relieved. "Exactly." I sat down beside him hard enough that I felt the rock digging into my bones and looked back out over the landscape.

After a long moment, he said, "Okay, then you have to go."

I didn't answer right away. I felt something new surging inside me and was a little overwhelmed at receiving any support at all. I gazed out again. There were a couple of tiny birds zipping past in the near distance, taking joy in their freedom of movement. For some reason, at that moment I thought of what we had learned in school about the loss of thousands of species in the last two hundred years, one of the largest mass extinctions in the history of the planet. Presumably, species were still dying off every year from the aftereffects. And here I was, not seeing anything of what was left of a once vibrant ecosystem. Stuck doing what? Farming? Teaching kids about things I'd never seen and never would? Diplomatic negotiations with the town of Kirkland Lake on stocks of cranberries? I was missing out on living while I was young and able. I was missing out on seeing what was left of Earth while there was still something to appreciate.

No.

"Yes, I have to go. I'll find Jay, and we'll travel together. It'll be safer that way. He hasn't had that big of a head start, and I'm in better shape than him. I know the route he's supposed to take; he showed me. And to hell with Cedar and her gang."

Oak stood up. "I'll help you round up some supplies. And my bike is in better shape because you're so rough on yours." He looked much more serious than usual. "I'm going to get in major shit for this, but it's the right thing to do. I love you like a sister, Birch. It hurts to see you so sad. Go see what's out there." He crouched down again.

At that moment I couldn't speak. I just put my head on his shoulder, and we sat in silence for a while longer.

X.

BARRIE

JAY

Elm turned out to be a very agreeable travelling companion. Despite her age, she kept up with me quite well and even set the pace at times, though she did slow a bit as the morning wore on. She knew a lot about the land of Ontario and even places far beyond it, that was for sure. Running into her and travelling with her may not have been in the rulebook, but I had a feeling this was a stroke of luck that would be greatly to my benefit. This woman had seen more than anyone I'd ever met and was willing to talk about it all.

There was a lot of overcast this day, but the clouds didn't look threatening, and since it wasn't as humid as usual and there was a surprisingly fresh breeze, we kept going without taking an afternoon break. Elm reckoned it would take six or seven hours to reach Barrie, a fairly large and sprawling city, now deserted, or at least it was when she was last there not long ago. The city had been the site of fighting during the civil conflicts, as well as decimation by pandemics, and was just north of a huge refugee camp, or "concentration camp," as Elm muttered. I figured I'd ask more about those later. It had been mentioned in our classes, but just as another example of the terrible chaos of the Ruin, not as something anyone we knew would have experienced directly.

Since it was cloudy, there were still swarms of biting bugs around, despite the breeze. Elm paid no notice to them at all, while I found myself constantly waving an arm around my head and almost unbalanced a few times. She didn't remark on that but did look amused each time it happened.

Along the way, when I could ride parallel to her, I quizzed her more about her long life on the roads. She claimed to have no regrets about any of it.

"The idea is we're building a new sense of community from the ground up, and the missions are just to provide the information necessary for the coming rebuild and renewal. I get that. I actually agree wholeheartedly. But we're all different. I was always a solitary kid right from the start, with parents who didn't keep an eye on me all the time, out in the woods poking around, making friends with forest beasts. I had no time for adult questions, no time for sports and parties. I needed to be alone to feel safe, as counterintuitive as that sounds. I'm surprised more kids of my generation weren't like me, to be honest. Our start in life was … traumatic. And then it got worse."

Her face looked a little grim, but I decided to press for more. The Elders were forthcoming about a lot of stuff, but their formative years always seemed to be off-limits for discussion.

"Do you mean the camps?"

"Yes."

"I mean, you don't have to talk about it, but we're supposed to be preventing history repeating, and that's going to be harder when we don't know stuff that happened in our own Elders' lifetimes and that they experienced."

She barked out a short laugh and stopped pedaling. "*Know stuff*? You don't know enough? Let me tell you, then, Jay, if it hasn't sunk in yet. When the last semblance of civilization was clinging on, people did what they have always done when they're frightened: they looked for strength to lead them. Any strength, any leader who seems tough enough. Humanity is a herd creature. They were terrified for their families, the world they knew was ending, and they'd believe anyone who would lie to them and tell them what would comfort them, someone who seemed to offer tangible protection for them and their families. And as always, that strength was often expressed brutally. They elected rulers who in the end did away with democracy altogether. Who enacted policies designed to keep refugees out, and those that got over the border they put in concentration camps, where they didn't feed them properly, or provide proper sanitation, or a hope of a future, and if the refugees tried to escape, they shot them. And then ... worse things happened. All of this within a decade."

I was confused. "But you weren't a refugee, right? You're from Ontario."

"Yes, Jay, born and bred, near Barrie, in fact. What you don't know, I guess, is that it didn't end with the refugees. If you lost your job, if you couldn't support your family any more — and there weren't many jobs when there wasn't really any economy left — they eventually decided to put people like that in the camps too. Some of the camps for 'upstanding' citizens had better food and shelter and were called relief camps, but they put you to work doing menial or backbreaking labour."

"Is that where you and your family were?"

"At the start." She squinted up into the monochromatic cloud cover, still straddling the frame of her bike. "But it was discovered that my parents were radicals, or what they considered radical, calling for democracy to return and the truth to be told about the climate crisis, which of course the government tried to downplay despite the obviousness of what was happening everywhere. They even tried to organize the labourers in the relief camp to support one another. We ended up in a refugee camp. I was just a little kid and didn't understand what was happening."

She abruptly mounted her bike again and started riding, deftly dodging gaping holes, cracks, and shrubs. "And I saw things there that I'll never unsee. I lost family and friends there. We only got to leave when the last vestiges of civilization dissolved and even the government thugs lost hope and dispersed, leaving us starving, diseased, and in rags."

I felt I'd gone too far in my prying. "I'm sorry."

She looked over and flashed a sudden, yellow-toothed smile. "It's okay, kid. You're right. They always used to say about the Holocaust of the mid-twentieth-century that we should never forget. But we did. And we do. Over and over. The Seekers are right about one thing: we must remember, and we must remind ourselves over and over again. The horror has to end sometime, or what's the point of humanity existing at all? What's so great about us if we *still* can't live together without war and oppression? Our original unofficial motto at the start was something to the effect of 'the only way out of this mess is to be fully present and awake at all times.' We got through it, but we needed more than just survival as a goal. So we chose renewal — but not unless it was done the right way."

There was a long silence as we skirted the fallen deck of a peculiar bridge that looked like it was made for pedestrians, not cars. For some reason, there was an early twentieth century rail car on the left side of the road amongst the debris of a restaurant.

"This place was famous for selling hamburgers. In the old days, people were absolutely bonkers for hamburgers, which was basically ground-up cow meat mixed with spices and onions and served on a bun."

"I know what a hamburger is, Elm."

"All right, all right. Anyway, people were absolutely obsessed with that dish. No wonder the rainforests were all cut down for grazing land. People on vacation used to stop at this particular hamburger stand as some kind of summer ritual. I suppose it must have had the best hamburgers in the province or something, or people were convinced it did. The rail car was an added gimmick."

"Did your parents ever go there?"

She smiled. "Naw. My dad always said people who did the things everyone else did were followers and hence dangerous and stupid. He instilled an independent, stubborn streak in me. And a cynicism. Though he had me beat on that. But it's probably why I've never been a comfortable Seeker. I started all gung-ho and bushy-tailed, but it wore off fast and caused a lot of conflict."

I sensed I was about to receive some wisdom more valuable than facts about popular meals of the olden days, so I stayed silent and focused on pedaling.

"Life on the road is simple as can be. Easy. Clean. Closer to nature. As far as we know, we're the only species on the planet that is fully sentient. Ever think about that? And thus the only one that can truly suffer, because it's the only one that is *aware* it's suffering; that can suffer an existential crisis. Unless there are still dolphins and octopi out in the oceans somewhere, and maybe they feel something like that. I doubt it."

"I guess I never thought about that."

She chuckled. "A scholar, but not a philosopher, eh? You tend to think about these things more as you age. When I'm by myself, I can forget that each person is an island of suffering, surrounded by an ocean of peace, of nature getting on with things. Nature contains suffering, but its sufferings are shorter and more merciful than ours. And no matter what we do to it, it eventually recovers and gets on with things again. While we continue to suffer; they used to call it 'the human condition,' and billions of pages were wasted on trying to figure out what went wrong with us, why sentience wasn't working for us, what purpose it served. Not to mention all the competing philosophies, political ideologies, religions, et cetera, that we use to convince ourselves we're more important than the rest of the life around us ... and other people around us."

I decided to venture another dicey question. "And this ... cynicism wasn't well received by the other Seekers?"

There was that harsh, quick bark again. "You could say that. I had other reasons to leave, too ... relationships there that became too hard. See? I sound wise, but not even I'm immune to the human condition. But like I said, I regret nothing. I've lived the life I wanted. I've lived to be old by anyone's standards. I've done what I felt was right. And what feels right at the moment is making sure your ass is kept safe for a while."

"Thanks... I appreciate it."

After that, she clammed up for almost the entire ride into Barrie but did some not-very-musical humming that I found more soothing than irritating.

• • •

As we neared Barrie, we saw more and more ruined houses and businesses lining the road. And soon the highway doubled in width. In places, the holes and crevices in the asphalt were so wide and deep that it looked like a bomb had been dropped on them. Maybe it had. Soon after that, we were surrounded by the ruins of big, multistorey buildings, similar to what I'd seen in parts of Great Sudbury but much more dilapidated. Up on the left on a rise were the blackened, skeletal walls of a clump of buildings that Elm said had been a hospital.

She had recovered her good humour, but in a macabre sort of way. "Welcome to the dead city! One of many, yes, but quite a few of your fellow Norbay citizens trace their roots back to this place. When it was destroyed and emptied, it had a population of nearly two hundred and fifty thousand people, though a lot had fled by the time it became a battle zone. This was in the late 2050s or roundabout, after any semblance of a government collapsed. People got a hold of actual weaponry, guns, army gear. Two factions fought over the city, which controlled a lot of the resources around here. The government and a breakaway group. Not that either of those groups would have been kinder to the refugees, so it ultimately didn't matter which side won. Within a few years, they had almost razed the place. The fighting was brutal. I know, because this is near where I was born."

I didn't know what to say. This graveyard had once been a flourishing, peaceful city where Elm's parents may have hoped to raise her in some sort of leafy suburban paradise, in the face of such stark knowledge. That outcome would never come to pass. It was chilling to think of the petrifying fears billions of people suffered during those years.

"C'mon, kid. We'll have a short tour. Why not?" Elm veered off at the next exit ramp, and we bumped down it onto a street that was totally taken over by weeds. Left and right as we pedaled, we saw the remains of a seemingly endless sea of fast-food restaurants and big-box stores, the prefab concrete of the latter crumbled or blasted away and only girders left rusting in the elements. Vegetation had almost taken over most of it. I could smell something odd mixed with the usual plant smells, something greasy.

There were vast amounts of rusty bits of cars and trucks strewn everywhere amongst the encroaching greenery, and downed wires were flung over everything.

A shattered plastic sign near us that was surprisingly intact, although lying on the street, said *im Hortons.*

"Ah, yes. Tim's." Elm shook her head like she was at the gravesite of a friend who'd met a tragic end.

"Yeah, what was the big deal about that place?" I asked. "Even in Norbay, you see signs of it everywhere, and in Sudbury too. Old trash, old signs. That place must have been weirdly important to people. McDonald's, too."

She snorted. "You could say that. It was a form of ritual. Social bonding. That's the nice way to put it. Though fast food existed because people of the past had no patience, and also despite the increasing automation of life, their lives got busier instead of less cluttered. They worked and worked and bought and bought, and when they had time to eat they bought over-packaged junk full of salt and sugar, and they bought them at these places because they'd come to feel at home there."

I really did sometimes find the people of the past confusing. "So they had all this technology they developed, and they thought it would make life easier..."

"For some, it did." Elm turned off this main road filled with the memories of ancient capitalism into the remains of a subdivision. "But for most, it meant they had to be even more productive, and the eyes of their masters were on them all their waking hours — sometimes even when they slept. And with their addiction to what they called 'social media' on top of it — I'm sure you've been taught all about that horror — and the knowledge starting to sink in that they'd screwed up the climate, they were a pretty miserable bunch. I guess they needed that sugar. But as to why they chose to patronize the same dining establishments over and over... I guess we'll have to chalk that up to conditioning and familiarity."

This subdivision we entered was full of larger houses, for the most part, than we had in Norbay. They had huge garages intended to be filled with multiple vehicles. In a couple of driveways sat the hulks of pleasure boats. Everything was completely wrecked, though, and some brickwork even seemed blackened by fires.

Elm looked grim. "This would have been a hellish scene toward the end. Likely, though, it was a storm or ten that helped flatten the rest of this place. Even before the twenty-first century, this area was known for severe weather like tornadoes and blizzards."

This made me curious about something. "So, Elm, if Barrie was a tenth the size of Great Toronto, and it was destroyed like this, then what is Great Toronto like?"

"I don't know," she said thoughtfully. "I used to. I haven't been there for so long... It mostly wasn't this bad — it wasn't fought over like this — but it's a really big place, so who knows? I do know that no one is going in there right now that comes back out. And there's those rumours about the place, the dark ones about what they're up to with that new government. I'm kind of maddeningly curious about it myself."

My blood quickened. "Does that mean…?"

She shook her head. "I don't know. Haven't made my mind up. We'll see when we get closer. Now, we should get out of here. Turns out you're only getting a short tour. The place gives me the heebie-jeebies, as my grandfather used to say." She turned her bike around to head back to the highway.

Just then, out of the corner of my eye, I thought I saw a shape moving, a human shape, about a block away, flitting around the corner of a side lot. Had I seen the long grass swishing in their wake?

"Elm?"

"I saw. Could have been an animal, but maybe not. I think we'd best be on our way. Everywhere *looks* deserted, but you never know who's lurking. And the people who lurk in a solitary way down here are usually people you don't want to meet. Not friendly old wandering hermits like me. I know a much safer place nearby with a secure, dry basement where we can bunk down. No fires tonight. Not safe enough. So we'll be eating cold food."

I didn't need to be told twice. I set the pace on the way out of the neighbourhood and looked forward to avoiding the place from this point on.

XI.

FREEDOM?

BIRCH

I wasn't what you'd call an early riser, but I knew if I was going to avoid a major scene with the dads that would inevitably end up with me staying, not because they'd demand but because they'd plead, I'd better be up at dawn. Fortunately, despite being so very into the whole farming thing, neither of them was up before six thirty most days — not exactly conforming to the old agricultural stereotype. But then there was no shortage of helping hands in the gardens.

It felt strange and inconsiderate to be sneaking out like this, and I knew I'd have regrets about that, but I was also strangely sure that I'd see them again. It wasn't like I never wanted to be in town ever again. I just wanted to be there on my terms, when I wanted. And that life would start now.

It was very dull and grey, though it was actually one of those days when it *should* have been bright. The pumpkin-shaded rising sun would soon try to penetrate the noxious smoke layer, but it wouldn't be very successful. That was about a third of the days from March through November, though not all of them were bad enough to be considered a "smoke fog."

I'd clandestinely packed what I could scrape together while the dads were out for a walk last night, mostly dried food, water, and a couple of changes of clothes; I'd laundered my clothes in a creek a few times while camping in the bush, and I knew that a pack could get really heavy, really fast. Best to travel light. Oak had backed down on giving me his bike, which he loved, but had promised to get me a better one (mine had a few dents from plummeting down the steep escarpment and was rusty as well) and a few other things. He'd also promised to have a word with my dads after I left. I covered for him by writing a note he'd supposedly find, addressed to him, explaining my actions and asking him to inform the dads.

I briefly stroked Violet, the fluffy grey cat who sometimes lived with us when she wanted company, sat down on the floor to put on my hardiest pair of boots, and slipped out the door of our house on Norman Avenue. I have no idea who Norman was or why he, or anyone else for that matter, ever deserved to have a whole street named after him. Just another example of the rampant egotism of the people of the old world, I suppose.

A five-minute walk through streets silent but for birdcalls brought me to Oak's house. Somewhere in the near distance, a rooster started crowing. The smog suffused the breaking sunlight with an eerie yellowy-orange glow.

Oak was waiting under the "carport," something people who couldn't afford garages for their car had installed. The town was full of them; maybe this hadn't been a very wealthy town.

He'd come through. One of those rare giant backpacks sat beside him, as well as a bike so well maintained, it practically gleamed in the weak light.

I crunched as quietly as possible up the steep, gravelled driveway.

"Only the best," Oak said proudly in a low voice.

"Nice wheels ... thanks. Where'd you get that?"

"Pulled in a favour. And..." He grinned. "You'll see that the crossbar is lower, which was the way well-bred ladies preferred their bikes back when they were more delicate creatures than they are today."

I punched him on the arm. "Maybe we should trade, then, you little shit. Thanks, though." I had started transferring my possessions to the big pack, reaching all the way down inside, when I felt something jutting out at the bottom.

"Careful, there!" Oak exclaimed quietly.

I pulled out a long, thin item and immediately realized what it was. "Holy shit."

"Be careful with that, please. If they knew I had that, they might use it on me."

I rolled my eyes. "I doubt that. They'd probably sentence you to a few years on the microfiche machine or lentil harvesting instead."

I pulled the knife free from its sheath. It was shiny and looked sharp.

"They used this for hunting. Now all of these are locked up. But a Seeker or Seeker-adjacent person can still get their hands on one if they really want to. I honestly hated the idea of Jay being out there unarmed, and I don't like the idea of you going that way any better."

I was moved. I threw my arms around him, and he slowly returned the gesture. "Thanks, buddy. I knew you cared. I don't know how you pulled all this off, but I owe *you* a favour."

After we broke apart, he stood back and scrutinized me. He looked sleepy still, but his gaze was steady and serious. "Are you totally sure you want to do this? It's just not safe out there."

"And why not me? Because it's not some official, noble 'mission'?" I challenged. "It's okay for all kinds of other people to be sent out there into danger, as long as it's part of our *mission*."

He hung his head sheepishly. "Look, I'd rather everyone stayed out of trouble if I had my way. But I'm helping you, aren't I? It's even more dangerous for women, right? It has to be."

"They should try something on me."

He raised his head and laughed. "True. But watch where you go, okay? There are some definitely dangerous people out there. And stay away from Great Toronto. There's all this weird news coming out of there. I've heard people talking about it."

I'd heard a bit too, but it was really vague. "Weird how? There's a cult that eats people?"

"Could you take things seriously for once?" His voice sounded strained.

"Sorry, sorry. Listening."

"A few people who were down there have managed to talk to people who live in the area. I overheard Cedar talking to Dad about it at the big send-off dinner the other night. They say that the Six want to revive the old world and have set up their own regime in the town. They want to start using petroleum and making plastics, people say; they basically want that world back, and anyone who disagrees with them gets imprisoned or gets put in a labour camp. They're the opposite of us in every way. They're dangerous. More dangerous than the gangs you've been warned about, or isolated hermits, or whatever. Don't go near there. I'm not sure what the Elders are going to do about it if Great Toronto finds out about us, but it sounds like it could be bad."

Honestly, I was tired of hearing all this and retorted, "First, all that sounds like bullshit. Plastics? And has it occurred to you that this might just be fear-mongering? That those people might just better and quicker at getting organized and getting on with what needs to be done than we have been, and the Elders don't want us to know?"

He stepped back a little. "What do you mean?"

I could feel my voice unwisely rising but didn't hold back. "All this gathering, all this talking and analysis … all the procrastination. All this living off the scraps of whatever we can find from a world that had all these wonderful things. But we condemn them for it all when we're more than happy to help ourselves to their stuff when it's useful. Doesn't that seem a little hypocritical to you?"

"Birch, I don't know…"

I had a head of steam now. "Maybe these people realize that the only way forward is to restart and try to figure things out as they go along. Maybe they're not that bad. But nooo, they aren't basically a community of cloistered monks, like this one, so they must be eeeevill. And yet no one's met any of them or even set foot in their community. Well, maybe I'll have to pay them a visit."

"Birch—"

I sighed loudly. "Okay, okay. I'm sorry, Oak. I just get tired of all this sanctimonious crap. I promise I won't go near the big, bad Six. I'm just heading out for a while on a journey of self-discovery. You know what to tell my dads. Tell them I won't be gone long. Even if I actually *intend* to be gone a lot longer. And you know no one's going to come after me and put themselves in danger. They'll just shake their heads, sigh, and go about their business."

I stowed the knife away, hefted the pack onto my back, and hopped up on the bike. "And thanks for the new wheels. I owe you!"

I pushed off down the driveway and decided not to look back to see if he was waving.

• • •

Unfortunately, things didn't go well. First, the guys at the entrance to town hailed me and came out to ask questions. At least they were doing their job properly. I told them I was just going on a brief adventure close to town to camp for a night and to pick some berries, no big deal. I'd known these guys since I was a kid, so they didn't ask any more questions, but they seemed suspicious about the size of my pack, so I figured they'd probably tell on me to the first person they saw.

Then, I made it to the knocked-down green sign for "Powassan," about an hour or so out and only about an hour away from the farthest distance I'd ever been from Norbay, and I was rejoicing loudly at finally seizing the freedom of the road when there was a major shift in the already hazy atmosphere.

I'd been riding in an almost dreamlike state, imagining what this road would have looked like in its prime: four lanes of perfect asphalt populated by gleaming vehicles that could whiz you to a destination hundreds of kilometres away in a few hours, full of clean, nice-smelling people with clothes they changed every year according to style, taking "vacations" and "getaways" from their busy lives. Majestic trees would have surrounded the highway, not the scrubby younger ones that struggled out of the ash fields and crawling shrubbery a lot of the landscape had been reduced to.

I couldn't help but feel mournful at these thoughts. I just wasn't made for this life of scavenging, chin-scratching, and vegetable gardens; I had the mind of a scientist and an adventurer, I was told, but those jobs didn't really exist anymore. There was study going on, but it was slow, methodical, and not very experimental. It was all analyzing, no action so far. All we could do was figure out how to use the remnants of their technology and make the best of things. Or at least that's how it would be for a long, long time to come if the Seekers had their way.

If I'd been born in, say, the 1970s, a *long* time ago, I could have been a famous researcher and cured some disease; I could have been a deep-sea explorer or a climate scientist. I could have been any number of things. Now I was just another member of a commune preparing for a life of building sheds and growing zucchini.

I started to smell it first: like a giant campfire. Then the sky grew hazy, and the tangerine-like sun was almost completely obscured. Soon it was almost like dusk; everything looked foggy, and even though the wind was up, everything was blanketed in smoke. This meant that a really, really large fire was burning somewhere close by, to the north and west, and the shift in weather patterns was sending its nasty fug down on our region. I mean, this happened about twice a month, but we could just lock ourselves in our houses and put on some good old-fashioned twenty-first-century plague masks, of which there were such large stocks that we would likely never run out, to filter the worst. Which didn't prevent a lot of the senior citizens in the community from having respiratory problems and cancers, but hey, no one said life after the apocalypse would be a party.

Anyway, this was a terribly bad smoke fog, and I could make myself sick just by exerting myself in it for an hour. This was shit luck. I put on a mask, one of the good N95 ones, which we tied around the back with twine — the original elastic bands had disintegrated long ago — and went off on a side road in search of some sort of reasonably sealed building. I wondered if Jay was doing the same somewhere not far down the road.

And I wondered if he was safe, or if he was scared and lonely. Some of my cocky resolve was already starting to drain away.

Great. I just got out of town and I'm already going to be choked to death, I thought.

That was kind of an exaggeration, but the smoke fog really was toxic and not something you wanted to be out in. But there was no way I was going to turn back.

Coughing, I saw a cluster of buildings in the hazy distance, almost totally encompassed by the forest, and fought the gusts to get there, feeling faint. I needed to find one that still had windows, or a basement that wasn't flooded, or at least a somewhat sealed shed. Worst case, I'd have to bury myself in the thickest vegetation I could find.

Fortunately, one of these turned out to be an actual house surrounded by collapsed outbuildings. Of course, there were no doors or intact windows. I stepped in, testing the floor, as we always did when entering a house. It seemed firm, so I went down the hallway and found the basement stairs. I was desperate to get out of the poisonous air, but I knew better than to race down rotting wooden steps. They held, and I found myself in a cellar, an "unfinished basement." Miraculously, there were no signs of flooding, and the light that seeped in through a cobwebbed window was filtered through unbroken glass. It still stank of mould, though.

I sank into a corner by a rusty metal shelving unit with stacks of paper covered in layers of grime, cobwebs, and dust. Not much of the smoke would get down here, but I'd have to keep my mask on.

This really was terrible luck. The wind could change again, and the smog could lighten, or the weather pattern could set in over the region for days and pour this stuff in as long as the fire was raging. In which case I'd have a choice to make: my food wouldn't last for days, and I wouldn't be able to leave to forage without taking chances, in which case I might as well just head home with my tail between my legs — or keep going and risk getting sick.

I made myself a bit more comfortable on the concrete and pulled idly at the stack of paper beside me. It turned out to be magazines. I peeled one away from the middle of the pile.

Of course, Norbay's archives contained a lot of magazines, usually ones about science and technology and economics and politics. This stained, ripped relic said *Hustler* on the cover. Opening it, I saw page after page of photos of naked women without body hair, their legs open, showing off every last bit of their anatomy. *Ew.*

I'd seen one of these before; kids were still kids, after all, and things like that got passed around … *for our education*, we'd all say if someone saw. I guess in the old world they had their own mating rituals, and things like this must have been part of them. It seemed bizarre. Maybe I shouldn't judge things I didn't understand. Still, I felt kind of nauseous looking at the images, so I tossed the magazine aside and reached for a different stack.

This one said *Architectural Digest,* and the photo spreads inside were of immaculately maintained, shiny, and new-looking properties larger than anything I'd ever seen in the selection of ruins we often visited in the Norbay area — larger even than the ones on top of the escarpment, where the upper crust used to live. These looked like white, gleaming fantasy castles to me, each surrounded by wide, emerald-hued, close-cropped lawns.

I guessed these magazines represented two different kinds of pornography, and I knew that the people of the old world had maintained a strong interest in many kinds of it. They juggled lots of addictions.

It reminded me that I probably shouldn't be quite so eager to romanticize the decadent, shallow civilization that chewed up and spat out my ancestors. Things were more complex than the black-and-white view my bitterness created.

I shook my head at the thought of the owners of this house enjoying both kinds of magazine. The people of the past were very strange … and there were definitely things better left unrevived.

I put down the second boring, surreal magazine, found a torn couch cushion to rest on, and settled down to wait.

XII.

THE CAMP

JAY

After my third night away from home — and it felt a lot longer than that — we rode on toward Great Toronto, the mighty, sprawling, glittering metropolis that once dominated the entire country. I learned more and more about Elm as she revealed more bits and pieces. She'd led an interesting life, to say the least. Her travels had taken her far over the former borders into places like Manitoba and Quebec; she'd even gone far south of Great Toronto, around the great lake there, and seen the giant waterfall that once formed the border with the empire of the United States. She said that even though its flow was a fraction of its former glory, the waterfall was a truly amazing miracle to behold, and all Seekers brave enough should head down that far at least once before they died. And she'd even ventured beyond that but wouldn't say much about it other than the destruction and death and the desolation left behind were even worse in those places.

There were some less educated people in our community who said the eradication of the United States was fully deserved, since that country was responsible for the economic philosophy of consumerism and consumption that had gripped the world and led to its downfall. In other words, they had it coming. The more educated, usually Seekers, felt compassion for everyone who had been seduced by the addiction of consumerism and knew it had affected all of the world's nations like a virus.

Elm's life of solitary travel had been punctuated by occasional rest stops in Norbay to visit friends, and it became clear from her anecdotes that despite her independent spirit, she still sometimes served as a kind of scout, providing helpful information about other communities and even occasionally acting as a kind of envoy. The land may not have been heavily populated, but it held a diverse array of different kinds of small communities, and it was important to avoid conflict between them. Norbay's influence had gradually grown in the last three decades, since we were so prosperous and well governed.

Given her age, I was curious about some of her connections, so I asked, "You must know the other Elders well?"

She chuckled dryly as her legs continued to pump out a slow, steady rhythm on the pedals. It was hot, but there was still some cloud cover and a relatively fresh breeze. The heavy, flooding fall rains and chilly temperatures of fall and winter weren't too far away. I was hoping to beat them home, but it would be close. Though a bit of cold rain might be a relief right now.

"Yes, you could say that. I knew some of them *very* well. Very well indeed."

A typically cryptic answer. I decided to press further. "Like...?"

"Well, I know your instructor."

"Cedar?"

"The very same. We basically grew up together. We have a long history. A *very* long one." There was an odd tone in her voice.

"Sorry, am I bringing up something bad?"

There was that dry chuckle again. "Bad? No." She stopped pedaling. The trees surrounding us here were very scrubby, I guess because this had once been farmland, and despite decades of growth, the land hadn't quite filled in to look like a proper forest. There were a lot more hunks of rust that were once vehicles around here as well; they were scattered everywhere. It seemed we were entering the heartland of what had been the province of Ontario.

"I can tell you're a very inquisitive sort. Probably a good thing, considering your choice of career. So, I'll be blunt without violating my own privacy. I may have left Norbay, but a piece of me is always there. A big, important piece. A long time ago, I had to make a choice between a settled life with someone who loved me and the life I thought I really wanted. And you know which I chose. Does that come with occasional regrets? Of course. But we can't go back and change our choices, and I've had a good life. I'm still alive and kicking after all this!"

"Do you ever think of heading back and settling down now that you're..." I trailed off.

Now her laugh was a full-belly cackle. "What? Say it, kid? Ancient? Decrepit? Infirm? Ready for the grave?"

"I didn't mean—"

"No offence taken, Jay. To someone your age I must seem as old as these bizarre remnants of the civilization that spawned me we see around us. And I actually am. Believe me, I'm listening to my body and my mind, and when the time is right, I'll decide what to do. But if you give up on yourself early and decide you're finished ... *that's* when you become old. At least that's been my observation. And that ain't happening to me. I'll do as I please as long as I can."

"I get it."

"Good. As for my old loves and losses, that's for me to keep to myself. You're good at reading between the lines, I can tell."

Instead of making me more curious about her life, the conversation had left me thinking uncomfortably about my own. As a Seeker, I was bound to go away every now and then, but otherwise my life in Norbay would be pretty settled, more of a scholarly one, unless our leaders decided something different. But Birch? I felt like I was now looking at a very elderly version of my promised. Would she feel trapped by me? Would she leave me because of it? Would I be able to accept that if she did? It seemed that when I got back, we'd need to have a chat to sort out some of this before we both ended up with a broken heart.

Only three days away, and I was surprised to find myself longing for her. Sure, we seemed very different, but at heart we loved the same things. I thought of her long face, flowing hair, and those pointy elbows, her sharp brown eyes, and high cheekbones in a way I'd never felt before.

I even missed Oak's constant teasing, my mom's pestering, and my dad's slow, measured lectures.

Elm snapped her fingers in front of my face. "Earth to Jay. I just realized there's something else I want to show you around here. Something crucial to your education. We'll be taking the next exit."

"What is it?"

"The best history lesson you'll ever receive." But the way she said it didn't make it sound like very much fun.

That was all she would reveal about it.

• • •

Our exit was at a place that had been called Bradford, and as we rode along, we saw more ruined subdivisions. We were entering the vicinity of the old "megacity." Here, the road was even worse, which was surprising. Entire chunks were missing to create what looked like craters, like there'd been an actual wartime bombing.

After twenty minutes on this chewed-up road, we came to the corner of an imposing grey metal fence that joined at a right angle, tall and thick and covered in rusty patches, and rode alongside it for a few minutes. The parts that still stood were topped with coils of barbed wire. Through the fallen gaps, I could see identical one-story buildings. The roadway led up to a wide gate with a stained sign hanging at a forty-five-degree angle. *Bradford Migrant Housing Installation,* it said. On either side of the gate and at intervals along the wall, which stretched far into the distance, were guard towers.

I stopped pedaling. "Is this what I think it is?" I was suddenly afraid, right down into the pit of my stomach.

There was no laughter in her voice this time. She sounded cold and distant. "Yep. Like I said, it's something you need to see. Be prepared." She walked her bike through the open gate.

There was a huge open area, all paved over, with dandelions sprouting through cracks in the pavement. Then the rusted walls of long, barrack-like buildings made of and roofed with corrugated metal stretched off into the distance in long rows.

"Come on."

All of Elm's usual dry levity was absent. She hopped on her bike and started riding slowly down one of the rows, then suddenly turned right at a particular intersection. She clearly knew precisely where she was going.

It was eerie. All these buildings were identical, and there must have been dozens or even hundreds of them. Above, on the fence, the collapsed guard towers loomed threateningly over us. The sky was cloudy, and there was a metallic scent on the breeze. It was like entering a new, disturbing world.

The only other signs of visitors were occasional faded, red-painted graffiti, things like *Bastards* and *Murderers* and *Repent, Sinners,* as well as indecipherable tags and expletives.

Abruptly, she stopped and pointed to the pile of metal in front of us. It looked like all the others; there was no window, just a yawning doorway and blackness beyond. "Fifteenth down from the left, thirteenth down from the right. This was where I lived — survived — for several years, well into my teens. Me, my family, and two other families in this little shack."

I swallowed. This had all suddenly gotten very heavy. "When?"

"It was around 2055. I was very young, I think about eight or nine, but I remember being here — I remember perfectly. It's seared into my brain, and as I age, I remember more and more. What I didn't know at the time, because I was too little to understand anything, was that the democratic government had collapsed and been replaced by a different kind."

She sighed and ran a hand down her face. "You see, Jay, as the world blew past all its climate targets, the emission targets and heating limits it seems governments never intended to meet, and as it became obvious that nothing was going to change about how we did business and lived, people started to get scared. They were terrified, in fact, but they still didn't change anything significant about the way they lived. It seemed they just ... couldn't. Then things started to happen on a larger scale and accelerate. Long, intense heat waves killed hundreds of thousands around the world. Forest fires chewed up whole towns. Every coral reef on Earth died. Higher water levels started to swamp the greatest cities in the world. The Gulf Stream vanished and the climates of whole countries changed and became unliveable. Refugees started streaming north from hotter climates, looking to us rich Canadians with all our land, for help."

I waved an arm around. "*This* was how we helped them?" I had never expected this, despite all the lessons. Seeing it brought it all home.

"Not at first. This came later. See, the strangest thing about the early years of climate collapse was how even though we *knew* what was happening and had irrefutable proof, not only did people refuse to change how they lived, but they also elected governments that denied the problem existed or just didn't act on it. Deliberately. And when that tactic wasn't going to work any longer because the evidence was too overpowering, they moved to claiming only they could protect the citizens; they'd make sure our countries weren't overrun by refugees, and they'd protect the resources we needed to survive.

"This happened all over North America and Europe. People elected strongmen who said they'd offer protection. And when things really got bad and people started to ask questions and protest … then there were no more elections. The strongmen ruled the way they wanted. They closed borders. They put in martial law. It was like being ruled by the mid-twentieth-century totalitarians. It was worse, actually, because it was everywhere. People were so scared of the effects of climate breakdown that they'd let those monsters do anything as long as their own families were protected. And Canada wasn't hit as hard as some places, so for a while it looked like maybe we could be kept safe."

I'd read about all of this, of course, and Cedar had described it much the same way. But the words had extra weight in this place. All the unbelievable stupidity of the people of the early twenty-first century... It was hard not to hate them.

She sighed deeply again, putting a hand on the metal wall. "Eventually the flood of refugees overran the borders and headed into the populated areas. The government's response was to use the military, police, and hired thugs to round them up and put them in newly built camps, like this one, saying they'd feed and take care of them. When dissidents protested, they'd put their whole families in here too. That's how I ended up here, along with Cedar's family and others. We lived with people from Nicaragua, Mexico, Florida, Texas … mostly brown-skinned people, because another myth of the twentieth century, along with progress, was that inequality and bigotry had been eradicated. It was all a lie. The rich white people still lived in air-conditioning, thinking they might be able to adapt to a hotter world through technology. Poor people just came north to save themselves and their children. They had a right to live. They had a right to be welcomed. We didn't welcome them. And when walls weren't enough to keep them out, we did this."

A few sparse raindrops started to fall. Elm didn't seem to notice. The rain felt like nature's bitter tears for the people who had suffered here. History was now feeling very real and present.

"Horrible things happened here as the camps got more and more overcrowded. They almost stopped feeding us entirely. There was no sanitation. Disease was rampant. They still wouldn't let us go. And then..."

I didn't want to ask.

She clammed up, jaw locked, picked up her bike, and moved on without a backward glance, and I hastened after her. Soon we were at the periphery again, in front of a big, wide-open space with only sparse weeds covering dead soil.

"See this?" She pointed angrily at the sketchy patch of land.

"Yes?"

"If you had a shovel with you, and you dug a little, you'd find bones. Many, many bones, in piles. Thousands and thousands of bones."

I couldn't breathe. I was stricken. "They massacred people? Or did people just ... die from hunger?"

She stared fiercely at the soil as if she could see the people buried there. "Both. And they did shoot them. Toward the end. When the camp got too full, if they received too many truckloads, or maybe they just felt like it, they'd take the infirm and shoot them on the edge of the pit, or if they were too infirm to move, just throw them in. The things I saw..."

A small tear descended her dry, wrinkled cheek. I wanted to put an arm around her but somehow knew I shouldn't.

Suddenly, she turned to me, the wind whipping her hair against her forehead, her eyes blazing. "So ... if you want to know why the Seekers are so intense about changing *everything* about the way people live, and why we resolve to find a way to make sure these horrors can *never* happen again, no matter how many times they have throughout history, think about this place. Think about how there were hundreds of such places around the world, and how the same things happened in every one of them. We can't allow a *trace* of a world that would allow these things to happen to return. It would be better to be extinct. Sometimes I wonder if that outcome might actually have been for the best."

She grabbed her bike again. "When everything collapsed for good and the strongmen started to fight each other, they couldn't even keep these places going; the guards left to take their chances elsewhere. We escaped and fled north, just trying to get as far away as we could. I remember those hardships too. But you know enough for now."

She hopped on and started toward the gate but turned back once to say, "And you had family here too, by the way."

"Oh, really—" I said, feeling my face blanching, but she was already pedaling away. I would have to wait to find out more about that.

As we retraced our path, I noticed something I hadn't on the way in: a small church with mildewy white siding, as damaged as all the other buildings around but with steeple intact. It stood only a couple of hundred metres from a corner of the camp's border fence. It chilled me to think of people blithely worshipping their benevolent saviour inside that church on a Sunday, so sure of the truth of their beliefs and the goodness of their god and its plan, while people were starved and shot just a few feet away.

• • •

And still, throughout this wasteland of broken subdivisions that increasingly surrounded us as we went south, we saw no signs of life. It was like all the most populated areas had been abandoned, except, apparently, for Great Toronto itself. This made me curious.

"Elm," I panted. It had become clear by this point that this septuagenarian was in far better shape than me, despite tiring a bit sooner at the end of the day. Now she was pedaling with a grim mechanism borne of traumatic memories. "What's the deal with Great Toronto anyway? Have there always been people there?"

"Yes, scavengers mostly. But a few years ago, people started to gather there again. Let's stop for something to eat. I should tell you this before we get there, anyway."

We took shelter under a tall tree from the occasional spits of rain that had continued to fall in the late afternoon.

"This is an elm, by the way. Let's hope that's good luck. Anyway … I haven't come completely clean with you, which is why I should tell you now." She tore into a piece of dried apple from my bag and spoke as she chewed. "I may seem a lonely, friendless wanderer, but I have connections. Places I go to get food and see friends, and not just in Norbay. Lately, on behalf of the Seekers, I've been consulting with smaller communities about the problem of Great Toronto. Something is going on there that's not good, and we need to find out how far it's progressed."

"I've heard the rumours about that. Granite knew."

"Well, we're still sketchy on exact details. All conjecture aside, we know about the gang that has taken over there and is running it like a city-state. Now, of course, they have every right to govern themselves as they see fit, of course. But the things we hear are troubling."

"Like what?"

"The rumour is they want to restore the pre-Ruin world, without checks on our behaviour. And that there's more than one such place; this is just the closest one. That they want to revive bad technology. They may have vehicles. Their government is supposed to be authoritarian and punitive. That much we have established. They take captives, and the citizens that come out of there are armed to the teeth and not to be approached. The perimeter is guarded. It's a shit-show developing, frankly. Nothing good can come of a community becoming an armed camp. Soon enough, it's human nature for them to want to expand. They can believe what they like, but they don't have the right to force it on others."

"Then what can we do about it? Nothing, right? I mean, we don't even carry weapons for our protection, let alone have an army."

She barked her laugh. "Well, all that remains to be seen, doesn't it? We don't have the information. Without that, we're armed with nothing. We need more. So, I'm heading that way at least to get a sense of where their border is set, see if there's anyone nearby to talk to, get some more intel, that sort of thing. Do what I can. Without, I promise, putting myself in danger. Lonely old wandering hermits tend to be invisible. And there's no tangible evidence they're looking to spread beyond their northern border — yet. It's just conjecture. But worth looking into. "

"And you want me to go with you?"

She grinned slyly. "Well, that's up to you. You could head east to a number of places now that we're this far south. The old Bradford Bypass is nearby. Highways 407 and 7 are options for you to stay clear of Great Toronto. So, you can head to Kingston and hope that the university there has books and DVDs that haven't turned to mush or dust and that no one has seen yet, just to get your feet wet … or you can do some real spy work with me on your first mission. We'll tell anyone we meet that you're just helping your pathetic old granny on her final journey. What's it going to be?"

I looked up at the roiling grey clouds for just a second.

My choice was obvious.

XIII.

CAPTURED

BIRCH

The blanket of thick white smoke didn't relent even slightly until late in the afternoon, so I had a choice to make when it finally did: either camp out in this raunchy, stinky basement for another twelve hours, or see how far I could get in the hours before nightfall. Being me, I chose the latter.

This was a bad smoke fog, just clinging to everything; visibility was only a few feet around me at times. Despite my mask, I was coughing, and my eyes stung, even now as the fog dispersed a bit.

I was lucky the wind changed… It could sometimes be a couple of days before smoke cleared.

It was about 4:00 p.m. when I left Powassan, according to the fancy wind-up timepiece Oak had given me. I figured I could at least make it to South River, a town I'd seen in the map book he'd also managed to pilfer for me. He really was a good friend. There was still a serious haze, but the smoke was mostly gone. I kept a mask on anyway. The sun glowed a surreal orange — almost cherry-red, as it sank.

By seven, the light was getting dimmer, and when I finally found the long, curving ramp to South River it was almost dark. I took shelter in the biggest, most intact building I could find — a brewery — wondering if Jay had maybe been there not long ago. If he had, there was no trace of him.

Despite having spent almost the entire day hiding from smoke, I was exhausted and fell asleep almost immediately after concealing myself behind the cash desk of the brewery gift shop. I could have sworn I felt a trace of Jay's presence there, but I told myself I was being silly.

My sleep was surprisingly deep, and I don't think I woke at all during the night. In the morning, I was up far too late, mid-morning, and everything seemed clear outside. No smoke, no people, nothing but dust and dry leaves blowing down the main drag of good old South River.

Today I would try hard to make good time, at least to Bracebridge, about seven hours' ride, or even farther. Of course, it all depended on the heat, as every day did. But I had plenty of water and was determined to get there.

The ride was uneventful, though there was a tense moment when, coming down a slope, I saw what looked like a group of people crossing the highway at a side road. I was a long way off, but I definitely saw a cluster of something large plodding across. They were pretty much just tiny moving silhouettes against the glare off the pavement. I guess it could have been deer, but I doubted it. I stopped and hauled my bike away under the trees until they had been gone for at least twenty minutes to make doubly sure they didn't see me. This was the first sign of people I'd come across; I'd been told and warned that Muskoka was by no means empty and safe, but now I knew. I'd have to keep an eye up ahead and even behind.

Still, nothing else happened, the heat wasn't too unbearable, and the seven hours went smoothly — well, it was more like ten, and toward the end it was dark, of course, and I had to pick my way by the thankfully strong moonlight and starshine. Not the smartest choice, and I was already cursing my impulsivity.

Eventually, though, I was able to make out the Bracebridge turnoff. There was no way I was going to be able to find whatever was left of the town on pitch-black, overhung sideroads, not to mention the frequent potholes and obstacles I could bash up against. Fortunately, when I was starting to think that I'd just have to curl up under a tree and endure the torture of the bugs and the dangers of the elements, I saw the shell of a fast-food restaurant, one of the ubiquitous Tim Hortons chain, not far off the highway.

Breathing a sigh of relief, I pulled up to it. It was long deserted, and though of course all the glass was caved in, the roof was mostly there, and I could take shelter. That was all I needed.

I pulled my bike into the kitchen, which had no windows, feeling my way around. I struck a match long enough to get situated and find some food in my bag. The ghostly shadows of all the food preparation equipment scattered around flickered into view for a minute until the match burned close to my fingers and I waved it out.

I told myself I'd have to be smarter if I wanted to avoid dying pitifully alone after snapping a leg or cracking my head on these lonely roads.

• • •

I woke groggily and peered at my watch to see it was 8:00 a.m., making sure to give it a good wind, too. This sleep had been fitful, with constant periods of dozing and a vague feeling that something wasn't quite right, and I hadn't really settled into sleep until early morning; the hard tiles under me didn't help. A beam of sunlight sliced through the kitchen doorway but hadn't been enough to wake me. At least I'd get an earlier start today. Despite the crappy rest on cold tiles, I didn't feel too bad. I decided I'd better scope things out a bit before eating.

I slouched out of the room, looked out the shattered front window, and instantly froze. Outside stood several human forms — large ones. I ducked behind the dusty counter and peeked out again. They all looked male, brawny, with bushy, jutting beards and very long, greasy hair. There were four. They were just standing around out there a few feet apart from one another, not even talking, just standing silently like statues.

I slunk back to the kitchen to gather my stuff. I needed to get out of there, immediately. Fortunately, a building like this would have a back door. I left one thing out of my pack: the knife Oak had given me. I gripped the sheath in my shaking right hand and the frame of my bike in my left as I approached the back door.

That heavy metal door was still in place and closed. I leaned the bike on a wall.

I took a deep, ragged breath and pushed gently on the bar. It screeched a little, but not too bad. Maybe I was going to be lucky today. I opened it just enough to slip through the gap.

There on the left, leaning against the wall, was a man.

"Hi there," he drawled. He was huge, well over six feet tall, with a prominent craggy nose over a puffed-out black beard streaked with grey. He had some kind of bandana on his head. His clothes were somewhat ragged but appeared mostly clean. Bulging biceps protruded from his crossed arms. His face was very lined and scarred. Even though he didn't seem to be that old, they were the lines of a person who has done and seen terrible things. He wore a calm but menacing smile, and his beady eyes were narrowed. He was violence personified, and every instinct screamed at me to run.

He maintained his casual position as he spoke again. "If you're thinking about taking off, don't." He uncrossed his arms to show a gun holster at his hip. "Watched you for long time yesterday. Shouldn't'a been out there all alone. It's dangerous."

"Yeah," I croaked. "So I hear. Thanks for the tip." I could feel my pulse racing, a painful thumping in my ears, and my bowels loosening.

"So..." He leaned forward and pushed off the wall, his eyes fixed on mine. "Now *we're* gonna protect you."

I backed up, and he smirked with delight. "Don't be scared, baby. What's your name?"

"That's for me to know." I continued to back up with the knife now in my hand, feeling a pounding my ears.

Now he chuckled. "Spunky. That's no good. Don't like 'em too spunky. Well, I'm Brent. You're gonna get to know me good." He pulled the gun from its holster. "Gimme the knife."

I weighed my few options. I could already tell going with this guy was going to cause me more suffering than I could ever imagine; his look and demeanour said everything I needed to understand that. But I also didn't want to die today. It would be better to surrender and watch out for opportunities than to go out in a blaze of glory. At least for a while.

"Okay." I put the knife in the sheath and extended it to him.

"Thanks." He pulled it a little way back out and whistled. "This is a good one. Happy to have it." He grabbed me roughly by the elbow. "Now you come with me."

He hauled me around the front of the store, my feet dragging, to where the other men waited. Four sets of eyes turned to me, looking me up and down. One whistled. "Nice catch, bud. Looks even better up close."

Brent gave that evil chuckle again. "You bet. Good work, boys. Know we were gonna do some huntin', but we struck gold with this one. Let's head back with her." He turned to me. "Go get your bike."

I was frozen on the spot, still feeling a painful pounding in my ears.

"Go. We'll be right here. You got nowhere to run."

I stumbled back into the store, my mind racing. I couldn't control the thoughts; I was shivering with fear now and felt myself mentally shutting down. I got to the kitchen and stopped for a moment to breathe. Finally, a dominant, rational voice said, *Get it together if you want to make it through this. Stay aware.* Someone, at some point, had said those words to me, and for some reason they now stuck in my head like a mantra. *Stay aware.* That's what I'd have to do. Keep a clear head and be in the moment, poised, waiting for the right reaction to make. Not fall into a daymare of panic and despair.

I grabbed the bike from the back hallway and slowly wheeled it out, taking deep breaths.

"Good," said Brent. "Now, we gonna start riding. See my bud Steve there? See that rifle? See Dwayne over there? He's got a handgun. You're going nowhere. Just come along, do what I tell you, and your life might not be that bad. Your *new* life." He leered.

That bad? What the hell are they going to do with me? Though I already knew.

The one called Steve managed to brush up behind me as he went to mount his bike and grab a handful.

I spun around instinctively with my hand up, only to have Brent grab it. The whole gang laughed raucously.

"Now, now," said Brent. "Play nice, sweetie."

"Fuck you," I hissed between my teeth.

A second later I was staggered by a blow across my face more painful than anything I'd felt since I'd fractured my leg racing down the escarpment in my early teens. I almost fell over but managed to keep myself upright. The blood pounding in my ears was gone, and rage was replacing some of the fear. Good.

Brent got up close, his nasty breath blowing right in my face. "You gonna learn *never* to talk back to me. Or *any* man."

He stepped back and turned to Steve, who was just a little smaller than him and had more grey in his beard. "You do that again, I'll cut you. This one's special. Not for you, fuckhead."

Steve seemed to pull himself up taller. "Oh yeah? Says who? You're not the boss."

Brent pulled out a knife — my knife — and stepped up to him. "Really?" He stared into Steve's eyes. "Wanna try me?"

After a few tense seconds of this alpha male stalemate, in which no one moved a muscle, Steve just shrugged and got on his bike, conceding Brent's dominance. That was the cue for the rest of the gang to do the same.

Brent gave that laugh again. "Good. Well, girl, we gonna know your name soon enough — gonna know *everything* about you, and believe me, you'll know *me*."

If I hadn't already realized what my capture meant, now I really knew. *You should have attacked him when you could, you idiot! You could have gone down fighting.*

"Steve, ride behind her. Best view you're gonna get."

They slowly started moving with three in front of me, three behind. My legs felt numb, like they weren't even there, but they somehow kept moving, pushing downward. My pack was still on my back, the dead weight of all my anticipation and enthusiasm for seeing the world now made to look very stupid and naïve. I could feel the morning sun on my skin, a light breeze, faintly detect the morning chorus, but it was through a paralyzing filter.

Stay aware, you can survive, said the voice of reason.

But I won't make it through this, I answered. *Not this.*

Now my jumbled thoughts turned to Jay and his kindly, thoughtful ways, and to Oak and his silly sense of humour, then to my dads and their wonderful guidance and the way they selflessly took me in when I was an infant nobody, and even to Cedar, who had gently tried to help me find my path. I even flashed back to patting the cat in the garden on a cool morning, her rolling around in the dirt to have her belly scratched. I'd never see any of them again. They'd never know about the terrible way I was going to live and die. And I'd been so stubborn with them. Now I'd never make it up to them. I felt tears gathering and blinked them away. That weakness made me angry; rage came pouring in.

No. No. Not like this.

I stopped. Even though we were going slowly, Steve almost crashed into the back of me. I leapt off the bike and looked wildly around, preparing to run. The forest shrubbery pressed in almost in a jungle-like way. If I could just make it to the edge of the road and get in there, I could lose them…

"Fucking bitch," Steve bellowed, righting his bike, his face turning red.

"I don't think so," Brent hissed. I whipped around to face him. He'd hopped off his bike and stood two metres away from me, reaching for the knife that was now tucked into his belt. "Guess you need a couple of scars to teach you not to act out, huh?"

The others clustered around in pleased anticipation. I prepared to put up the best fight I could. He'd have to kill me.

The moment the knife left its sheath and was raised, I thought I heard a bang and Brent's head … vanished. In a blink. I felt a light patter of something wet striking my face.

I watched in horror as his almost headless body toppled over onto his bike. Then the guy next to him reeled, screamed, and fell after something hit his shoulder, causing blood to gout out of it. This time I'd clearly heard the gunshot. He lay on the road writhing and crying like a baby, clutching at his wrecked shoulder.

The three remaining men spun around aimlessly, looking for the source of the shots. I was frozen to the spot, unable to comprehend what was happening.

"Hey!" a voice called out. I couldn't figure out where it was coming from, but it was loud.

We all just stood there. The remaining men had their guns out but didn't know where to point them.

"I said *hey*!" bellowed the voice. "Do you know what kind of weapon I need to be using to blow up that asshole's head like dropping a pumpkin? Put your fucking guns down, *now*!"

The three exchanged blank looks and then one by one put their pistols and rifles down on the road, then just stood there with their arms hanging loose, completely stupefied by the turn of events.

"Here's what's gonna happen. You're going to get on your bikes and start riding. Leave the girl. Try to touch the girl and I'll cut you down. Leave all your shit here too, including your weapons. When you get home, tell your buddies what happens to anyone who comes this way. Got it?"

They didn't move, still peering around at the trees on both sides.

Another shot rang out, this time hitting the guy on the ground in the chest with such force it threw him a few inches to his left. He was spattered in blood, and his keening stopped.

The others, including Steve, wasted no time in dropping their bags, guns, and knives, jumping on their bikes, and pumping madly away from the scene without looking back.

I just stood there, dumbfounded, with a man's brains all over my face and clothing.

A minute later, a figure came out of the trees about twenty metres down the road. It had on some sort of camouflage raincoat with the hood up and was holding a massive rifle, the kind sadistic pieces of shit once used to shoot endangered animals at vast distances. No wonder it had that devastating effect.

I was too shocked even to register a feeling, let alone move or make a decision about what to do. Suddenly, I felt my jaw aching from the blow I'd taken probably only about ten minutes ago, though it seemed like hours.

The figure slung the gun over its shoulder and stood watching for a minute until the fleeing figures had receded far into the distance and rounded a wide bend in the road before turning to me.

I ran to the side of the road and emptied the acid and small amount of food I'd ingested from my stomach. I could still feel the stickiness of Brent's brain matter all over me, along with a horrible smell of so much blood.

When I looked up, I wasn't surprised to see the lined face of a woman. She pulled her raincoat's hood back to reveal a head of salt-and-pepper black hair. I'd put her in her fifties.

Her mouth twisted into something of a smile. "You're welcome."

Suddenly, I could feel my limbs again, and my brain chugged back to life. "Thank–thank you so much," I said foolishly, like she was a gardener who had just handed me my order at the vegetable stand at Lee Park Farm in Norbay. This sudden deliverance had left me even more confused than the way my day had started.

The woman turned away and started rifling quickly through the packs the men had dropped. "We don't have forever. They won't be back soon, but they'll probably be back … with reinforcements. You'd better come with me. Not sure you're in any condition to take care of yourself right now. I know the look on your face."

She extended a bottle of water to me. "Here, dump this over your head and clean up a little."

As I gratefully accepted the water, she piled up the weapons and any food she found on the pavement — including clear plastic bags of what looked like raw meat — then started stuffing things into her own large pack. When she straightened up, it was bulging, and she now had another gun slung over her other shoulder. Even so, she stood straight and didn't seem to feel the extra weight.

"C'mon. Pick up your bike. We're going the other way." I walked silently with her while she turned around every thirty seconds or so to make sure no one was coming. She even pulled out a pair of binoculars and peered through them for a while before making a noise of satisfaction.

"That was good, the way you stopped short there. I'm a good shot, but that gave me a perfect target. You've got guts, I could see. Made it more fun to help you out. Not that I'd need a reason to shoot at those fuckers. I should have killed them all."

This woman may have been rough around the edges, but she exuded confidence and an easy familiarity with this environment.

Just before we got to the restaurant where I'd been captured, she vanished off to the side of the road and came out with a rusty touring bike.

Before I could ask, she said, "I'd been tracking those assholes for a while to see what they were up to, how close they'd get to my territory. Too close. I had a side errand for a day, and by the time I caught up with them early this morning, they were here at Tim's. I knew something was up by the way they were just hanging out there. Then I saw you, and I thought, *Oh shit, I know where this is going.* Normally I'm not much for doing strangers favours, but that's one thing I'm not letting happen."

"Th–thanks again," I said.

She laughed, a nice, surprisingly musical sound that was a contrast with her expletive-laden conversational style and hardened appearance. "Funny, you don't look like a woman of few words. C'mon, I think you'd better come with me until you get back to normal. That was a big fucking shock, I'm sure, waking up that way."

She hopped on her bike.

At that moment it hit me just what I'd avoided and how insanely lucky I'd been. I owed this stranger *everything.*

I mounted and followed her back toward the highway. It probably wasn't even 9:00 a.m.

XIV.

"WONDERLAND"

JAY

We didn't actually get very far after we left Bradford and the miasma of its lingering bygone horrors before a stop became necessary. While for me the palpable sense of doom lifted from my shoulders with each pedal stroke we took away from the place, the emotionally taxing visit seemed to have left Elm older and wearier. Her burst of energy was short-lived, and for the first time she appeared genuinely elderly and had a lot of trouble keeping up with me. She barely said a word for some time. Still, she insisted we at least make it to the top of sprawling Great Toronto by day's end. It didn't help that the cloud cover had thickened and the wind had picked up, a shift that usually preceded dangerous conditions.

The entire flat landscape was now the seemingly endless skeletal remains of subdivisions, row upon row of almost identical townhouses, their empty upper windows glaring at us like the eye sockets of ancient skulls, though often obscured by masses of greenery, almost fully filled-in forest in some places that grew in front, in between, and sometimes even inside them. Each former lawn was now a miniature jungle of shrubs, bushes, and trees.

There were no signs of habitation, though we saw several murders of crows flapping overheard as we rode, possibly curious to check out these two relics, last of a lost species, slowly picking their way down the broken road. Maybe the corvus would be the next intelligent inheritor of the mess we left behind.

After about two and half painfully slow hours, just as the force of the wind really started to worry me and slow me down, and I was about to suggest the urgency of stopping, Elm gasped, "Over there, on the left."

I saw bizarre structures silhouetted against the grey sky, looming over the trees; for a moment, my eyes deceived me with the skeletons of dinosaurs from one of the palaeontology books that captivated me when I was young.

Then I realized what they were: another kind of mythical creature I'd only seen in a few pictures, newspapers, and in magazines. It was yet another remnant of the time when middle-class people's lives were so free from danger and fear that they had to deliberately seek those instinctive, visceral experiences in a closed, controlled, and safe environment: an amusement park. Cedar had once devoted a whole lecture to twenty-first-century humanity being so totally disconnected from their inherent nature as animals that many people would seek the stimulation of fear through extreme sports, mountain climbing, daredevil activities, and the less adventurous through things like the rides at amusement parks. For a small fee you could pretend for a few moments that you were about to plunge to your death and be reminded that, yes, while you will die someday, right now you are still very much alive and kicking. *Carpe diem.*

Then they'd go stuff themselves with sugar and fat to reenergize and go do it all over again.

An exit ramp leading to this temple of controlled fear and joy was presumably where Elm wanted to head, so I made my way over with the full force of the gale smacking into me from my right. I'm not sure she'd even have heard me if I yelled. A couple of minutes later, as I crossed a huge parking lot, dodging several towering trees that had erupted through the pavement, I turned around to see Elm was some distance behind me, struggling badly. I turned back. There wasn't anything I could do to help other than stay with her.

Fat raindrops started to whack my face, driven by the gale. We both dismounted and staggered on until we were through the broken gates. Inside, it was a surreal scene. While some of the rides, the ones I could see from the highway, were miraculously still standing, some leaning precariously, many had fallen, crashing into each other in expansive piles of metal wreckage, track meshed with track like you'd find in a fossil bed. I could imagine such a graveyard of massive plant-eaters taken out by the meteor that books told me had destroyed all of their kind. We passed what would have been fountains, and then right in front of us was a small, crumbling hill of concrete that had presumably been shaped to look like a mountain peak.

We had to dodge the gigantic steel frames of fallen roller coasters as we headed for whatever safe place Elm had found here. But we were running out of time.

Now the wind had reached such force that it was blowing us off our feet, and the rain had become drenching.

"No more time," I heard her croak.

A shed, maybe a ticket booth or food stand, loomed on the left, and she ducked through the door into the blackness, tossed her bike to the side, and sank down, drained. I could hear snapping and metallic booming as things flew around the park. The roof of the shed rattled frighteningly. Well, it had somehow survived the better part of a century without maintenance, so maybe it would make it through today as well.

I pulled the light blanket from my pack, dropped it against the wall, and then helped Elm to sit against it. She closed her eyes. The life seemed to have been completely sapped from her, and I was worried. I'd only known her a couple of days, but already the prospect of losing her was hard to bear; not to mention we were nowhere near any hint of medical assistance. For two days, she'd been bright-eyed and quick-witted, but I barely recognized the person in front of me now.

I got out some dried food and squished millet bread from my pack to share. At that her eyes did open, and I was glad she sat up to partake a bit.

Finally, over the howl of the gale and the gunfire of heavy rain on the roof, she spoke weakly. "Oh, don't look so spooked, kid. I'm okay. I just forget sometimes that I'm not your age anymore." I couldn't hear it but saw her shoulders shake a little as she chuckled.

I breathed a sigh of relief and looked out the doorway at the apocalyptic storm. Just as I did, a big, heavy tree bough — or maybe an entire small tree — swooshed by, so powerful was the cyclonic force. We had storms like this on a regular basis in Norbay, sure, but a couple within a few days was really bad luck. Things were bashing deafeningly against the metal walls of the shed, and I could see them shaking. It was scary to think that some storms like this were just the remnants of even bigger super storms down south that left few things alive in their path; they weakened over land before they reached us.

"It must have been nice to live in a time when weather like this never happened, and every season was predictable."

She laughed again, louder this time. "Hell, every day. They could predict the weather every damn day, or close to it. That's a science we could use right now."

She sat up some more and became more audible over the roar. "Now, good. I'm feeling a little better. I'm sorry to have worried you. I admit that I probably shouldn't have inflicted the memories of that place on myself, but I *did* need to inflict it on you. I buried a lot of that time for years. You can imagine why. You've led a sheltered life, and I'm happy about that in some ways, but if you're going to spend time on the roads, you need to know that those evils happened in the not too distant past and could happen again. Hence, the next stage of our journey has to be approached with caution. It's also hotter down here, so travelling by day won't necessarily work every day. We'll sleep here tonight, no matter what the weather's like, and reevaluate tomorrow."

I was feeling very reflective after taking in all these sobering sights. "I wonder if the whole planet is like this now."

"Like what?"

I took a quick swig of water. "You know, mostly depopulated and full of dangers from the weather. I mean, I know it is … but it's incredible to see everything ruined. How much is gone. Or how much there was. How many people there were. I try, and I've seen footage, but it's still hard to imagine what it was like to be in those crowds and for that to be normal."

"Yes. I guess I'm used to seeing all this, and I was alive for the last gasp of it, but looking through your young eyes, it must be confusing, especially when nothing new is growing from these ruins other than plants — not yet. But there's hope."

I shook my head. "I know. I believe it. That's why I joined the guild. But it's such a huge job. Are there people like us elsewhere? Or is everything just … lawless out there? Where do people live?"

Elm took a few moments to pull off her scuffed boots, revealing socks with multiple holes. "There are settlements, like I told you, beyond the few you know. In Ontario, there are many small ones. I've seen people everywhere, just getting by, learning to farm and hunt again, mostly just trying to keep their heads down. There are those who prey on others, of course, as it always has been when there's no rule of law. There's been no rule of law for a *long* time, so the sheer persistence of any human decency and a sense of community is a victory unto itself, if you think about it."

That was true; I'd never thought about it that way. Even in the ashes, the best of the human spirit struggled to stay aflame, so we weren't the only ones. But what about Great Toronto?

She broke into these thoughts. "As for the rest of the world … I'm not sure. And I guess your Elders haven't brought you into that knowledge yet. We have radios, and sometimes there's contact with other places. But I'm not up to date on how that's been in the last, well, in many years. We know some things, though. The equatorial regions became too hot for human habitation for large parts of the year — all year in some places — a very long time ago. Millions of people once lived there. Most of them died or fled, and many of those who fled still died. You've seen a small piece of that history here. Entire civilizations are now gone.

"But it wasn't just the hottest regions. There was this thing called the Gulf Stream, a warm ocean current that parts of Europe happened to depend on to regulate their climate. When the polar caps melted for good, it just … vanished. That means the environment tens of millions of people depended on was gone, and the climate in those places drastically changed. The chaos was incredible, I'm told. That was before contact with them was lost."

Her voice was becoming weaker and quieter as weariness took hold.

"I believe there was sporadic radio contact from there, but not anymore. Same with anywhere equatorial, Australia, Africa... If there are people left, they're mostly clinging to the boreal regions, I assume, like we are. Maybe the last of the species. Are there thousands? Millions? Tens of millions? We don't know. Another reason why the Seekers' mission is so important. Live properly or die with dignity; either way, be properly *human*." Her voice strengthened a bit with the conviction of her statement.

It was bizarre to think that Britain and United States, the two places that had dominated the world's economy and pushed around so many other peoples for hundreds of years, were now just ... gone. Not just in terms of the political entities themselves; as far as we knew, *all* of those were gone. But the people, too. Our historians in Norbay called all of this the "Anthropocene Extinction Event," which was ongoing and far from complete.

I decided to change the subject to something I'd been curious about ever since we first met. "Elm, you were one of the founders of Norbay, right?"

She shot a glance at me as if she knew where this would end up going.

"My grandparents are all dead... I don't remember them. Who were they? Were they founders, too?"

She frowned disapprovingly. "You mean Aspen hasn't told you *anything*?"

"Not much, to be honest."

"I knew your grandparents. On your father's side, they were Martin and Jane Morrison. They were in the camps with us. They survived, but they weren't well afterward. Jane was well enough to give birth to your dad, mind you. But she was never in good shape. Martin was sick too, physically broken in some ways. He died just after you were born. Aspen should have told you. I don't even remember what names they took. But I remember them."

Some of this fit with the precious little my dad had told me.

"Your maternal grandparents were Rajiv and Adya Lal. I didn't know them well because I was on the road a lot at the start. They weren't founders. They weren't original citizens of Norbay either. I don't remember where they came from, but they came, and they stayed and were by all accounts model citizens. But Rajiv died of cancer. Adya lived longer, and I don't remember what she died of."

Now a very vague memory of a woman with long, dark, grey-streaked hair started surfacing, but it was fleeting and her face was blurry.

"All good people, but I can't tell you much more other than Martin and Jane were fighters. They weren't leaders, but they were fighters, and they were very useful in the early years. My memory's a bit foggy other than that."

"Thank you for telling me," I said.

Elm fell silent, having run out of strength again, and lay down with some of her outer clothing for a pillow.

The main storm had passed, including some funnel clouds I was pretty sure I saw through the doorway, but was followed by wave after wave of thunderstorms and torrential rain.

We settled down, made ourselves as comfortable as possible, and waited out the night in the mustiness of this metallic cave. Elm seemed to fall asleep almost instantly, which I was happy about, but I lay for a long time listening to the shrieking wind, over which I was sure I heard the howling of many dogs, but maybe that was just my imagination.

• • •

I woke up hot, very stiff, and grouchy. I could see strong sunlight outside, putting it at midmorning. I could tell this was going to be a scorching day as a new high-pressure system followed the storms; they generally did. It was also soppingly humid. Not atypical for the middle of fall, but it was certainly hotter the farther south you went.

I groaned as I forced myself up onto my elbows, which woke Elm. She stretched, looking much more composed and sharp-eyed, almost back to her normal self.

The first thing she said was, "I have to apologize, Jay. I wasn't myself at all yesterday, which is why we ended up in this uncomfortable place in the middle of a deluge. It wasn't like me. I usually travel in better style than that."

I was busy trying to find a variety of dried food in my pack. "No problem. I was just worried."

Elm placed a hand on my arm, the first time there'd been physical contact between us. "Thanks, kid. It's been a long time since anyone was worried about me. It almost feels good and necessary." She stood up and looked out the door. "Now, today is going to be *hot.* I doubt we can travel more than one or two hours before we'll need to take shelter again. No amount of hydration can combat that kind of heat. Anyway, we'll be near Great Toronto by then, and we'll have to start being a lot more careful. I suggest we move again at dusk. But first, let's get out of this memorial. It's going to get very hot in here today. I can feel the echoes of the people's happiness, and it reminds me of their suffering too. That's enough of that for a while!"

I felt suddenly guilty at the way I'd judged all those millions of people who had come to this park; if anything, it should probably be considered a place of joy and, as Elm implied, a memorial to the sun-drenched nostalgic memories in the lives of our forgotten ancestors. I hoped some of that joy had soaked into the metal and concrete of what was now a memorial to the age of "fun." Just because I'd never experienced it, that didn't mean it had no value.

We washed up with some rainwater that had collected on the corrugated metal outside, then got ready to depart.

As we went through the front gate, I turned around and tried to imagine excited, carefree children scampering around on a clear, sunny day, and you know, it wasn't that hard an image to conjure.

• • •

However, the lessons weren't over yet. As we rode back across that giant parking lot with heat already visibly radiating from the pavement, we passed a badly mauled and mostly consumed deer carcass that hadn't been there yesterday. A giant swarm of flies encompassed it, and the tang of blood was thick in the air around it. I blocked my nose.

Elm stopped and cursed, glaring down. "We were lucky ... again."

"Why?"

She pointed at the carcass. "Did you hear anything last night?"

Then I remembered. "Yeah, I thought I heard dogs."

"Well, there you go. There are huge packs of wild dogs down here, far more than up north, and I was so tired that I forgot that. They're the descendants of domestic pets; people in the early twenty-first century had a mania for keeping dogs. If they'd found us sleeping, we'd likely have been torn apart. I'm being stupid on a regular basis… I'm losing it, kid. We needed to barricade that door or find somewhere else, maybe somewhere elevated. So, learn from my stupidity."

I didn't know what to say at the vehemence of this self-recrimination. "It's okay, Elm."

She looked at me fiercely. "No, it's not. Learn from me, both from my wisdom and my errors. Where we are now, we can't afford any more mistakes. We're heading into Great Toronto."

XV.

NING

BIRCH

I barely remember the ride to my rescuer's home. I think it was a long way, but I was nearly catatonic, only able to focus on following her. I knew we did cross the highway and set off on another rural road, this one even more overgrown and shadowed by an almost menacingly thick canopy. It was cloudy and dim under there, and the bugs were bad, I remember that too, but otherwise my head was enveloped in a fog.

Everything had changed in the space of an hour, and neither I nor the way I viewed the world would ever be the same. Of course, we all realized we lived in a world that once had laws and organization and safety and now had none of those. We had been told over and over, warned as kids, that outside our utopian bubble life was often a brutal fight for survival, and there were people that would take your life in a heartbeat. *If you stray too far from town, the bandits will get you,* my dads had warned, *and they may even eat you!* It seemed ludicrous even when I was very little, but now I knew it was true.

Turns out there were worse things they could do than eat you. Despite my put-on cynicism, without realizing it I'd had a very naïve view of human nature.

So, there was that, plus the shock of the things I'd just witnessed. I'd never seen anyone die; in fact, I don't think I'd seen *anything* die beyond squished mosquitos, dead deer picked over by scavengers, and the chipmunks and birds the cat would catch, which we'd have to finish off in a mercy kill. (I always cried when I had to do that.) I'd attended lots of funerals — the healers could only do so much with herbs and pieced-together remedies, after all — but never *watched* someone die.

And now I'd seen a man's head explode in front of me. I couldn't imagine a more visceral reminder of our fragility. The seat of what little intelligence he had ... vanished in a second. The scene replayed over and over, and it was amazing that I kept my legs moving consistently enough to propel the bike. Bile kept rising, but somehow I didn't throw up again.

My new companion didn't say a word; she just led the way. Every now and then, she'd glance back inscrutably but seemed to know better than to try talking to me. Not that she seemed the chatty type.

Eventually, we turned off onto what had once been an even more remote dirt side road and was now almost entirely taken over by undergrowth. It might not even have been there for all a passerby might realize. You could still pick your way along it, and she seemed pretty good at it — maybe there was a faint trail she'd left before that she could see — but the branches and stems clutching at my wheels and pedals constantly threatened to throw me down.

The fight to stay upright helped to snap me somewhat out of my painful reverie. Rain started to spit, a few scattered drops penetrating the canopy, and the bugs got even more vicious. Since I was riding, I couldn't do much to fend them off. My companion seemed unfazed but secured her hood tightly and ploughed on ahead of me.

Finally, after what felt like hours but could have been less than one, she turned off onto an even more overgrown path, barely visible as a road at all. Now I really couldn't stay upright, so I dismounted and slogged on, losing her in the undergrowth.

Finally, I entered something of a clearing that was inhabited by a moss-covered log house, and I mean it was the old-fashioned kind, not a wooden shack: logs stacked up and expertly locked together, with what looked like cedar shingles above. The windows were long gone but now covered with thick sheets of translucent plastic sheeting.

My host was by the door, rubbing the ears of a mean-looking, untied black dog that eyed me suspiciously but didn't make a sound.

She turned to me and sized me up. "You look like shit. First time seeing someone get killed, huh?"

I nodded and swallowed, the image rising again with my gorge.

She grunted sympathetically. "You never forget it, but you get past it. As for having done the killing, well, that's a whole other trip. You get used to that too." She flicked her head at the dog. "This is Night. She's harmless … to friends. Let's get away from these little bloodsuckers, speaking of murderers."

She opened the wooden door, she and the dog slipped in, and I gratefully slid in too and slammed the door behind me before too many mosquitos could flood in.

The woman removed her camo poncho and went over to a woodstove. "Make yourself at home. Take the load off."

Within minutes, she had stoked a fire and set water on to boil. "I'm going to make you mint tea with honey. You need something to settle you down."

I had gratefully sunk into a rickety wooden chair. "Thanks."

"I'm Ning. That apparently means 'peaceful' in my ancestors' language." She chuckled bitterly. "My parents were being ironic or overly optimistic when they gave me that name. I've been anything but peaceful, and the world's even fucking worse."

There was a pause.

"And you are?"

"Uh, sorry… Birch."

She scrutinized me some more and then said, "Ah. That would make you one of those Seeker people, huh?"

I shook my head. "No. I mean, I come from there, and we all get names like that, but I'm not in the guild."

"Then what the hell were you doing out there on your own, on a bike? You got lost and headed hundreds of kilometres in the wrong direction?"

I tried to think of an answer that would sound sensible; I felt like my brain was computing in molasses. "Um … I wanted to … see things, I guess."

She laughed uproariously for several seconds, less musically than she had before. "Fuck me, you're kidding. Well, now you've seen stuff all right. Don't they give you any training?"

"Well, the Seekers get some, I guess." I was starting to feel and no doubt look defensive. The irritation was reviving me a touch, and I sat up straighter.

"Okay, okay, I'm sorry. I actually get it, I do. Really. Why do you think I'm out here on my own? Can't play well with others, am I right?" She handed me a pleasant-smelling metal mug, and I held it under my nose to let the steam enter my nostrils.

"Well, I'm not the friendliest person myself, but you've had a shitty day so far, you're in shock, and you can't be going anywhere until you get over that. So, you're staying here today and tonight."

"Uh … thanks." I couldn't seem to find my voice again. I slumped back, drank some tea, and looked around the room, trying to avoid the images that kept crowding back, but also dwelling on the fact that the wryly smiling woman sitting in front of me, delicately sipping her tea, had cold-bloodedly killed two men just over an hour ago. She almost seemed to have enjoyed it. Hanging in several places were animal pelts, which gave me a bit of a shock, because you hardly ever saw that in Norbay; they only harvested the fur of animals they found dead.

On a table by the bed was the only piece of modern equipment in the place, right beside an overstuffed bookcase. I couldn't make out the titles of any of them but was interested to see what kind of taste in reading my host had. But the radio was more immediately fascinating to me.

"Is that … a radio?"

She grinned. "Yep. Surprised? Ham radio. Used to be a hobby some people had, talking to other people around the world. I power it with a small solar panel outside. It's the one thing I took with me when I left … where I lived. I took all my stuff in a cart attached to my bike, but this was most of the weight. Works great." She walked over and showed me the handset, holding it to her mouth.

Her last remarks made me curious, but I decided it would be best not to ask for the moment.

"I'm sure you have these where you live?"

I shook my head. "I guess. The leaders probably do. I've never used one, but I wondered sometimes if anyone had made any contact with the outside world." I leaned forward excitedly. "What do you hear?"

Ning put down the receiver. "Not much, to be honest. I've talked to people on the prairies, where it's hotter than here. Life is hard. Makes Ontario look like a party. I've spoken to people close to the east coast. Even some from the south. And farther."

"The south? I thought no one lived there."

Ning's laugh was now surprisingly gentle. "No one? In all that space? Of course people do, in the higher elevations and forests, in places where it's not so hot. Small pockets, doing what we do. Surviving. No cities. Once or twice, I heard people speaking in other languages that sounded what I imagine Asian languages sound like."

"I guess you don't..."

"I may have a Chinese name and background, but who would there have been to teach me? And once..." She grew serious. "I once had a talk with someone from Europe, and she told me some terrible things. As bad as it got here, it was worse there. And I don't just mean the climate. There were huge wars, even rumours of nuclear weapons being used ... vicious dictators and giant camps, way bigger than here. Slaughter of migrants. Millions dead. There was a meltdown at some neglected reactor in Russia that poisoned thousands of square kilometres. Listening to that wasn't a fun history lesson. And then, after that, I never could get in touch with her again. That was about ten years ago."

I wondered how long she'd been living here by herself, but as if anticipating and deflecting the question, she said, "I think it's almost lunch. How about it? But first ... you should finish cleaning up."

I suddenly realized I was sitting in a shirt that had been soaked with blood and brains. The shock was finally starting to wear off a little.

She levelled a sympathetic gaze at me. "Head outside. There's a rain barrel on the side of the cabin. Have a wash. Leave the shirt out there. I'll burn it. I have plenty of old shirts to give you here. The outhouse is about thirty feet away on the edge of the bush. Stay away from the apiary if you don't want to get stung."

"Thanks," I said, getting up. "And I didn't say … thanks for … for what you did."

She flashed her lopsided grin. "Actually, you did. A couple of times. Don't worry about it. I'd have done it for almost anyone. And it helps me out too — eliminating potential threats and scaring the crap out of the rest. Those cowards never go anywhere without their posse. I just thinned out the pack. And I'll do it again if I have to."

I couldn't think of a good answer to that, so I went outside to clean off as much of the horror as I could. I was sure the memories would take a lot longer to wash away, if they ever would.

• • •

I reentered with wet hair and wearing a faded light blue shirt with the peeling words *Blue Jays* emblazoned across the chest. This made me think of Jay, naturally, and the urgency of catching up while he was probably still nearby. But now I found myself really tired —annoyingly, excessively tired — like the atmosphere was weighing down my limbs.

There was a strong but pleasant smell hanging in the air and something boiling on the wood stove. Ning seemed to notice that I was still kind of floppy.

"Sit down, kiddo. You look cleaner but still kind of miserable."

I sank down into one of the wooden chairs and slowly pulled off my boots.

She pushed whatever was boiling and emitting that smell around the pot with a metal spoon for a minute or so, pronounced it ready to eat, and then spooned greyish lumps with bits of herb sticking to them onto two metal plates. She extended one to me, and I took it cautiously.

"What … is this?" I moved it around the plate.

She frowned in amusement. "What d'you mean what is this? Rabbit! Or hare, to be specific. You mean you've never … oh, wait. Right. It's because you're one of *them.*"

I defiantly took the plate. "I'm not one of anything." But when I looked down at the steaming mass of meat and took in its smell, my gorge threatened to rise yet again as the image of Brent's head blowing apart seized me. "Sorry, I'm not sure I can do this right now." I rose quickly and put the plate on the side of the stove. "I *would* have eaten it." Though I wasn't convinced of that.

"Sure, sure," she said. "Well, if you've never eaten meat before, then maybe it's just as well. You'd be puking one way or the other, and I've seen enough of that outta you today. You're just lucky you ended up with me and not one of those people who survives on scrounging up eighty-year-old half-rotted cans." She took a healthy bite off her own fork.

"Sorry. I appreciate all this. I'm just not feeling good."

"I get it." She placed her own plate down after throwing her dog a chunk from the pot; the animal devoured it in a split second. "I can make you some kind of salad … no shortage of dandelions around here. And I grow a few things out back." I shook my head. "Well, let's have some stories then. Tell me why I found you out there, defenseless and hopelessly naïve."

I fought back the urge to protest and just launched into an abridged version of my background and motivations for leaving Norbay, leaving out the emotional stuff, though whenever I mentioned Jay, she gave sort of a half-leer that wasn't hard to interpret.

When I was done, she sat back and took a swig of the tea she seemed to drink incessantly. "Well, I appreciate your candour, though you were leaving out a few things. Since we have time, I can tell you some stuff that'll help you out. First, my story in a nutshell, since I'm sure you're curious. I come from Parry Sound. You must know about that place."

The silence that followed was clearly supposed to mean something to me, but it didn't.

She frowned, this time without amusement. "No? Nothing? Fuck, they don't teach kids much up there. Well, Parry Sound is a community that, like most communities, inhabits what's left of a town that once existed there. There are similarities to your Norbay, which is why I'm surprised you haven't heard of it. The people who founded it in the 2040s were a group who called themselves 'eco-Stoics.' They realized the extinction of humans was inevitable and isolated themselves in an abandoned kids' summer camp. When everything went to shit, they eventually occupied the town, too."

This was fascinating stuff. "That does sound similar."

"Yep." Ning reached down to scratch the dog's head. "It was, except your crew are utopian and cultivate that touching optimism, while the eco-Stoics decided to welcome the end. The old world was unworthy, yes, and we had it coming, so there was no future. Just live as best you can, stay away from everything, try not to have any kids if you can help it. They'd isolate themselves, get back to the land, hunt, fish, forage, live as close to what they felt was the 'real' way for humans to co-exist with nature.

"See," she leaned forward, eyes glittering, "back before the Ruin, there was an unpopular idea amongst some radical environmentalists that humanity is a sort of disease; we haven't evolved into some glorious god-like being, but instead we were a virus slowly eating away at the rest of nature, which all existed in perfect balance until we developed our consciousness and spread all over the planet, destroying everything as we did. Very inspiring, gives you a reason to get up every day, huh?"

I nodded. "Well, to be fair, that makes as much sense as anything else I've heard."

She smiled wryly. "Sure it does. Can't argue with the results, huh? Well, anyway, that was the founding principle. We had to de-virus ourselves. Purify, humble ourselves. When everything fell apart permanently, the community survived. And that's where I was born, sometime in the ... 2070s, I guess. One of the few kids born there."

"How long have you lived alone, though?"

"Maybe twenty years. I'm lucky things worked out for me. I've been healthy. I don't need company. I don't like it, either ... generally."

"But why did you leave?"

She sighed and reached for the dog again. "Traded quite a few pelts for this trained pup. I guess I needed a friend after all. Well ... a community based on the idea that humanity is a cancerous growth isn't a fun place to live. And our leadership was harsh. The second generation was harsher than the founders. It became less about living in accordance with nature's laws and more about keeping people in line. I even had to learn to read in secret; learning about things not related to immediate survival isn't *natural.* There weren't many births, like I said; few people joined us. When people got sick, they didn't get much care because everything had to be as *natural* as possible. My mother died of pneumonia when I was small, and I believe to this day that if we had some kind of healer, *any* kind, she would have had a chance. Of course," her voice got very brittle, "as I aged, I couldn't help but notice that our leadership got better treatment, better food, better everything, than the rest of us. So, even in our community, our basic fucking flaws as humans couldn't be kept at bay."

"I'm sorry."

"Yeah, me too. Well, anyway, I put up with it a long time because, I thought, where else could I go?"

"Norbay?"

"I'd never heard of it. Our leaders wouldn't let us travel, wouldn't let us find out what was out there. Barely educated us; like I said, not even reading for most of us. I didn't find out about your community till much later. After my dad died, the next day I packed up what I had, hooked up the cart, and left. Scouted around for a while, found this place, which was perfect for me. Unlike you, I was sure I wasn't going back. Ever. There wasn't anything for me there."

"Is the community still there?" It didn't make much sense to think that it was. I was sure I'd have heard of it. Maybe Jay had.

She shook her head. "Yes and no. I never really travel in that direction. North, east, a little south, but not west. I don't want to see the place or be near it. Last I heard, it was down to a few dozen people at best. Maybe it's done now. There are gangs like those assholes you ran into today out there, and the last people left in Parry Sound would be easy prey. I don't care, anyway." She fell silent for a couple of minutes, gazing at the milky plastic sheeting of the windows.

"Well, now you know my story. I look after myself. I trade with a few people I've met. I catch or grow my food… I forage more of it — they taught me *those* valuable skills, anyway. Then I got hold of this radio and the power for it, and that's my connection to the human species. It's been a couple of months since I saw another soul up close, until I was out on the road and was lucky enough to see those pieces of shit in the distance, making no effort to keep quiet, acting like kings of the world. Sub-humans. Literally nothing left of their fucking humanity. No ideals driving them, just their instinct to dominate." It looked like she was going to spit on the floor. "Especially those physically weaker than them. If you'd ended up in their clutches, you'd have been used for breeding and abuse. If you even lived that long. My gang may have been deeply flawed, but we had principles, at least. We kept our dignity. And yours do too. Good for them. If we don't, then we may as well all be dead after all."

I would have asked more questions, but the intensity of that rant shut me up.

Finally, after more staring into the distance, she finished her plate, splitting it with the dog, and gestured to the bed.

"Now, I have more work to do. Cutting wood, a little foraging nearby. The heat's not too bad today. The cold season is coming. So, you need to rest." She gestured at her bed, which was made tidily. "Sleep. I won't be back here for hours. No one knows about this place. It's far enough from anything that even the chimney smoke isn't noticeable. You're safe. Rest."

She didn't wait for a response, just slung a smaller rifle over her shoulder and headed for the door with the dog at her heels.

I realized I was more exhausted than I had ever been in my life. I dragged myself over to the bed and dropped down. There was complete silence except for the occasional pop from the embers in the woodstove.

I took in a big breath, smelling the wood all around me. Soon my eyes closed.

• • •

I roused from a dead sleep in the late afternoon, unable to remember any dreams, feeling a lot better. Ning was right. I'd never totally get over what I saw and the fear I'd experienced, but you know what? Those guys had it coming. She was right about that too. Without the rule of laws, we could only depend on our basic human decency, and those fuckers had none of it. I wouldn't let this scare me, and I wouldn't let it stop me.

She showed up later with an armload of wood and a full pack that didn't contain anything dead, for which I was grateful. I wasn't up to watching her dress a carcass.

We ate quietly, me eating a "salad," as she called the mixture of dandelion greens and mushrooms, supplemented with some dried lentils from my pack and some apples.

Then, as it got to twilight, she stoked up the fire and lit a couple of candles. They had a strong mixture of scents.

Ning noticed my nostrils quivering, about to sneeze, and laughed. "Sorry. When you're scavenging, you take what you can get. People used to love nasty fake stink. Fucking bathed in it. I don't even notice it anymore."

Then she thrilled me by offering a demo of the ham radio. She tried lots of frequencies and called out on many of them, but there was nothing but static. She tried for a while, and then she let me try for about half an hour, but there was no response, which she said was typical. I was disappointed, but it was exciting too. For maybe the first time in my life, I felt like I might possibly connect to a wider world.

"You need a lot of time and patience. I've got lots of both. Even if it's months, if I find someone to talk to, it's worth it. It makes me feel that yes, there is still a world out there, and yes, we're worth preserving."

I shot her curious look.

"What?"

"You sound more like a Seeker than an eco-Stoic, frankly."

She laughed. "I see sleep restored your sharpness. Well, yeah, for sure. If I wasn't so old and set in my ways, I'd consider joining up with you all. But I *am* old, and I *am* set, and I'll die here, happily alone. Anyway, it's worth the patience, like I said. Last month I talked to someone in a place called Alberta, believe it or not. That's a long, long way from here. Even there, there are pockets of communities doing what we do here. Getting by."

This did make me feel somewhat more hopeful. Sometimes it felt like Norbay was the only safe, sane place on Earth. But now I'd met this inspirational hermit *and* learned about others of her kind. It didn't really make a close brush with becoming a sex slave worth it, of course, but it did make me feel better.

She had nothing that even resembled a guest bed, and when she offered to share her bed rather than have one of us sleep on the rough wooden floor, I accepted. By now I completely trusted her. She slept facing the wall while I lay on my back with the dog, Night, half-draped across me, sighing and licking her chops every once in a while. She was very heavy, but I didn't mind.

Now, it took me a long time to fall asleep. A sliver of red light escaped the door of the woodstove, and I could hear the cacophony of crickets blasting outside. I knew I was ready to resume my search for Jay.

• • •

I woke to find Ning crawling over me to get out of bed. "Sorry." She dropped roughly to the floor and stretched, then disappeared outside to return a few minutes later with her hair wet.

"No matter what time of year it is, I always start my day by dumping cold water on my head. That gets me going."

I hauled myself out of bed and did the same, stripping down and splashing cold water from the barrel all over myself, slapping at the hungry mosquitos that came calling for a meal. I was happy to get more of the previous days' stink off me.

Then we ate (and I still avoided the meat), and it was time to get ready.

She gave me a sharp look as I rose and headed for my backpack. "You sure you're okay to do this?"

I turned to face her. "Yes. Thank you so much for saving me and for all of this. If it's okay, I'll come back and visit someday."

Her look softened. "You know, Birch, in twenty years I've never welcomed anyone here as a friend. But you and me, we're the same in many ways, I can tell. You're welcome here any time. But you have to do what you have to do. I understand."

I got my stuff ready, including the hunting knife that I made sure was secured in its sheath, but before I headed out, she went to a chipped, scratched chest of drawers that contained all her clothes and other worldly possessions.

When she came back, she held a small, black object. It was a pistol, or handgun, whatever they were called. I'd never even seen one outside of a picture before yesterday.

She held it out to me. "This doesn't belong to one of our asshole friends, though that would be poetic justice. I got this a long time ago, and I won't tell you how. You need to take it." She extended her other hand, which held a box of ammunition.

I made no move to take either. "I–I don't know how to use that."

She laughed heartily. I was already missing that laugh. "Of course you don't. You're going to delay your trip for a little lesson."

There was no point in arguing, so I followed her outside. "Too dense in the forest for target practice, so we'll just have to do it here."

She showed me how to load the handgun, how to point it, how to make sure the safety was on, and what to expect when I pulled the trigger. I took a couple of practice shots, which were terrible because my hand jerked so much, but Ning said ammo was at a premium in the world, so I couldn't waste any more. The mere threat of a loaded gun would keep most dangers at bay — human dangers, anyway.

Then she accompanied me to the end of her overgrown lane and pointed me back toward the main roads.

I was surprised when she gave me a quick, tight hug. "You've got guts, Birch. I wish you safety. And the good sense to be more aware of your surroundings now. Eyes fucking open — all the time."

I smiled. "I will." I rode off onto the pitted larger road with dead pines pressing in around me, accompanied by a new sense of resolve.

It was time to find Jay and face the wonders and perils of this lost world — together.

XVI.

NOW

JAY

Looks like we're out of time again! It's a consequence of listening to elderly storytellers… You need plenty of patience. Well, I think we have a longer block of time available tomorrow. We'll need it all, the way this is going. You all want to hear the end of this? … Yeah? Good.

BIRCH

Very touching, that last part, huh? I know how to tell that part really well. Had a lot of practice.

JAY

Touching? Not sure violent death is very touching, Birch.

BIRCH

Let's not bicker in front of the kids, okay? You know what I meant.

JAY

Fine, then. Tomorrow you'll find out about Great Toronto, at last, and what Elm and I found there.

BIRCH

And what I found too.

JAY
I hear there's a dinner tonight at Trout Lake. Who's going? I'm definitely thirsty after all this storytelling.
BIRCH
We'll see you there! I hear Sparrow and all her apprentices will be there too to lead the music, so it should be a lovely time.

XVII.

GREAT TORONTO

JAY

Elm and I continued cautiously and slowly that day. It was scorching, easily in the high thirties or low forties. We'd have melted into sticky red puddles if we tried to push it — or the pavement might have gotten so hot that our tires would just gradually disintegrate right under us. I'd heard of that happening.

Fortunately, now that Elm was back to being quick-witted and sharp-tongued, thanks to her scouting we were quickly able to take shelter in the basement of the least ramshackle-looking house we found upon exiting the highway. This place had been called Vaughan, but frankly I don't know how the citizens of Great Toronto had been able to tell one subdivision from another; despite their varying states of dereliction and the massive plant growth encompassing them, I could tell that every single house in this sprawling suburb had once been identical.

We settled down for the afternoon in that stuffy room, which still had some furniture in it that didn't smell too bad. The house looked like it had never flooded, which was why Elm chose it. The heat was still suffocating, but it was several degrees cooler down in this dank room, and after sitting silently for a while, watching dust motes dancing in the rays through the cracked ground-level windows, I did manage to doze off.

Elm woke me around six for a meal. My supplies of dried food were still holding out well, but at some point, I knew I would have to apply the foraging skills I'd been taught. Of course, that would be difficult in these urban areas, but maybe there would be berries or the remnants of abandoned gardens to pillage. I'd ask Elm about how best to go about that after we got through this dangerous part of the journey. My curiosity was strong, but I was also getting very nervous.

"So," she said through a mouthful of dried fruit, "this is where things get interesting. What I want to do is get close enough to feel out a sense of the place, if possible. Which doesn't mean we'll get *that* close. I want to see if the rumours are true that the city is now basically guarded like a fortress. That in itself would tell us quite a bit — something negative. People who act like that are either defending themselves from a threat or are preparing to *be* the threat. We haven't heard anything about the former, so it's probably the latter. Anything we can learn will help the council decide on a response, if any."

This was starting to sound serious, but there was no way out now without feeling like a coward. "I'm in, but after we do that, I need to head for Kingston. I have to fulfill my mission."

She nodded. "I understand perfectly. Your first mission is important. Without that, you won't feel like a true Seeker. I wouldn't mess with that for the world, I promise. As for what I'll do next myself — that depends on what we observe.

"There are two reasons why it's best to travel by dusk and even night if we can. First, on a day like today we don't have a choice. Second, the less they see of us as we approach, the better. We're near a big street called Steeles Avenue that goes east to west. I don't trust taking the old 401 mega-highway across the top; I suspect that's what they'll be using as their border or safety zone. If we go across higher and then sneak down for a peek or two, that should be enough. You can join the 401 outside of the city, where it's safer, then I'd suggest taking Highway 7 instead for a while. It's a doozy of a detour to the north, but much safer."

I was glad to be travelling with someone so experienced. I didn't know if I'd have had the sense to take the smaller but parallel Highway 7, which we would pass on our way to Steeles Avenue, toward Kingston, or whether my curiosity would have brought me down to the 401 anyway. But it was far better to do that with Elm.

She glanced out the window, where the warm golden light of early evening was starting to fade. She got up. "Well, it's still going to be roasty out there, but we'd better check it out and get moving if we can. Dusk is our best bet for travel."

• • •

The trip down to Steeles Avenue only took about forty-five minutes, but they were brutally hot minutes, even though the sun was nearing the horizon, casting the broken, jungle-covered anthropocentric landscape in an eerie reddish glow and huge shadows. You could easily imagine that not only humanity's time on Earth, but also the life of the planet itself was nearing its end under a swollen, spent sun.

The buildings were gargantuan here, larger even than anything I'd seen in Great Sudbury, and I gawked at them as we passed. Some of them probably had at least twenty storeys! And some you could see right inside, since the glass they were once covered in had fallen away long ago. They lined the highway in stretches, like sentinels with their ancient corporate logos hanging off them; a couple of them were caved in as though hit by a tornado or a bomb. Every now and then, there were big roadside signboards that once held advertisements, but those had peeled away decades ago, and now they just sat there blank and grey. Downed power lines lay across the road, long dormant and harmless. Once, we had to pick our way around the girders of a fallen electrical pylon.

There were also a couple of unpleasant and frightening moments.

About twenty minutes after we were back on the massive 400 highway, which the 11 had become upon reaching Barrie — it had to be at least ten lanes wide, and I could only imagine the tens of millions of cars that had once crowded it — in the failing light I saw a peculiar object on the road on the left side of the crumbled median, something that wasn't debris or vegetation.

"Elm? What's that?"

She stopped pedaling and gazed intently over at it for a moment, frowning. "I'm not sure we should find out, Jay."

But I was already moving. I leaned my bike up against the median and hopped over it. I could hear her sighing loudly behind me. "Jay..."

As I approached the object, I could see it was long and shaped like a person. And that's what it was. I stopped about ten feet short of it. It was a human form, still dressed in long sleeves and jeans, lying on its side, though I couldn't see the front of the torso. The hand that stuck out from the sleeve and the side of the face that I could see showed bones penetrating ... dried, pecked, almost absent strands of flesh and skin. This person had died some time ago, and scavengers had done their work. It was so dried out that there wasn't even any odour. I just stood there, frozen in place. I'd never seen a body like this, just forgotten, abandoned. It was so undignified.

I heard Elm just behind me. "Looks like they've been dead a little while. A few seasons, maybe, but maybe not long enough for our comfort. We can't say how they died. Could have just given out. Could have been violence."

I turned around, glad to look away from the sight. "Do you often see dead people on the road?"

She shook her head and put an arm in the small of my back to push me back toward the median. "No. I mean, I have seen them, yes, and sometimes a lot fresher than that. Sometimes ancient. Sometimes piles of bones. Millions of people don't just disappear entirely without leaving some traces, and life for people who don't belong to a community can be hard and short, and there are lots of predators and bandits, so untimely death is a frequent reality of this world, Jay. It can't be avoided. I guess you just learned another lesson."

Having fully restored her uncanny vitality by now, she nimbly hopped over the median, and I followed suit.

As she mounted her bike, she said sternly, "It's okay to be shocked and horrified by the things you see on your first trip. That's what this is for, really, not just being schooled in some arcane knowledge that will change everything. It's about growing as a person. You've learned in class about what the world was, and what it is, and what it *can* be. But you have to see it to believe any of it and find out how you will deal with it, emotionally. Not everyone can handle it."

She started off without another word.

Soon it was getting dark, with just a band of orange on the horizon in the west, a darker band of blue above that, then a gradation to night-black, and we were nearing the place where we'd leave the highway.

I was probably paying too much attention to the eerie beauty of the city skyline in the distance, silhouetted against the vivid colours, instead of the way ahead when Elm hissed from just in front of me. "Stop, get off, and move to the side of the road."

"What?"

"*Now.*"

She was already rushing over to the side median about ten metres away.

I rushed to do the same, my pulse racing. Whatever it was had to be very dangerous to elicit this frenzied reaction.

We hunched down against the shadowy metal fence, and she pointed ahead.

They were far off, but I could see a group of moving forms. They were holding lights that waved from side to side, but they weren't the flames of lamps or torches. *Flashlights?*

"Not good, Jay," she whispered. "They must patrol this road; it was the main way into the city. Get ready to jump over this low wall in a second. We'll have to leave the bikes to them… It'll make too much noise if we try to put them over."

I held my breath as the forms slowly neared, but for some reason, before they even got within shouting distance or we could make out their exact numbers, the cluster of people stopped and then slowly turned around and retreated.

I slowly let out my breath and gasped in a fresh one. I heard Elm do the same.

"They must have reached the limit of their route. We got lucky. And I was stupid yet again," she said quietly. "We have to assume that party was on official business. Let's get off this thing. Steeles is just ahead."

• • •

We clambered slowly and painstakingly down a grassy embankment and past another strip of elevated parkway that had long since collapsed; if we'd realized it was there, we could have used it as a ramp to coast down off the highway to Steeles Avenue. I had no idea what was below and couldn't see my way at all, so each footstep was a step into the complete unknown.

This road was in even worse shape than the highway, completely chewed up and full of shrubs and grasses. Within a few decades, roads like this wouldn't even exist anymore. Eventually, the whole city, as unbelievable as it seemed, would be buried like the cities of ancient cultures under layers of earth and vegetation, but this time maybe no archaeologists would be left to dig up its secrets. Nature could reclaim and swallow up any environment, even a completely artificial one, given time. This scene made that very clear, and the end was in sight for the buildings and roads of Great Toronto.

Even though it was now quite dark, there was a glimmer of moonlight through the clouds. I would have been completely lost without Elm leading; she told me her night vision was very keen after so many years of avoiding the full heat of midday. We were surrounded by waist-high thickets of what I could tell were mostly ragweed.

Other than getting a bad fright from a group of raccoons that ran out in front of us (Elm told me a group of raccoons is called a "gaze"), we spent a quiet half hour ploughing our tires through the grasses and over hummocks, but the terrain got too rough, and we eventually had to walk, swishing along in silence as she picked our way forward.

I could feel more than see the looming black wrecks of seemingly endless stretches of industrial buildings on either side, concealed by trees, and I could understand why Elm had chosen this route. No one would have any reason to be out here at night — it was totally, awesomely desolate and lifeless, other than the occasional hoot of an owl and the perennial calls of crickets. It was slow going, and I was already yawning. It was also still very muggy, so I was covered in sweat.

Eventually, she filled me in on the plan, her voice drifting back a few feet in the darkness. "Up ahead is what used to be the city's main street, Yonge.

Once we're there, we'll see what the scene offers. If it's as dead as this, it'll be safe to head down toward the city. We'll just take a quick peek at the 401, which is just south of here, bunk down — not sure where, but I'll find somewhere comfy enough — get a few hours of sleep, then use the earliest part of dawn to take a better look. Surely, they can't be monitoring every last kilometre of empty highway. Then we'll decide what further risks we're willing to take or just go on our way."

She fell silent after that, and I just listened to the crickets and mysterious rustlings in the underbrush around me. I wondered what kind of predators had occupied the city; at the very least, there must be packs of coyotes. I thought I heard a few growls, but it was probably just my heightened imagination. Occasionally there would be clearer patches of road and we would mount our bikes and delicately ride for a while, very slowly but faster than walking. She stopped and scanned around her at major intersections, but everything was black and deathly silent, aside from nature's night sounds. We didn't take any breaks, and I was about to ask for one when we neared another big intersection. On the right was a patch of forest that may have been a parking lot, completely overgrown.

Elm allowed me to have some water and a bit of food. I gratefully sank down onto my haunches to eat.

She remained standing, clearly still irritated with herself for the near run-in with the patrol. "Okay, kid. We haven't tripped over anything and broken our heads. So far, so good. Yonge looks disused up here too. A little longer to the south, a quick look, and then we can rest for the night."

She turned right, and we made our way through what appeared to have been a more residential neighbourhood. Leviathan, crumbled condominium blocks looked awesomely ancient, lonely, and forbidding in the waxing moonlight. I took advantage of the illumination to check my watch: 11:00 p.m. I wasn't going to make it much farther. My legs felt like lead, and my hands hurt from gripping the handlebars and guiding the bike around obstacles.

Finally, after what could have been hours of this near-agony and larger and larger buildings hemming us in on both sides, we could see an elevated highway coming up.

"The 401," she announced quietly. "The big one."

"Thank frigging god," I muttered.

"I heard that," she said. "Now, be slow and *silent.*"

We carefully made our way up the ramp on the right, which still stood; the one on the left had collapsed.

I almost bumped into her as we reached the top and stood to her right. She was staring off into the distance. "My goodness," she said softly.

I followed her gaze ... and there, far away, surrounded by an infinite pool of inky blackness, we saw lights. The lights of a city! It wasn't a huge area, maybe a few kilometres square, but they were electric lights, nonetheless, scattered around like glittering stars in the firmament. Far more than I'd ever seen. Sure, in Norbay we had enough solar and wind to power a few lights in important places, but this was a sight I was sure I'd never see in my lifetime: signs of a living, functioning outpost of real human civilization in the middle of all this ruin. A civilization everything I'd learned had told me was lost forever. Astonishing!

"Amazing," she breathed. "They must be able to generate a *lot* of power to do that."

If it was enough to impress Elm, then it *must* be something new and unusual.

She turned to me to say more when another light blazed out — much closer and very, very bright.

We spun to our right in unison and lifted our arms to shield our eyes. Two points of light were blazing at us from not far away.

A voice rang out, metallic, as though through a bullhorn. "Intruder, stay where you are. Don't move, or you'll be shot. I repeat, don't move. Raise your hands."

I felt like my bowels were turning to water, but something new took hold of me. Some protective instinct, or sense of chivalry or honour, I don't know. I did raise my hands, but instead of standing still, I walked forward.

"Jay! What the hell are you doing?" Elm whispered hoarsely.

I turned my head and said with surprising calm, "Get back down the ramp, Elm. It's right behind you."

"Jay! I'm an old person," she hissed urgently. "Let them take me instead."

I stopped for a moment. "It's too late for that. Run!"

I continued forward a few paces, finding I had stopped breathing, hoping she was doing as I said.

"Intruder! Halt *now*! I won't warn you again," the voice called, this time with extra menace.

This time I stopped, dropped to my knees, still with my hands raised, and didn't move again.

XVIII.

THE SIX

JAY

I was in a car! An actual, functioning, motorized vehicle. It was so surreal that I almost forgot to be afraid. It was a very quiet one, so I assumed it was an electric model; after all, where could they possibly have obtained petroleum? The torn, worn upholstery even had its own smell that I couldn't place, something from the industrial past. It was like seeing the bones of a long-extinct beast reassemble into a skeleton and start walking around in front of you.

I was sitting in the back with one man beside me. Two rode up front. All of them wore uniforms, another thing I'd never seen before. I couldn't quite make out what the two in front were wearing, but it seemed the uniforms were mix-and-match, presumably assembled from scavenging. All three of them were clean-shaven — yet another thing I'd rarely seen. Trying to keep a razor sharp and avoiding cutting yourself with it were things that weren't deemed necessary to daily life in Norbay.

The one beside me looked stonily ahead from under bushy eyebrows, and while I could have tried to ask him the obvious questions racing around my mind, I was sure he wasn't going to answer them. So, instead, I decided to take in whatever sights I could make out at night.

I wondered what had happened to my pack, whether they had it or if Elm did. I'd been shoved firmly and quickly into the car. I also desperately hoped Elm had gotten far from that place; there was nothing she could do for me now. I could see a holster on the belt of the guy next to me, and I had a feeling they weren't averse to using their weapons.

Whatever was coming, I'd have to try to keep an open mind about it. After all, I only had rumours to go on about this place.

I would have expected the ride to be very bumpy, but it was surprisingly smooth; I could only assume they were somehow maintaining this part of the 401. After a while, the car went down a bumpier ramp and onto a street that again was surprisingly smooth and completely free of the obstructions of vegetation and rubble.

It being about midnight, there wasn't much to see for some time, just yawning, glassless storefronts. This part of the city didn't appear to be populated. At one point the lights of another vehicle approached, and as it passed us, both drivers lightly tapped their horns. I jumped. So many firsts tonight!

I spotted a slight glow in the near distance, and I leaned to the left as much as I dared to look through the windshield. The guy next to me didn't shift.

Now the wonder of wonders: there were streetlights! The car slowed down at a shed that had been placed in the road with barbed wire on either side of the roadway. As the driver stopped to chat with the guard there, I was able to see a road sign with extremely faded lettering: Eglinton Avenue West. This must be the northern settled extent of the city-state of Great Toronto.

My eyes were glued to the side window as we moved forward. After a while, we started to pass buildings that looked occupied and maintained; light beamed through many windows. And there were people in the streets! Not a lot of them, but they were strolling unhurried; some alone, some in groups of two of three. A few smaller figures looked like children, despite the lateness of the hour. We were passing through commercial areas, and while most storefronts were dark, a few even seemed to have shops or restaurants in them.

My established view of the world was being blown to pieces right before my eyes. There we were in Norbay, living decent, clean lives as best we could, but without most of the conveniences people of the early twenty-first century had enjoyed, while four hundred kilometres to the south a modern civilization seemed to be flourishing. What nonsense had Cedar and the others been selling us all these years? I shook my head, which was spinning, and the man next to me glanced over. *No.* I needed to reserve judgment. I couldn't be so easily seduced and impressed by these wonders without seeing more. Much more. I'd been taught critical thinking, and now was the perfect time to use it.

Finally, about forty minutes after we'd left the highway, the car pulled into the lot of a building with a rusty but intact sign that proclaimed *Toronto Police Service — 52 Division.*

They all got out, and the one from the passenger's side opened my door. "Out."

It was the first word they'd spoken to me since pushing me into the car. I obediently pulled myself out, holding on to the doorframe, and he prodded me toward the entrance. As we went in, I had to put a hand in front of my face at the sudden bright glare of the interior lights.

I was led with one guard on either side and one in front down a hallway into the bowels of the building, occasionally passing others also in a motley assortment of uniforms of different colours, but each wearing some kind of pass around their necks.

In a hallway lined with identical heavy metal doors, the lead guard opened one and gestured. "In."

I thought it might be a good time to venture a question. "Um, what is going to happen to me next?"

He looked right at me for the first time, his ice-blue eyes cold and expressionless. "Don't know. You'll find out tomorrow."

The cell contained a bed, basin, and toilet. I wondered if the toilet actually worked. I would find that out soon, too, I supposed. There was a faint chemical odour in the air.

They shut the door, and the light went out for a second, replaced by a slight dull illumination from the ceiling that at least allowed me to feel my way to the bed.

My mind was completely overwhelmed by everything I'd seen and questioned in the last hour, let alone the last few days. I had no idea what was next, but surely people who could achieve all this must have some goodness and reason in them?

• • •

Despite all the overstimulation, I did sleep, and it was so dark and silent in the cell — at some point even the faint light in the ceiling had been put out — that I was wakened by the cell door opening. A guard with a slightly darker skin tone than the previous one entered, carrying a tray.

"You got fifteen minutes to eat this and do whatever else you need to do before you leave." To my surprise, he went back into the halfway and returned with my pack, which he hefted onto the floor as well. "It's all there. Nothing of interest."

I eagerly opened it and saw that everything was indeed there: my clothes, food, *The Plague,* the CD cover of *Gord's Gold.* Everything except the maps, something I found odd. Didn't they have their own? And, of course, I had no idea what had happened to my bike.

The food was decent, though there was a glistening fatty, reddish strip of what appeared to be meat, which I avoided. The fruit was fresh, which had to mean they were growing it or had access to trading.

I was just finishing when the guard came back. "Okay, time to go."

"Go where?"

He ignored the question and gestured to the door. I had no reason to refuse; all things considered, their treatment of me so far had been humane — for a captive.

We went outside, and I was put back in what appeared to be the same car. My watch read nine o'clock. It was blindingly bright despite the whitish haze, though the surrounding tall buildings cast long shadows in the morning light. There were more people on the street, and many of them glanced curiously at the car. There were no other cars on the street, though the pedestrians seemed to stay clear of the roadway. As I had noticed last night, some buildings appeared to have been repaired or maintained, while others were shells, though it also looked like the more precarious bits of them had been taken down to avoid them falling into the streets.

Only a couple of minutes later, the car pulled up at a wide, open, weed-free plaza outside a peculiar collection of buildings: two curved towers, covered in moss and vines but otherwise intact, and a smaller domed one that sat between and in front of them.

I was hustled out of the car. There were no pedestrians in the square, only guards stationed every few metres around the perimeter, standing stiffly, like photos I'd seen of the guards at the king's palace in England scores of decades before. I noticed these guards' uniforms were colour-coordinated and matched perfectly.

We went through glass doors, then to another doorway, where no fewer than four guards stood, bearing large rifles slung over their shoulders.

The guard who had taken me from the police station said, "You're about to be questioned by the Six. Don't approach. Stand where you're told. Don't move. Don't talk unless they speak to you first. Got it?"

For some reason my fear had dissipated instead of heightened. This was all so absurd. Who in this world was so important that they needed all this protection and pomp? What was I going to do to them? I nodded. "Sure."

Two of the guards opened the doors, and I walked into a capacious, echoey room with long desks forming the curve of a half circle around a podium. The room was lit by electricity, even though it was daytime, which again amazed me. The sheer abundance of it here!

I was led right to the podium in front of the half circle and turned around. The guards stepped away a few metres on either side of me.

Facing me was the first semicircle of long desks, and only six people sat there. I scrutinized them, and they did the same to me for a few long moments.

There were three male and three female figures, all looking to be about my father and mother's age or older. None had full beards; all had heads of hair. They were a mixture of ethnicities, from what I could tell. Two wore eyeglasses, and one had a moustache. They were all dressed in what I could only describe as twentieth century business attire: suits, including the women. It looked very much like a uniform, kind of a silly one, when seen all in a row like that.

After a few seconds, a middle-aged man with a moustache, glasses, and tight, curly hair, finally spoke. His voice was deep and slow.

"You're called before the Six, stranger, for trespassing into the territory of Great Toronto. You are to give a full accounting of yourself so we can decide what's to be done with you."

The woman beside him, who had shoulder-length greying brown hair, said in a gentler tone, "Tell us your name, son."

I cleared my throat. "Um, Jay."

"Jay what?" said the man on the end, who was pale and had a very thin, intense face and a penetrating blue-eyed stare. His hair was slicked back.

I turned my head to him. "Just Jay."

He leaned back and tented the fingers of both hands. "Huh. Just Jay. Well, *just* Jay, that was the last clue we needed. For example, my name is Craig Kelly. First name, last name. Nothing special. Normal. Civilized. You, on the other hand, are named after a kind of bird and are not a man named Jason, I assume." His voice had taken on a mocking tone.

"I guess," I said. "Where I come from, we don't have last names. We choose names inspired by nature. We just like it that way." I had no reason to lie, and besides, that didn't come naturally to me. Anyway, I didn't think they wanted me to go into a digression about Norbay's naming conventions.

He leaned forward. "You're a Knowledge Seeker, from Norbay. You were sent to spy on us. That's what your crazy little cult does, right? Spy all around Ontario? You think we don't know all about that?" His voice dripped with disdain.

The woman on the far left, who had very short hair and a smooth-looking face, intervened. "All right, Kelly, we'll get to that." She looked at me in an almost friendly way. "What actually did bring you this far south, Jay?"

Again, I had no reason to lie to these people; the basic truth seemed harmless. "I'm on my way to a place called Kingston. It's my first mission."

The thin-faced man, Craig, scoffed. "*Mission…*"

The kindly-looking woman shot him a look. "We know what your 'missions' are and what they're for, but you deliberately entered our territory. You didn't just wander by. What's more, you were in the company of another person who eluded our guards, with your assistance. If you have nothing to hide, why did that person flee?"

"I was alone."

The moustached man laughed scornfully. "You were not. But don't worry, we don't practice torture to get confessions here. Not generally, anyway. The lie doesn't look good on you, though. If your friend took off, that was the smartest thing to do. And they'd better run far and fast."

Another woman, who had her grey hair scraped back into a bun and seemed the oldest there, put in, "Are you really suggesting you were just innocent passersby?"

Deciding it might be good to withhold a bit of the truth after all, I nodded. "Yes, ma'am. I thought the 401 was the main way around. I didn't even know you had ... territory. I didn't know anyone really 'owned' this land. Or any land."

Now Craig Kelly let out an ugly hoot of laughter. "Right. You don't *own* anything up in your utopian paradise, if memory serves me. You're true primitive communists or something. You seem so naïve, I'm almost inclined to believe you. Almost."

I shifted uncomfortably. "I don't know what to you tell you. I was just—"

"On a *mission,*" he interrupted.

"Craig, that's enough!" the kind-faced woman snapped.

He leaned back again, scowling, but fell silent.

"All right, Jay," said the man who'd first spoken. "Assuming that you were just passing by and not spying on Great Toronto on behalf of Norbay — and we don't believe that for a second — you still trespassed, and here you are. So, tell me, what do you think of what we've achieved here in Great Toronto?"

I felt all their eyes boring into me. "Well, honestly, I'm amazed. I never thought I'd see cars, and so much electricity, and so much organization." This praise was genuine; I was still in a state of mild shock at it all.

The woman with brown hair laughed gently. "See, Craig? He's a good kid. Go on, Khalil."

"I'm glad to hear that. What we've achieved here was won at great cost of blood, sweat, and tears. But it's just the beginning. Just as Great Toronto was the leader of a great country before the Ruin, so will it be again in the future." This sounded almost like a rehearsed recitation of a creed. "For too long the survivors of the Ruin have suffered without hope, without civilization, without anyone to care for them. It's time for humanity to rise again. And Great Toronto will be the standard-bearer of that rise."

There was a rustle of approval from the other five.

I took a half step forward. "I'd be happy to tell people at home about what you've done. I'm sure they'd be interested and want to start a dialogue about the next steps forward we can all take, together."

Craig laughed bitterly. "Dialogue? Not a chance. We know all about your cult; we have more effective spies than you. If you had your way, we'd be stuck living in medieval conditions for hundreds of years because of your misguided principles. You've hoarded all kinds of power sources and equipment and don't even use them properly. Most of them you don't use at all. You're a danger to the future."

The kind-faced woman shot him another look. "What Craig is trying to say, Jay, is that there are serious philosophical differences between us. A gap that probably can't be bridged, by all indications. Though I admit no one's tried yet."

Khalil interjected again in his rhythmic, melodic way, "We have spent many decades existing in squalor as lowly scavengers while the number of people living in a civilized, dignified way has declined. Now, under *our* leadership, we will restore civilization in its best and greatest form. We have enough knowledge. We have the will. The time has come to act. To *make* things again. To hew and mine and shape. That's what humans do. We are not scavengers by nature. We think and act and build and grow."

Craig cut in again, "Before we took control here, your Seekers had already ransacked our schools and universities for precious knowledge that we needed. It may have added years to the time we wasted getting things going here."

A dissonant note had definitely sounded against my initial, cautiously positive feeling about this crew and their achievements. I could feel my stance becoming more assertive as I stood up straighter. "Took control? May I ask how Great Toronto is ruled? Are you elected officials?"

Craig just laughed.

"No, Jay," said the older woman. "The people aren't ready for that, and they don't want that. Not yet. They want security and prosperity. The people you see here in this room today came to control Great Toronto through hardship and conflict that we don't care to revisit. We are the rulers here, and we rule for the greater good. We always have the people's best interests at heart. Someday, maybe, the people will be ready for something like democracy again. Do you think that's unfair?"

She levelled her gaze at me.

"Well ... frankly, yes. That sounds like an authoritarian government from the old world. And that's what we have to avoid, and what we avoid where I come from."

Khalil's brows drew together. "Yes, yes, we know all about your little community's utopian idealism," he said impatiently. "Nothing from the old world that could corrupt should enter the new one. A naïve and unrealistic view. Ridiculous. Unworkable. Human nature cannot be overcome," he boomed as though this was a debate he'd engaged in many times before.

The one person who hadn't spoken yet was the oldest, a man as pale as Craig who looked at least seventy. Now he chimed in, his voice dry and cracked. "Son, you aren't old enough to have known anyone who could really tell you about that world at its height. About its wonders. Its abundance. But you can see the signs all around us here in the city. Do you truly understand what we've lost? I think if your leaders were more honest with you, you might understand better."

"With all due respect, Elder, we are provided with a very thorough education in history."

He smiled thinly. "Yes, I'm sure you are. With a certain bias. Do you not have people in your community with disease? Cancers? Viruses? Do people die young from illnesses and infections that were easily curable a hundred years ago? Is that tolerable to you? Do you have a variety of food to eat?"

"We do what we can, and we're happy the way we are," I proclaimed defiantly.

"Because you're *told* the people of the past were evil; that their motivations were greed and lust for possessions. Yet you see signs of their glory everywhere. They could travel anywhere they wanted on the globe, within hours. They lived safely in climate-controlled environments and ate a wonderful variety of food. When they were sick, they would very likely be healed by the great developments brought by science. When people had a disability or a sickness, they were supported. We can bring all that back."

"*A few* of them lived that way. Most of the world didn't. A tiny percentage got to enjoy all those great things," I shot back. "What about the poor? Were they healed and supported? I can tell you where I come from, everyone is supported, no matter who they are. Everyone plays a role in the community. You don't need technology to care for others; you just need empathy and the will to help. We have some medicine and care for the sick and dying with dignity. And the destruction of the environment helped *cause* things like cancers and viruses and inequality," I added boldly. "You can't argue that isn't true. Look at the twenty-first century and the billionaires that ran everything exclusively for their own profit until there was nothing left to run. Do you want to go back and finish that job?" It was like all my education and pride were rushing to the surface to give me an eloquence I didn't know I possessed.

"We'll do better!" Khalil said heatedly. "We will be taking on the role of leadership. Most of Earth is not habitable... This is one of the last remaining centres of civilization. We have a duty to take on this role. We can't allow voices contradicting this with cowardly propaganda, slandering the great civilization we're reviving. The mistakes of the past won't be made again."

"Our ancestors were almost able to fix all these problems you mention before it was too late. With a little more time, technology would have been developed to end the climate crisis and heal all illnesses," the older man said with absolute certainty. "Any other view of history is painfully naïve." He seemed to have tired himself out with his arguments and leaned back in his chair.

"I guess we do disagree about a lot, then," I said. "The price of progress was almost the end of our species and caused the extinction of thousands more. What good is extending a few rich people's lives through technology when it was tied to so much destruction?" I was honestly surprising myself with the intensity of my defense. "And you want to plunge back into that. Is that just?"

Khalil and Craig looked apoplectic at all this defiance from some rag-wearing whelp from the sticks, I could tell, but even Craig had lapsed into angry silence.

Well, if I'd ever doubted whether the Knowledge Seekers were making a difference, I wouldn't doubt it any longer. Clearly, these people felt we and our ideas about taking care and time during reconstruction and a new, more benign role for humanity on Earth were a threat to their grand plans. They weren't prepared even to talk to us. What were their plans, then? Presumably not just to sit here in their half-ruined city and leave the rest of us in peace.

And now Khalil had made that most arrogantly notorious statement of all, the one statement that was anathema to our entire view of the world: history would never repeat, because *this* group was somehow better and wiser than all the greatest minds of the past.

My initial benign view of the Six of Great Toronto had turned very shadowy in the last few minutes.

"So, you want to just bring back ... everything? Fossil fuels? Capitalism?"

Khalil waved a hand dismissively, having calmed himself a touch. "That's a future discussion. We're nowhere near that. Right now, we need to organize and revive what we can. Living scattered like this, we'll never get anywhere. You know this. The views you've been taught have a certain nobility on paper, I admit, but they're childish and impractical in practice. An incremental approach will never restore humanity to its rightful place."

"I see," I said, now wondering where this was all going to lead for me, personally. "Well, I still think you could just talk about it with our leaders, if you see us as some kind of threat. We're not. I'm sure they'd be happy to talk. There's always room for compromise. An exchange of ideas."

Khalil sighed. "More talk won't—"

Craig broke in, "May I ask why we're wasting our morning debating with a teenager from some commune in the northern bush? It's tedious. We need to decide what we're going to do with him."

All eyes fixed on me. "Yes, what will we do with you?" the kind-faced woman said. "You're not our usual variety of trespasser."

The calm I'd felt earlier suddenly washed over me with the force of total conviction. "The fact that you won't just let me leave when I want to, call me a trespasser for even going near your city, look down on where I come from, and need to have armed guards everywhere tells me everything I need to know."

Khalil ignored my admonishment and instead rumbled, "I'm going to explain this to you carefully, because you now have a choice. It's clear you've got guts. You're smart. You can be a useful addition to Great Toronto. You can be part of the future we're building here and benefit from it, along with the rest of the citizens — if you can deprogram yourself from these cult-like beliefs that have been wounding our ears for the last several minutes."

"And if I don't want to?"

Craig made yet another angry noise and scraped his chair back but let Khalil pass judgment: "Whether or not you agree, you will stay in Great Toronto for the time being and assist us, like it or not. You will not be allowed to return to Norbay with the intelligence you've gathered here so that they can spread your propaganda against us in the north. You clearly can't be trusted."

"So," the brown-haired woman put in, "you can stay as our friend, or as our captive. I know I'd prefer the former. You should consider it."

Khalil gestured to the guards. "Take him back to the lock-up while he thinks it over."

XIX.

BIRCH AND ELM

BIRCH

Turned out I got most of the danger and trauma out of the way at the very start of my journey, I suppose, because the next two nights on Highways 11 and 400 were quiet. Mostly. The first night after leaving Ning's, I was unable to find a decent shelter by the time twilight fell. I had to avoid exposing myself at all costs and looked anxiously around for the best spot. I did finally come across a place not far off the road where two huge trees had fallen into one another, creating a sort of cradle where giant fallen trunks met. It wasn't exactly comfortable, but it was nice to know, as I hauled myself up the couple of metres with considerable difficulty, that neither predator nor prowler would likely be able to get at me. I'd hidden my bike in the always present thick shrubbery that clogged the forest floor.

The bugs were absolutely horrific, plucking at my flesh to the point where I wanted to tear my clothes off and run away screaming, so I swathed myself in sleeves, pulled my hood over my head, zipped up everything as best I could, and tucked in my chin in the pitch black, listening to the rustles, hoots, and odd little chirps of the night life. The canopy was too thick even for stargazing. There was no wind at all, not even a breath, and I eventually dropped off from sheer boredom.

I woke at some point in the night to snuffling and cracking below me. This couldn't be good. Cautiously putting my head over the side of the trunk, I could just barely see a large black form, a blob slightly darker than its surroundings, wandering around under there; either this black bear had smelled my pack and its food rations … or it had smelled me. I knew that bears were capable of climbing, so I gently readied the gun Ning had given me, drawing it out of its holster as silently as possible. It would be a terrible thing to have to kill this beast, but my Norbay holiness didn't extend to sacrificing myself as some hungry bear's midnight snack. Even nobility and principle have their limits.

Fortunately, after a few very tense minutes I heard rather than saw it wandering loudly off into the brush. I listened to it crashing away until silence reigned once more, then slept fitfully after that. Despite the interruption, I still managed to get an early start, since the days were getting hotter as I headed south, and I needed to maximize the potential of each day. If I snoozed away the morning, I wouldn't get anywhere.

Early that same day, however, I saw people again as I was picking my way down a long, sloped straightaway nearing Barrie, heading down into a dip where the two four-lane highways met, the 69 and 11, to create the 400 mega-highway. On either side were forested hillocks. These people were far away, as much as a couple of kilometres, blurry in the heat haze rising from the ancient asphalt, but even from my distant vantage point I could tell they were human forms, at least two, walking. The grass was so high where I was, poking through giant potholes in the highway, that I was easily able to drop my bike and hunker down, peering over the fat seed heads. If they came my way, I'd have to slink right off to the side and desperately hope I hadn't been seen. Again, I felt the gun digging into my side. It should have made me feel more powerful and confident, but instead it just felt … evil. Like it was a malevolent entity waiting to corrupt me into violence and the loss of my soul. I didn't know if I would even be able to bring myself to use it on a person. Once again, memories of the slaughter of Brent and his buddy intruded, my stomach lurched, and I shook my head to try to get back into the moment.

I was lucky again; the small, dark cluster didn't turn onto the highway. They moved slowly away and onto some side track. Their slow pace made me wonder if they were really a threat at all. Not everyone could be that bad, surely. I wondered what the hell people could be doing wandering around these forsaken lands, but then again, I remembered those scavengers who had tried to take me as some kind of forced breeder. I waited a good half hour longer before moving, straining my ears and eyes, but there was nothing but the breeze whispering through the tall stalks all around me.

Eventually, I resumed wending my way down the highway, past the ghostly evidence of Barrie on either side. I'd have loved to explore these ruins, but I'd lost time and felt the urgency. I didn't want to have to chase Jay all the way to Kingston. And I definitely needed to catch him before he headed east, if that was still even possible. I knew I had several options for that stage of his trip — if he hadn't already left the 11, and if he had, my chances of finding him were almost nothing. Well, then I'd be on my own and would make the best of it. There was plenty to see.

There was always the choice to just go home, too, but I didn't relish going back there so soon with my tail between my legs. Oak had stuck his neck out for me, and god knows what my dads and Cedar would say about all this. I was going to see this adventure through one way or another — get "my money's worth," as the old expression goes.

The day was sweltering, of course, but I pushed on and took just the occasional break in the trees. I knew I was risking getting dangerously dehydrated. The second night, I took shelter at twilight behind the counter in a gas station on a side road, not directly on the highway, and was undisturbed. It wasn't the safest place, but I'd exhausted myself. There was evidence of recent heavy storms in this area, judging by the amount of vegetation strewn around, stripped and torn from the trees and whipped by tornados and hurricane-strength winds.

The weather alternated between windy and rainy and overbearingly hot the next day. Smoke was mercifully absent, but I knew it wouldn't be long before the wind blew some in from somewhere. It was definitely worse here than it was up north.

I made quite good time during the more overcast parts of the day, and it was late afternoon, heading by some place called King City, when I saw movement ahead. I cursed; I'd been pushing myself so hard, so focused on avoiding obstacles that I hadn't been looking ahead at all. I could see a human form coming toward me.

This patch of road was too clear for comfort, no grasses to duck behind, so I was about to rush to haul my bike over the crushed metal barrier on the side of the road when something caused me to stop: this solitary figure was on a bike.

Now, Seekers were of course not the only people using bikes to get around at that time — my captors had them, after all — but something about this figure seemed different. The bike was wobbling around as though the person was either very new to cycling or very tired. This wasn't the focused determination of a potential attacker.

I had a feeling something was different, but I also wasn't going to be stupid about it. I unholstered the pistol, took off the safety, hefted the weight of the weapon in my hand, and waited. This time I'd face what was in front of me.

The cyclist didn't even seem to notice me until they were almost right on top of me.

I raised the gun and pointed it.

A beam of sunlight broke through the roiling clouds of the afternoon sky and illuminated a shock of white hair as the person noticed me and stopped, regarding me blankly. It was an elderly woman. She was panting, red in the face, and even from where I stood, I could see sweat pouring down her cheeks and glistening on her forehead.

"There's no need for the weapon," she croaked, dismounting with some difficulty, almost getting entangled with the frame. "As you can see, I'm no threat."

I kept the gun raised. "Who are you?" My voice was surprisingly steady.

"My name is Elm. This may seem a strange question, but your name isn't … Birch, by any chance?"

I felt my jaw drop, and a chill went up my spine, but I didn't lower the gun, though I almost dropped it. "How — how can you possibly know that?"

Now she cracked a small, weary smile. "Lucky guess. Nice to meet you. I think we have a mutual friend."

My arm dropped. "Jay?"

Her smile widened to a grin. "One and the same."

And then she collapsed.

• • •

"I've been riding for a day and a half, not sleeping much. I normally never travel in the heat if I can help it," Elm said.

I'd revived her by pouring some water onto her face, enough to get her up and standing, draped her arm over my shoulder, and helped her off to the side of the road into a copse of tall trees, then went back for our bikes. Now I had managed to get some food into her too, and she was looking better.

She had a long face, like mine, lined but not overly so compared with some elders I knew in Norbay, despite having the ochre skin of a person who had spent years outdoors. She had sharp eyes and a pointed nose; in fact, she seemed like a more outdoorsy version of Cedar, which would have bothered me a few days ago but now seemed comforting.

I was dying of curiosity but knew my first duty had been to make sure this old woman didn't expire in front of my eyes. Now that it was clear she wouldn't, I asked, trying not to sound desperate, "So, you've met Jay?"

"Yes. I've been with Jay for a few days. Last saw him two nights ago. I'm a Seeker, by the way… I mean, you probably figured that out. You won't know me — or of me. Maybe I'll tell you about that part later. But right now, you need to know about Jay."

When she was done with her tale, I could tell my face registered total shock. Jay had fallen into the hands of the heavily armed guards of some kind of new city-state? A place full of electric lights and … cars? But I shoved aside my amazement. Jay had been captured and taken to a place from which we were told people never came back.

"Why were you heading north then, if he's still back there?" I asked suspiciously.

She harrumphed. "Look at me, Birch. I'm not what I used to be. Back in the day? Sure, I might have concocted some plan to get him out of there on my own. Something heroic and crazy. Now? There's no way. I can't even successfully run away from some people my own age anymore. My best hope was to head to Norbay and hope that something can be done."

"Like what?"

She sighed. "I don't know, Birch. It's my first hostage situation. Some kind of negotiation? I've been in a few scrapes, lots, over the years, but never anything like this. I don't know, maybe there's a possible diplomatic solution. Either way, I needed help, and I only knew one place to get it."

Despite my anxiety, I was touched that she would undertake this arduous mission on behalf of Jay, someone she'd only known for a couple of days. And from the look of her when I found her, it might have ended up being a fatal mission. "I'm sorry. I didn't mean to sound like that. But that's a long way, riding like that in the heat. You could have killed yourself!"

She laughed, a deep, raspy sound. "Yeah. You're right. A fool's errand for an elder, I guess. Had to do something, though. Jay's a good kid. But — it led me straight to you, didn't it?" She sat up straighter and fixed her eyes on me, scrutinizing me. "But now here you are, like it was fated to be. And maybe it was. I had a strange feeling when he told me about you. So, what are we gonna do, kid? Opportunity knocks now that we're together."

I had been so engrossed in amazement at her story that I hadn't even started to think of that, but there was no doubt at all in my mind. "We have to get him out."

Elm slapped her palm with a fist, seeming energized. "That's the spirit! I don't know how, but we can figure it out on the way back down. It's not like there's a wall around the place. And I can tell you're resourceful just by looking at you. Don't even tell me how you got that gun, though. And don't be waving it around in front of me."

I was ready to jump up and go right away, but Elm was already lying down with her head on her pack. "Sorry, kid, I'm totally worn out. I'm going to need to some sleep first. And we'll have to do without a fire tonight. We're too close to the road."

"Uh … right. Of course. Sorry."

"I can see you're wired now, so you can take the first watch. We're in places where you have to watch your back now. Someone must be awake at all times."

She turned on her side without even removing her footwear. Evening was falling rapidly around us, and the tall trees that protected us from the road's sightline no longer cast shadows. The calls of the crickets had intensified.

I settled in against a trunk for a tense vigil. I wanted to go, *now.* I knew almost nothing of Great Toronto. I knew nothing of what Jay might be going through, what they might be doing to him. It didn't bear thinking about, so I tried to shove those thoughts aside, since they were of no use. I knew life without Jay wasn't a tolerable prospect, but I'd had enough of traumatic thoughts rattling around in my head. Action was the only solution.

After a couple of minutes, Elm stirred. "Birch?"

"Yeah?"

"I haven't asked you yet… Why did you come after him?"

"What makes you think it was all about him?"

She gave that raspy laugh. "Okay, sorry. What made you leave, period?"

I thought that over for a few seconds. "Well… I just had to. Following him just gave me a goal."

She turned over on her back, and I could see her eyes glinting at me.

"That's the right answer, kid."

A minute or two later, she was snoring, and I watched the few deep lines on her face relaxing as the light faded.

XX.

AN ULTIMATUM

JAY

Back at the cells at 52 Division, the door clanged shut behind me and I slumped down on the cot. The experience had left me bewildered and unnerved. My initial amazement and hope at seeing what had been achieved here had been badly damaged by what was said by this strange group of people. It sounded like a lot of "the end justifies the means," not to mention a total rejection of anything resembling our more careful, reasoned approach to rebuilding. While the tone some of this so-called Six had taken was often reasonable, their total scorn for the ideas of my community was troubling. And the belief that given more time, humans could have invented their way out of the problems they created with more technology was the ultimate intellectual sin to Seekers.

At the same time, other doubts crept in. Could they be correct, at least partially? How long was long enough to wait to try to reconnect people and restore some of the lacking technologies? Was knowledge and education alone enough to avoid falling down the same hole? Could people outside Norbay ever be taught to have a more empathetic and humane attitude toward the environment we shared? And were there even enough people now in the world to cause any trouble for the environment, no matter what we did? It was possible that our utopianism was impractical.

Most importantly, was Norbay's veneration of all life and the idea of humans finding their proper place in the ecosystem rather than dominating it just a bunch of philosophical hot air? These were things I'd believed my whole life: that humanity had gone astray when it became hypnotized by technological development, fully equating every aspect of it, no matter how problematic, with progress and never considering its negative aspects. We pushed boundaries and exploited resources until we ceased to be mere sentient primates and instead took our rightful place as gods, so we considered ourselves, then thought we could continue to spread forth to colonize the universe. An insane goal of endless expansion on a planet with finite resources, soon exhausted.

Was human-caused climate change just a glitch in that development, something to be overcome, rather than an ending? Could we come roaring back and do the same things as before, but better and cleaner? The Six appeared to be counting on that.

But then I thought of the thousands (or millions, for all I knew) of species that had been made extinct, the untold suffering and violence, the mounds of smartphones that were piled up at the old landfill site outside Norbay that I'd seen on educational field trips. The uninhabitable areas of the planet. The storms, the smoke, the floods, the toxic waste areas that people had learned to avoid. I thought of world wars and nuclear weapons. No. That the world *had* gone mad was a gross understatement. We were a total failure as a species. This was the only correct interpretation. What was actually worth salvaging from that world, just to risk starting the cycle all over again?

And then there was the nature of this new city-state. If the population really was on board with it, why would six oligarchs hold all the power? Why all the guards and guns? Were citizens all just happily going along with the program here in exchange for protection, steady food supplies, and electrical power? I had yet to talk to a regular citizen to find out if this community had been established based on some kind of consensus or whether all these ideas had been generated by the six people after they somehow seized power.

They radiated a sense of arrogant certainty that was deeply troubling. What was wrong with a little dialogue?

Well, it seemed I'd have the opportunity to learn more, since I was going to be their captive guest for the time being. A guard had left another meal tray holding some bland food, again featuring a kind of mystery meat that I avoided despite being very hungry. I still had some of the dried food in my pack to supplement the meal.

As I ate, I thought about Cedar, about Birch, my parents and brother, and Elm. Only the latter would even know what happened to me, and if she never got the chance to tell them, they'd never know — if I didn't make it home. Somehow, that possibility still seemed remote, despite my current predicament. I could only hope that Elm really had gotten away; the presence of all these guns and guards meant that sometimes they must really use them.

Getting tired of my own smell, I washed up in the thin stream of cold water that came from the metal sink, changed my clothes, then sank down on the cot, sighed, and idly sorted through my things. Rather than just sit and stew about my situation, I decided to read. My dad's gift was suddenly a godsend.

Apparently, this Camus character was associated with a philosophy called "absurdism" and advocated that we try to create our own meaning of life in a seemingly meaningless, godless world, which entailed making our own values based on our common feelings. The existentialists often wrestled with the meaning of consciousness itself. I guess Dad thought this would be helpful for me to ponder. I managed to get a fair way into the book — almost finishing it — which was quite moving, philosophy aside. It's about a town that is isolated by quarantine during an outbreak of plague and how each person has to come to terms with that isolation along with the closeness and hopelessness of impending death. You can figure out each person's character and the values they've created by how they respond, some with generosity and nobility, others with selfishness. I started to see some parallels between that world and the one I was living in. Faced with an impossible situation, what do you do?

The only way to survive is to face it head-on and live through it, and to be open-hearted in the moment — that's true courage. That seemed to be the message, or at least it was what I took from it, and it fit well with everything I'd been taught.

I decided that I'd observe carefully while here in Great Toronto to determine what kind of people were holding me. Were they generous at heart and just doing what they thought was right for the people, even if it could seem harsh and arrogant? Or were they only interested in wielding power over others and becoming unchallengeable rulers of a new empire they'd create from the ashes?

I read the book right up to the moment the lights went out and I was plunged into pitch black.

• • •

I slept surprisingly deeply again and was roused in an ungracious way by the ceiling light flickering on and the door clanging open. Once again, I was hustled out the door without even time to splash water on my face, ushered out into the blinding sunlight of midmorning, and then taken in another silent electric car to the city hall. And once again, I marvelled at seeing well-groomed people, adults and children, going nonchalantly about their daily business down tidy streets. A few cyclists even zipped by.

Minutes later, I found myself blinking sleepily in front of the same six people, all wearing similar clothes as the day before. Khalil levelled his gimlet eyes at me and said, "Jay, we hope you have used the last twenty-four hours to think this over. You can be a useful addition to our citizenry, or you can choose to be a dissident. You have knowledge to contribute, even if your perspective has been skewed by propaganda. We have business to attend to, so let's take care of this now."

"So, I guess letting me go still isn't an option?" I quipped.

Craig Kelly made an irritated sound but surprisingly didn't say anything.

The older woman, who had seemed most reasonable the day before, spoke up. "No, Jay. We can't risk it right now. What we're doing here is too important, it's still too early in our project, and we need to finish what we've started establishing before others learn about it. We need you to decide."

"He's using up food and taking up a cell for no reason. Let's just do what needs to be done," Craig put in.

I risked poking the bear. "Honestly, I haven't even seen how this place works, what the people who live here are like, or anything that would tell me I should *want* to stay. How am I supposed to decide like that?"

"Because we have all the advantage here, you little shit!" Craig shouted, almost leaping up. This man had taken a serious dislike to me, that much was clear. I wondered about his history and what had made him so angry all the time.

"Kelly, will you just calm down?" the middle-aged woman said curtly. "Jay, here's the situation. Craig's right in his own particular, if unsubtle, way. We can't waste resources. So, if you need more time to think this over, fine, but not for long. And in the interim, you'll work. And the work that needs to be done isn't easy. If you join us officially, the work will become a lot easier and more pleasant. Do you understand?"

I nodded. "I'm not afraid of work." Maybe this would allow me to get out and about in the community and meet some real people.

"Fine," Khalil rumbled. "You asked for it, remember that. You're going to be put on teardown detail. You'll see what happens to people who are on the fence about what we're achieving here, or are resistant to it."

"Khalil..." said the kindly woman with the smooth face, frowning and speaking for the first time today. "Is that necessary?"

"Enough, Sydney," Khalil said firmly. "We've wasted enough time here. We have business. Take him to teardown detail number 2 at Bathurst and Bloor. He'll have plenty of time to think this over while he works."

Craig Kelly was looking disturbingly satisfied by this development, so I had a feeling it most definitely wasn't going to be easy work. But I wouldn't be in a cell, and it was a chance to see some more of the city, one way or the other.

I just nodded and smiled defiantly at each of them in turn as guards flanked me, grabbing my arms, and marched me from the hall.

• • •

The car traveled smooth roads, past some buildings that were clearly in use and some that had already been torn down or were mere façades. At least the guard in the back with me was a little chattier than the others had been so far. He was round-faced, almost doughy in a youthful way, dressed in a blue shirt with a black cap with some kind of gold emblem on it. The shirt read *Safeguard Security* across the pocket. The guards in the front wore different makeshift uniforms, one white shirt, one black.

"How big is the occupied area of the city?" I asked him, and he surprisingly looked back at me with a half-smile and acknowledged my words.

"Pretty big. It goes as far as Bathurst, up to Bloor here — and even further, up to Eglinton downtown — east to the river, and down to the lake."

Those words meant nothing to me, so I shrugged at him.

"Bathurst Street is a couple of kilometres past where we are now. We're expanding our borders, but we need work details to make sure things are safe — falling brick and glass, flammable materials, and things like that. Tearing down crumbling buildings that can't be saved."

"I see. And people get paid to do that work?"

He hesitated, looking uncomfortable. "Some of it. The less dangerous work."

I was starting to get the picture. "Ah. And the dangerous work?"

He looked even more uncomfortable. "You're about to find out, bud."

"Ah," I repeated and changed tack. "And do you like living in the city? Did you grow up here?"

He just looked at me, presumably debating whether to engage further or tell me to shut up, when the car came to a stop.

"Teardown detail number 2," one of the guys in the front announced, a little too loudly.

They hopped out and opened my door.

"Good luck, man," my guard offered with what seemed to be sadness.

"Thanks," I replied. I got out, stretched my arms, and took in the scope of what awaited me. This had once been one of the city's grand intersections, a mixture of ancient brick twentieth century storefronts and looming condominium blocks. I had yet another shock when I saw several battered but clearly still functional giant trucks, what used to be called dump trucks, full of small chunks of concrete and rebar, standing on two adjacent corners. The rumbling of their idling engines was something I could never in my wildest dreams imagine I'd ever hear. It might have been like experiencing the roar of a Tyrannosaurus rex.

From what I could tell at first inspection, two of these larger damaged buildings were being disassembled piece by piece, almost brick by brick. Lines of people extended from the entrances to the trucks, handing along pieces and baskets full of concrete, wood, tile, rebar, wire, and other waste. None of the people were wearing any protective headgear, masks, or even had gloves on. The work appeared to be happening slowly but deliberately, and guards were everywhere, some standing laconically with their hands on their hips, others fingering the stocks of their rifles.

None of the guards were standing within a wide radius of the buildings, though, except for the entrances, because every now and then a chunk of concrete or brick would come sailing down from many floors above to shatter noisily on the pavement. If you got caught within ten metres of the place, you might be dead within minutes.

A red-faced man in a yellow plastic hat marched up to me and my guards. He was stocky and paunchy and sweating profusely; the day was already set up to be scorching.

"Who the hell's this? He's not on my detail, whoever he is," he grumbled and spat loudly to his right. He was brandishing a clipboard.

"He is now," said the guard from the passenger seat on my drive over, a hulking guy with a square jaw.

"For fuck's sake," said the foreman. "Can barely keep track of the labour without springing soft-looking skinny kids on me out of nowhere." He stared at my face. "Yeah, soft. You got a name?"

"Jay."

"Jay what?"

"Just Jay."

His face got redder. "Fuck it. Fine. Okay, Just Jay, welcome to the fun zone. Not sure what you did to get here, but you shouldn't have." He glared at the guards. "You guys can fuck off now." He made a shooing gesture, then scribbled something, *Just Jay*, I guess, on his clipboard.

The guard who had spoken stepped a little closer. "You better watch your mouth, Tyler. You think you're not replaceable?"

Tyler just spat again, ignored the threat, and pointed to the nearest multistorey building being demolished. "Get the fuck over there. Someone'll tell you what to do. Like I give a shit."

He marched away without a second glance at any of us.

I marched over, flanked by guards, to the gaping opening of what would once have been a lobby, where another person with a clipboard was eyeing the workers. They were a sorry-looking group, covered in grime, dust, sweat, and a few trickles of blood. None of them even looked at me.

"Um, I'm supposed to work."

The tall, very thin woman glanced up from her clipboard and looked me over. "Are you, huh? Lucky you." She nodded to the left. "There's a staircase. For now. Take one of those and head to the top." She indicated a pile of heavy-looking sledgehammers behind her. "Don't even think about starting something. Those guys will shoot." She pointed a slim finger at the guards nearby.

I smiled. Might as well stay out of trouble. "I wouldn't think of it."

Her heavily lined face suddenly grinned and laughed, a surprisingly pleasant sound. "Good. An attitude like that might keep you alive."

I hefted the sledgehammer, which was a heinous weight, up onto my shoulder and edged onto the staircase, lined with people passing the bits and pieces down. It looked ridiculously inefficient. There was no equipment beyond sledgehammers and baskets in use. Some people grumbled a bit as I brushed by, enveloped by the overwhelming stench of unwashed, perspiring humans.

I passed several floors before suddenly coming out into an open, unroofed space with some wall left around it, maybe just above waist-height. The current top floor of the building was spread around me, and I had an open view on one side. I gaped in awe. First gas-burning trucks, and now this? Far off to the horizon I could see the deep blue of the great lake. That was amazing enough, since I'd never set eyes on it before. Nipissing, the lake Norbay was situated on, was big and wide, but this expanse looked like the ocean! The distant aquatic horizon met a deep cerulean skyline of almost the same hue. It was painfully beautiful to my eyes.

Inland was a sea of skyscrapers in varying states of collapse and, closer, new forest encroaching on two-hundred-year-old homes that were gradually disintegrating and returning to the earth. To the east, in the inhabited parts of the city, I could see evidence of the results of the demolitions and the clearing of the trees.

But then my eyes were drawn to a solitary needle-like object piercing the sky, standing above the other remaining skyscrapers. This was the CN Tower! Of course, I'd seen photos of it, many times. But like everything from before the Ruin, it had changed. I'd say the top third of it was missing. There had once been a doughnut-shaped observation deck, but that was gone, smashed to pieces on the ground, and now there was just a concrete pillar that terminated jaggedly hundreds of metres in the air. It looked more like a weapon than a symbol of pride and progress.

I felt a stab of regret, remembering how badly Birch longed to see things just like this. It didn't seem fair that I got to see it first.

"Hey, you! Work! Malik, get this idiot working," barked an armed guard I hadn't noticed yet, cradling his rifle. That brought me back to the scene.

All around me, people were hammering unenthusiastically at inner walls and outer ones, exposing rebar and concrete, nibbling away at the building piece by piece. A man sauntered over, taking his time.

"Who's this, boss?" he said. He was about my height but looked double my age. His face was covered by a greying jet-black beard, and he squinted from under bushy brows.

"Dunno ... must be new. But he can't stand around staring. Get him working."

"No problem. Come over here, kid."

I followed Malik, whose olive skin was sweating as heavily as the others under the sweltering late-morning sun, and he told me just to hammer away at anything I wanted except the floor and the front wall of the building, being sure not to smack anyone in the process.

"That's it?"

He stared at me. "What the fuck you think? You waiting for a presentation about it? Just do it."

The guard left, and I noticed the activity around me slowed considerably the moment he did.

Suddenly, Malik supported himself on the handle of his sledgehammer, letting out a slow breath. "Might as well take a break." His tone had immediately softened. He regarded me shrewdly. "You aren't from around here."

"How do you know that?"

He shrugged. "Can just tell. If you're on this 'detail'—" he emphasized the word with sarcasm "—you must have pissed someone off, committed a crime of some kind, or wandered over the border. They don't like any of that. They're totally paranoid."

"Who? The Six?"

"Yeah, those fuckers." I thought he was going to spit, he looked so pissed off in that moment. Then the spark died from his eyes. "So, how'd you like our utopia so far?"

The guard's head popped up in the roofless hole from which the staircase emerged, so Malik hefted his hammer and headed over to an interior wall. "C'mon."

I did the same and started aimlessly whacking at the cinder blocks, which started chipping and cracking.

As bits fell, every now and then others would butt in to gather the pieces whole if large or in baskets if small, occasionally with the help of a broom.

"I haven't really seen anything yet. I just had a couple of visits with your leaders. I got grabbed at what I guess is your northern border, uh ... yesterday, I think." I was already panting from the exertion and heat.

"Take it easy over there. Most guards don't push us too hard. Working harder doesn't get you anywhere. It's bad enough that they don't feed us properly or give us enough water. Some of them are still human, though."

"What if someone gets sick or hurt?"

He laughed scornfully. "People get hurt every day, bad. People collapse. Sometimes they fall. They take them away, but I don't know what happens to them. They don't come back."

The full picture of this place was getting darker by the minute.

"There's paid work, of course, for honest citizens who keep their heads down. They brought back currency, believe or not. Must have found a stash of old coins and bills, and now you get paid in them." He lifted his hammer to deal a mighty blow near the top of the wall, creating a crack across three blocks. "Worthless anywhere else, of course, but here that's how you get food and shelter. Helps control us."

"So, the citizens do the easy work. Then who does the dirty work?"

He gave that ugly, bitter laugh again. "Criminals. Dissidents. That's what they call us. People who commit real crimes, sure, but also people like you who wander in and, I guess, aren't gagging to join up right away. And people who resist their leadership. Not that this work has any point other than keeping us busy. That's how it was, anyway ... to a point. Now I wonder if they're getting less picky about who they sentence to this shit, or maybe even going in search of labour. Getting shit done isn't the point of this, as you may have figured out by now."

"So, do they raid other places and capture people?"

"We think so. I've talked to a few people here for long enough to get a sense of that. It may just be to build up their army, though. That's their real interest."

To our left, a gaunt woman had gone down on her knees, panting heavily, with a hand on her head. Everyone was ignoring her. The guard watched her coolly, unmoving. I made a move to go over, but Malik shook his head. "Don't."

After a few minutes, she pulled herself together enough to stand and weakly resume hacking at the outer wall. She somehow managed to stay that way for the rest of the day.

Malik fell silent after that, and we worked through the afternoon with only a few short breaks to be given some of that mysterious grey meat, which I forced down, feeling nauseous afterward, and some water, but not nearly enough. We ate sprawled out under the unforgiving rays of the midday sun. The rainy, chilly season couldn't come soon enough for me and these other unfortunates. I already coughed constantly from the dust.

Eventually — it must have been late afternoon — a whistle was blown, and everyone slowly, agonizingly, lurched down five flights of stairs, me included.

Transportation was not provided. We were herded, with several guards observing us closely, down one of the two major streets of the intersection a mercifully short distance until we came to what would once have been a grand grey stone building, maybe a school, and then through the doors.

Malik had stayed close to me and now grabbed me by the arm. "Stay close, kid. I've got your back."

He guided me into a room that had presumably once been a classroom, now filled with rusty cots. There were only about ten of us in a room that had thirty cots, including the woman who had almost collapsed. She fell right into her cot like a dead weight and didn't move. Everyone else just slumped down onto the thin, stained mattresses with groans and sighs. No one talked.

Malik plunked himself down on the cot beside mine, pulled off his barely wearable ragged sneakers, and rubbed a bare foot.

"So," he said, "normally I end up like these poor people every day, lying here wishing I was dead. But I'm curious as hell about you. Let's trade stories. That's all the entertainment we're gonna get for the time being, anyway."

"Okay," I said, rubbing my left arm, which was so sore, I thought it might fall right off. "You first."

XXI.

MALIK'S STORY

JAY

Here, I'm going to read from something I wrote down later. I'm paraphrasing some of this. I'm hoping Malik wouldn't have minded. I wrote all this down not long after meeting him and hearing his story, while it was still fresh in my mind, to honour him and because the information about his life and about the Six are both significant. I tried to capture his voice as well. Curses and all.

MALIK

I was born in 2080 — I think. It was around that year, anyway. You can tell by looking at me that I'm middle-aged, so I know that much! I grew up in … you ever heard of a place called Stratford? It's way to the southwest of here. They say it was a really fancy place for tourists at one time, which was, you know, people travelling around doing stuff and seeing stuff just for fun. Can you imagine that? Zipping around in their personal cars, buying things just because they wanted them, not because they needed them, going to places like Stratford to see plays, which was what the place's economy was based on. That and farming. There were all these wrecked stores and fancy theatres around, so it must have been quite the place back in the day.

Anyway, what I was told when I was young, and of course I've confirmed it since then, was that around 2045, things totally fell apart, everywhere. There were parts of the planet where people could barely live anymore, and billions of people were on the move, desperately looking for somewhere safe. Governments fell apart and were replaced by dictators — ironically, kind of like what we're dealing with right now in Great Toronto. Everything was beyond fucked up, and you didn't know whether you'd still be alive by the end of the day.

My parents were born right after that. Everyone was scrounging and scavenging if they couldn't get a job, and then soon there were no jobs because there was no economy and no money. The whole world had depended on the climate acting a certain way for the economy to work, and when things changed and became unpredictable, no one could handle it and it all fell apart, fast.

I don't even know what happened to my grandparents. Or I've forgotten somehow. I don't have memories of them, so they must have been dead.

When Stratford emptied out, my parents had no choice but to move to Waterloo, a nearby city. It had a massive concentration camp, the biggest one in Ontario, until about 2055, and after that, from what I was told, the guards who'd run the camp ran the city, and they ended up killing thousands of people. At that time, there were huge numbers of people pouring in from the United States ... like, unimaginable numbers. You'd never know it now. I guess it doesn't take long for a dead body to break down...

Waterloo was a bad place, but it was sort of organized and you could get hold of some food, at least.

I don't know why my parents thought it was a good idea to have a kid, or whether I was a mistake, but anyway, there I was somewhere around 2080, and they had to take care of me. I guess they tried their best in Waterloo, but it was getting more and more violent there — mainly if you looked a certain way, but also if you just looked at these guys the wrong way. A few bad people with lots of weapons and a whole army of thugs ran the place, and if you didn't do what they wanted, they killed you. They kept people fed — basically, but that was it. People were running away from the place like crazy, but that didn't stop these guys or make them act any better.

My dad died protecting us from a gang, or at least that's what my mom told me. They'd been practicing Muslims up to that point — you know what that is? It's a religion from Asia — but I guess what happened to my dad was partly done because of our race. Mobs and the scumbags running the place blamed anyone who wasn't white for the way the country had been overrun by refugees and for the "end of Canada," whatever the fuck that meant. Canada was long gone and didn't mean anything by that point, so I'm not sure what they were mourning. My mom just stopped with religion after that, but I've read some stuff about it since then, and I kind of wish she'd kept it up and taught it to me. It would make me feel better to know that there's something watching over us that has a plan for us, and that all this shit we've been through might actually *mean* something, you know?

My mom was really brave. After my dad died — I was about five — she fled with me in the middle of the night, and we walked and walked. Sometimes I have memories of it … really hazy ones. It's almost pitch-black, and we're just kind of stumbling along some road, and I can feel the fear pouring off her … she's holding my hand so tight, it hurts. You don't forget that. And missing my dad, though now I can barely even remember what he looked like. But he was missing, that protector we needed.

I can remember the roads being full of refugees, though maybe my mind's blown it up. It's a long time ago, thirty-five years at least, or more. But I remember hearing all these different languages I didn't understand, people crying, people lying by the side of the highway. Just like I remember the smell in Waterloo when they were burning bodies … but I don't want to get into that right now…

(…sorry, I had to take a break there, man. It's been a long time since I've thought of all this shit. It's harder than I thought it would be.)

Anyway, so, somewhere between Waterloo and Stratford, she must have collapsed, and the rest is really hazy, but I know that we were taken in by some people who called themselves Mennonites. They were a Christian group that had always lived in a back-to-land kind of way, rejecting the technology that fucked everything up, and so since they didn't rely on technology to live and actively avoided that shit, they were in a better position to deal with the collapse. They knew how to grow food naturally and all that.

Some of them, anyway. There were lots of them around this place, and somehow a few groups of them managed to keep going, under the radar, way off the main road, and they kept worshipping and farming like they always did.

I don't know why they took me and my mom in, I really don't. If they took in everyone who needed help, they'd have been totally overrun.

But they did, otherwise I wouldn't be here talking to you right now.

So those were my people, I guess. My mom went to work in the fields, and an old lady, Mrs. Fischer, who had been a teacher, taught me how to read and add things up a bit. I'm still not good at math, but I kept up the reading. Most people can't read much now, but I can. We're surrounded by signs and moldy books, and hardly anyone can read them. I bet you're good at it, though, where you come from. You're educated, I can tell.

Anyway, we'll get to that, right?

So, I was raised by these Mennonites for ten years, and they weren't bad people. They didn't make any effort to convince us to worship their god; we were too foreign for that. We just made ourselves useful, and that seemed okay with them. My mom even started to smile again after a while. The hard work seemed to be good for her. Somehow, things had started to die down. You saw less and less people coming through on the roads. You started to see less and less of the bodies — you used to see fresh bodies all the fucking time. The weather was dangerous a lot — tornadoes. We would hide in their strong brick cellars when those came along. It was too hot to work some days, so my mom would come and sit with me in the cellar while I read. That's the happiest memory I have right there, her sitting and helping me with my reading, a mixture of yellow candlelight with a little natural light coming through the window, Mrs. Fischer there drinking her herbal tea and correcting me when I read aloud, down in the damp of that cellar.

There were storms and floods and tornadoes, like there are now, and lots of smoke that came from up north, and sometimes raiders would come by and steal our crops or hold us up for whatever we had, but they usually didn't hurt anyone too bad.

We heard there was no government at all, anywhere, but the Mennonites didn't mind that, since their ruler was God, they said — funny, now that I think about it some more, that they never made any effort at all to convert us. I guess we were worth saving physically, but maybe too different, or exotic or something, to preach at.

But things got worse again. The raiders came around more, and they were more violent. But these people didn't do much to defend or protect themselves; they figured it was God's plan and they'd end up in Heaven anyway if anything happened to them. My mom and me, we were scared, though. I was only about fifteen, but I tried to speak up, and the elders shut me up quick, saying I didn't have the right to advise them about it, since I wasn't a true member of their community. That hurt.

But we had nowhere to go, so we stayed and waited.

Well, not long after that, the shit came down. A huge group of them raided in the middle of the night. They had cars, which was already really rare by that point. Like, gas ones. I guess you could still get hold of that or use something else for gas, I don't know. And don't ask me how the fucking Six are running those dump trucks they use. That's a mystery.

Anyway, so, they came ... dozens of them. I remember seeing the lights of their cars, lighting up the night and blinding us as we ran. And they didn't come just to steal a few carrots. They came to finish us off, too. When my mom woke me, I was scared shitless but I wanted to fight. I was ready to grab a knife, or pitchfork, or whatever. I was fifteen, after all. You could see barns on fire all around, hear the animals and people screaming, gunshots... I was in a rage.

My mom begged me to just run with her. Her eyes were so scared, and she was crying, saying I was all she had left, and nothing was worth dying for.

So, we ran out into the fields out the back door, I guess leaving Mrs. Fischer and the other villagers to die or to run themselves. There wasn't any time to think about them.

My mom fell just as we were about to cross the back fence. I grabbed at her, but she didn't move. I rolled her over, and I felt her blood on my hand. They shot her right in the head. In the light of the fire in the house next door I could see her eyes were just staring and her mouth was open, like she died trying to say something.

I couldn't see where the shot came from, but I had no choice. I took off.

(...yeah, I'm okay. Thanks. I've only told a few people here all this shit. It's rough, but we've all got stories like that.)

So, the rest? I wandered around, scavenging, stealing from small settlements I came across, did a few things I'm not proud of and I'm not going to tell you about.

The land was fucking empty. There were still bones and sometimes fresh corpses everywhere you went, and you didn't stay long in urban areas like Guelph or Hamilton if you could help it.

So, I ended up drifting up here. I mean, I had no destination, you know? No purpose, no friends, no community. I was turning into an animal. Other people I saw were no better off. You stayed away from the dangerous-looking ones, and you didn't help the friendlier ones; you were just grateful they didn't want to hurt *you*.

I ended up here in Great Toronto in 2112. There wasn't anything great about it, just fucking ruins as far as the eye could see. But so many people had lived there that you could still scavenge a few things. People's gardens still had vegetables, and there were as many rats and dogs and cats as you could catch if you tried hard enough. You could even find old canned food, if you were brave enough to try eating it.

I just stuck around here, living like a dog, but there were others doing the same thing, and we ended up helping each other out, making friends, trusting each other, and starting something like a community, I guess.

We got organized enough to get those gardens going and to catch things like coyotes and rabbits, not just rats. I had friends for the first time in my life … good people. We brought each other back to life and to being fucking human, man.

We were free and alive and grateful for it.

Then, as things got more organized, people started joining us, lots more people. And it became a *real* community.

• • •

JAY

I had sat quietly and listened, as I was taught to do from childhood when someone had a story to tell, but at this point I interjected, "So how did the Six end up in charge, then, if you had such a good thing going?"

"I was about to get to that, man," Malik continued. "Those people were originally just part of the community. They weren't even original members; they came a few years later. But they had an advantage … they were a lot more educated and smarter. They knew stuff or were good at figuring it out. They knew about politics and society and engineering and fixing things. Running things and shit. They had come from larger communities that dissolved, and they were mostly a little older than us, and they were strong personalities. They were good for us at first. They helped out and formed a kind of natural leadership. We trusted them. I knew them all well. Then I guess they got talking between themselves and came back with bigger ideas."

I nodded. "Let me guess: they think Great Toronto is going to restore the best of the old world without any of the worst, and they're the ones to do that because of their success here. And they want to expand."

He gave a twisted smile. "Guess they were forthcoming with you, huh?"

"Actually, yes."

"Huh." He looked a bit shocked. "You must be important, then."

"I'm important because they could tell I was from another community. Norbay."

"I've heard of that place. What's that all about?"

It was time for me to tell my story; I had no reason to mistrust Malik, who had told me about his traumas so openly. It was valuable to have another first-hand account of what people had gone through. The younger people of Norbay were truly lucky; I'm not sure they realized it. Now, I did.

When I was done, he whistled through his teeth. "Well, Jay, I can tell you that you getting caught was *not* a good thing. For you or for your people."

I knew what he meant, but I said, "Why's that?"

"These people, the Six, have lost their minds, man. They're what was once called, mega — uh, mega something … power-crazy. They're not the same people they were in the start."

"Megalomaniacs."

"That's the word for it, yeah. So, you talked to them, right?"

"I did."

"Khalil's especially bad. Craig's just an asshole who likes to boss people around and has a sadistic streak, and the others seem to try to moderate them, but Khalil has crazy plans. Well, the same shit they started spewing years ago, they're still spewing it, but now they have their private army to put it into practice. It's not just harmless dreams anymore. They did a good job at first, like I said. They got power going by collecting up all the solar panels and wind turbines they could and figuring out how to fix up some power lines. I mean, imagine that! Real electrical lights. We would follow them anywhere after that. They organized food production and trading and sanitation — all that shit. But then after a while, people started asking if others could get in on the decision-making, because we had ideas to share too. They didn't trust anyone else's ideas. They stopped listening to other voices, and if you kept talking, they silenced you. After a while, they started gathering more and more weapons and arming their goons."

He lowered his voice, seeming to remember he was blaring out all these bitter complaints with some of those goons lurking around.

"Like, more and more of them. They surrounded themselves with bodyguards. They told us that if we wanted to keep the power on and people's kids fed, we would do what they said. So, we did. Even I did, and I always spoke up for myself and for others. But in the end, they went too far when they started up these 'work details' and made prisoners out of the people who criticized them. I'm a reader, like I said, and I've read some history books about the twentieth century. I saw what was going on.

"And that's why you and me are sitting having this conversation right now in this shithole of a dorm. I spoke up one too many times, and now here I am, years later, wasting away on work detail, waiting for my time to fall ten storeys or speak out of line and get beat to death or just die from malnutrition. I'm on my way. I can't weigh myself, obviously, but I used to be a lot fatter than this. I'm tired all the time. I've been breathing in concrete dust and other shit from these buildings for years. The guards may seem okay, but if they catch you running, they just shoot."

"I'm sorry."

"That's not the worst of it, Jay. They aren't just building up this army of guards to protect their crappy empire here. You talked to them. You know what they think their purpose is. They're going to try to expand their territory. And who's gonna stand in their way? What's between here and your town? Anything?"

I shook my head. "Not much. No one, really. Just the distance."

"Then what you represent is the only threat to them that they know of. Another place that's self-sufficient but actually *works* for everyone, based on what you told me. Where there's democracy and people seem to care about each other without being forced to, and there's no work details or guns. And your ideas are different. That's an even bigger threat. Man, I'd be worried if I were you. You need to get out of here and warn your people."

I nodded. Twilight had crept into the room. The others were motionless on their cots. There was no light on, just an eerie stillness, a moldy smell mixed with body odours — it appeared the washroom was a bucket in the far corner of the room by an open window — and a muffled silence that seemed to pervade the entire building.

"But how?"

"I'll help you. We'll find a way to distract them or something. It's possible. Maybe I can come with you."

"Some of the Six seemed more reasonable … kinder. Can't they be reasoned with?"

He stifled a laugh. "Jay, Jay … no. They *seem* that way, but in the end they're capable of anything. Sure, Craig and Khalil are the worst of them, but they'll all do whatever it takes to stay in power and bring back the world they're obsessed with restoring. Or die trying. Or kill whoever they have to, more likely. They're not letting you go. They're not going to admit your community is a competitor, or an equal, or any of that shit. You have to get *out*."

XXII.

RECONNAISSANCE

BIRCH

Travelling in the morning and then sleeping the afternoon away in a place called Vaughan where Elm said she'd stayed with Jay just a couple of days ago, we made good time and thankfully didn't see any people, just packs of dogs or coyotes in the distance, birds of prey coasting overhead, and of course plenty of bugs. The cooler season could start at *any* time, thanks. I was done with constantly being thirsty and itchy and eaten. This woman clearly possessed a lot of stamina, though; she already seemed completely recovered from the day before. She was an excellent role model of exactly what I would want to be like in fifty years.

For some reason, even though I'd only known this serene, wind-burned sage of the road for a day, I had instantly trusted her leadership. Her clothes were well cared for, despite being ragged. She walked with a very slight stoop, nothing for a person her age, but with confidence and a sharp awareness. She rode the same way. Her eyes were bright and blue, and her words were never wasted. Elm was a true Elder, and I kind of wished I'd had, or accepted, the guidance of someone like her before now. Maybe there was still time to change that.

We had made it to the outskirts of the suburbs of Great Toronto, endless broken houses and lush growth, and we sheltered in a clean, dry-ish basement in a stretch of townhouses. I honestly don't know how they could tell one place from the other. Or what they got out of living there.

After we'd released our sore feet, stretched out on the warped wooden floor, and checked out our combined food stores, Elm suddenly asked, "So what're you going to do after we get him out?"

I narrowed my eyes at her. I'd been hoping to be the pry-*er* in tonight's conversation, not the pry-*ee*. "What do you mean?"

"When we find him and get him out, which we will, what will you do after that? You wanted to get out of Norbay to have an adventure, I presume?"

"Well ... that's one way of putting it, I guess." It sounded kind of juvenile when it was expressed that way. And she was far too good at reading me.

"You know Jay has a mission to carry out. I can tell he's the sort of person who will want to complete that first mission successfully, or he'll consider himself a failure. Will you go with him?"

I hadn't thought about it so specifically, but of course I would. Where else would I go? "I mean, yeah. But won't that break some kind of rule? They're supposed to do the first trip solo, aren't they, to show they've got what it takes?"

She laughed in a way that sounded kind of bitter. "That's *one way* of putting it. A sort of rite of passage. But yes, I suppose. You're not exactly speaking with a rule follower right now, though."

"Yeah, about that... I'm really curious about how you ended up in this life. You're a Seeker, but you don't seek. But you didn't stay at home to study or farm either. I'd never heard of you before."

She bit into some dried apple and chewed on it for a while, just looking at me. "Fine," she eventually said. "I think it'll be instructive for you, and I do see something of my younger self in you — a lot, actually — so I'll tell you some history that I haven't told anyone in a long time, if ever."

"Great!" I leaned forward.

She sighed at my enthusiasm, but in an amused way. "Well, hold your horses. We have to go back a long way. Fifty years or more. Sometimes I lose count. I was in a concentration camp. I think I told you that already.

And when we got out of the camp, I was a teen, and we wanted to get as far away from them and from 'civilization' as we could, those of us who had believed we'd survive and wanted to plan for some kind of future. 'Civilization' had failed us in the most fundamental sense — it had persecuted us instead of protected us. I showed Jay that camp, by the way. Wish we'd had more time, and I'd have done the same for you. It really helps in grasping the significance of the things I say. Anyway, there were several families, or remnants of families, that had been close and helped each other survive as best we could through those terrible years. So we gathered together and headed out on the road, always going north, always staying together no matter what. We kept each other alive and didn't lose a single person on the way, even though we were mostly starved and sick.

"The farther north we went, the fewer people we saw, which suited us fine. And the natural world was everywhere. It was everything that we hoped to preserve, just endless beauty as far as the eye could see, even if a bit ravaged.

"Eventually, we came across what had been a small city, North Bay. It wasn't our destination, but it seemed meant to be. There were still a few hardy people hanging on there, but not many; the years of deprivation had largely emptied it out. It was by a beautiful lake that was still mostly healthy, with an escarpment on one side, lots of places to grow things, lots of shelters to fix up. Somewhat defensible, if it came down to it. So, we stayed. And once we stayed, we needed to figure out what to do with ourselves — to organize. To heal from all our traumas as best we could, organize, and figure out how we would live and what we would live *for*.

"There were several among us who were natural leaders. I wouldn't necessarily count myself among them, but I played my role. We had meetings, and we decided to be both pragmatic and idealistic. Everything was gone, everything good about the society that had spawned us — but everything bad, too. Viewed the right way, it presented a golden opportunity. This could be a clean slate for humans to rid ourselves of divisions, religions, ideologies, philosophies, hatreds, habits. To start anew and discover our true nature at last. We knew one thing for certain: the people of the future could *not* repeat the mistakes of the past. If populations grew again, at least in the most habitable places like Ontario, we had the opportunity to start living in accordance with the ways of nature, in cooperation with it, not dominating and enslaving it. We could treat each other as true equals, no matter what kind of person you were. We could decide what technologies were useful and benign, then do away with the rest."

I had a feeling Elm had given some variant of this speech many times before, but most of the information was new to me, so I just kept quiet and waited for more.

"So, we organized ourselves democratically; there'd be an elected council, but it would rotate members. That was an unbreakable rule. Anyone showing too much personal ambition would get dismissed from the council for good. Truly antisocial, hurtful people who wouldn't reform or couldn't be reasoned with were exiled out of town; that was probably the harshest thing we ever did. People with specialized skills would work in the appropriate areas, but otherwise everyone would work doing whatever they wanted, and everyone would receive in return. There were few enough of us to make this function well, you see, without anyone making trouble or dissenting. We were of one mind. It was surprisingly harmonious right from the start. We managed to assemble enough renewable power sources to give us that semblance of civilization, though only enough for essential use. Eventually, other refugees came to join us, and seeing what we were achieving, they joined whole-heartedly.

"Over time, we added the second goal: to make sure we did things right, we needed knowledge, often beyond what our founders possessed… After all, we were mostly pretty uneducated, having grown up in concentration camps. And there was another reason: all those repositories of knowledge were being destroyed by weather, by fire and wind and water, and by people, too. Eventually there'd be nothing left, nothing useful, nothing to serve as a warning. We needed to help save what we could. And now that we had a home base, we could gather things and keep them safe and study them. That's how the Knowledge Seekers started — those of us who were adventurous and willing to go back into risky situations. When seeking first started, everything was all untouched, lying around, whatever had survived the destruction. We hoarded as much as we could and educated ourselves — for our own sake, but also, we thought, for the future of the whole species. As far as we knew, even by listening on radios, there were few communities as organized as ours. At least not that we could detect; mind you, the world is a huge place.

"I was one of the original Seekers, and my friend Zara was another."

"Zara?" I interrupted. "Who's that?" It was an odd name for a person from Norbay.

"I was getting to that." She harrumphed. "Another thing we did, which may seem fanciful now, but it stuck around, was clean another slate: names. Our names were part of the decrepit, corrupt world and represented things we didn't want to remember. We decided to take new ones as part of our fresh start. Just symbolic, sure, but sometimes you need to do those things. Names from the natural world. I took the name Elm. No surnames. Those represented the old world too. Old prejudices, old tribalism, old ways of thinking."

I had to interject again. "What was *your* name before?"

There was a long pause as she rubbed one arm. Then another sigh, this time less amused. "Catherine Fenton was my name."

"Catherine ... that's a nice name."

She smiled gently but with some wistfulness. "Yes, it was. My father was George, and my mother was May. I haven't said my own name in decades."

I put a hand over hers. "I'm sorry if this is painful."

"Painful? No. Wistful. Poignant. Not painful. It's been too long. Time dulls pain. It's one of the advantages of a long life."

"Okay, so who is Zara?"

She looked right into my eyes. "You know her as Cedar."

Wow. Now this was some good information!

"We were the two main founders of the Seekers, in some ways. We both had that drive, almost messianic, to serve our cause. We didn't just want to be farmers; we needed more. We needed humans to do more than survive and then possibly proliferate again and just restart those destructive cycles; the way we lived in the future would make restitution to the Earth and its myriad beings for what our ancestors had done. Zara — Cedar — and I were inseparable in those days. We were young and full of energy. We undertook many missions together, and we had a lot of scrapes, I can tell you. She was tough. But maybe not as tough as me, as it turns out.

Though I'm sure that's a matter of opinion. There are different kinds of strength."

I could tell there was a lot being left unsaid, so I pushed a little. "Inseparable?"

She smiled again. "Okay, Birch. Yes. It's what you're thinking. You happy? She was the love of my life. And I was the love of hers." Her face darkened. "But that didn't last. Clearly. And that's what's actually relevant to you about this whole story, as a matter of fact, so I may as well follow through on the whole thing."

This was unexpected. "Yeah? How so?"

"Because after a while, maybe ten years, Cedar lost her taste for it. She was tired of danger, of sleeping in stinky basements, of avoiding gangs and bears and storms and smoke just to retrieve and haul back a few artefacts. She wanted to be a bigger part of molding our community and making sure it was running smoothly, with the compassion that we dreamed of. She was still dedicated to the ideals but wanted to play a more organizational role for the long term. And, to her credit, along with others, she did that. I'm proud of her. But me ... I had developed a taste for life on the move, even beyond the missions, and so we had to part ways."

Her head drooped. She looked profoundly sad, despite her bravado.

I put my hand out again. "I'm sorry. That must have been hard."

She looked up. "Yes, Birch. And life *is* hard. But we made the decisions we needed to and lived our lives the way we wanted. We're both lucky to be alive, wherever we are. I'll admit openly that one of the reasons I'm infrequently in Norbay is I sometimes find it hard to see her, to this day. But I still love her and admire her. That's not my point here in all this, anyway."

I had some idea of where this was going, but she'd been generous enough to share, so I decided to be gracious. "Okay, lay it on me."

"Birch, I see the same situation developing here. Jay is tough in his own way, but I can see gentleness in him. This life won't be for him in the long term. He's a scholar at heart. You're tougher. You have fire. You're like me, always wanting to see what's over the next hill. And the one after that. I mean, correct me if I'm wrong; I've only spent a few days with the kid. He's good, I can tell. Pure of heart. But in the end, you will have to decide whether your paths will truly travel together. You don't have to decide any time soon, but the time may come. You don't have to be a Seeker, but you're not the type to be happy staying in one place. Of course, you'd have found out in the end, whether or not I told you my little story. But it's the privilege of the elderly to inflict their stories on the young."

We both chuckled at that.

"Thanks, Elm. I appreciate you sharing all that. It means a lot. I hope I'm as tough as you say."

She lay back to get ready for sleep. "You are, Birch. You'll have to be. Otherwise, with your nature, you'll never be truly content."

• • •

The next morning, we finally made it to Great Toronto. You already know the route that Elm and Jay took. That had ended up going badly for him, so this time she took us down by a different route, trying to avoid patrols. We hid out for the afternoon in yet another shell of a building, this time a cavernous, echoey warehouse of some kind filled with dust- and moss-covered rusted machinery as well as the constant cooing of flocks of pigeons. At twilight we made our stealthy way down and across the top of Great Toronto via a rubble-strewn and vegetation-choked street called Wilson to a road she said was Bathurst Street.

Like I said, Jay has already given you a description of what he saw in that dead suburban city to the north of the 401 highway ... and it was truly amazing to see these places where so many people had been crowded into so little space. With each new sight, a little more of my admiration for the energy of our ancestors dissipated. What had life been like in these anthills?

We got to Bathurst Street at nightfall, which worked out well because there were no people to be seen and no sign anyone had been here for many years. We took the extra precaution of stopping just north of the highway, which went over the top of Bathurst Street, and listened and waited under cover for at least half an hour. We saw nothing other than a fox that scampered across the road and some bats flitting around.

"Okay," Elm murmured. "We're going to take Bathurst. Once we're under the highway, I think we're officially in their territory, though I think this area is uninhabited. Obviously, they don't have the manpower to patrol the entire metropolis, and why would they, anyway? We need to keep silent and stick to the shadows. I won't make the same mistake twice."

Great Toronto was a jungle, almost like a photo of rainforest ruins in an archaeology book that used to fascinate me and Jay. There was enough room to manoeuvre the bikes, if we were careful, but it was difficult by night, since there was only a bit of moonlight to see by. If there had been smoke or cloud cover, I wouldn't have been able to see at all, and we'd have had to walk our bikes — not that cycling at this pace was much faster.

The buildings got closer together and the neighbourhoods denser as we went farther south, and from what I could see, the buildings were also older. Elm said this was once the heart of the city's west end, the liveliest part of Great Toronto, full of "bohemians," a word I didn't know, but I assumed it meant interesting people. I tried to imagine all the street life, all the shops and diversity of pedestrians, but it wasn't easy; at night, these ruins were downright creepy. We were going steadily downhill the whole time toward the lake that I could occasionally see gleaming faintly in the distance.

It took about an hour, and it had to be midnight by the time we hit a street Elm said was called St. Clair Avenue. We took a break behind a clump of shrubs.

"See that faint glow over the rooftops? That's electric light. We can see that somewhere not far beyond here, that must be as far as their settlement is lit, which means that's probably as far as they're living and as far as they're patrolling. Unless they have the manpower to wander around in the dark out here, but I doubt that's the case," she said quietly.

"Okay, so now what?"

"Once we get to Bloor Street, which was the main street of this part of the city, we'll head east and be *very careful* as we scout."

We had some water and then finished the journey to Bloor Street. It became obvious as we neared it that this was the edge of the settled area. I tried not to gasp loudly when I saw the diffuse glow of streetlights not even a kilometre away. It seemed a waste of precious power. In Norbay we had some electricity, sure, but it was rationed out: each house had its own supply of solar and wind power, but the council didn't waste the town's power supply on needless luxuries like streetlights.

"It's something to see, huh?" Elm whispered. "Even I haven't seen that in decades and decades. It makes me feel funny. I've thought it over and decided our best bet is not to approach by night, but instead to enter the town by day, on foot, like regular citizens, see if we can go unnoticed while we scout out the territory and find out where things are right under their noses: where they keep prisoners, where their bosses hang out, that sort of thing. It's not *that* large a place. We'll try to find somewhere secure now and get some sleep."

"Okay," I whispered back, still a little dazed at this spectacle from the distant past, something as simple as lighted streets. What other wonders awaited my eyes? I reluctantly peeled them away from that glow. I couldn't see any signs of life stirring up ahead, but there had to be some kind of guard presence, and we couldn't take the chance that there wasn't.

We backtracked a few streets and then onto a narrow side street. With a bit of searching around, we found a somewhat intact and safe-looking house. We crept in, careful not to trip over any debris, and settled in the first available room, just going to a corner and curling up without any further conversation. Elm, who almost always seemed unflappable, was snoring within minutes.

I didn't know if I'd be able to sleep at all, wondering what the day would bring and if Jay was all right, wherever he was. Was he nearby? Was he suffering? People who had done all this couldn't be *that* bad, could they?

XXIII.

SENTENCED

JAY

I was exhausted enough to sleep, but only fitfully. Whenever my sleep is interrupted, the early-morning hours tend to be fully of surreal, unpleasant dreams, and for obvious reasons this night was full of disjointed imagery from Malik's story and scenes of lurid violence.

Malik had passed out almost immediately, depleted by malnutrition, exhaustion, and the emotional impact of imparting his biography to me, and as far as I could tell he was dead to the world the entire time I tossed and turned. I was shaken by his story: those people I'd spoken with, the Six, had seemed both intransigent and incorrect, but now that I knew and had experienced the things they were capable of in defending their position and their goals, it was clear Malik was right. I had to get out, or this story would end tragically for me. And if I could help Malik too, I would.

But I'd have to wait for the right moment. The big question I had to ask myself was would I continue to allow myself to be enslaved like this for any length of time? Could I? Malik looked like a defeated, sick man whose health would soon be broken for good. I couldn't allow that to happen to me, because I needed to get home and warn my people of this threat. Who else could do that? Elm might be on her way there now, but she didn't know the things I did. Having heard Malik's story, there was no doubt in my mind that Great Toronto's resurgence was no miracle revival. It could be the start of everything we feared and everything we were working to prevent. The Six might be delusional with their visions of grandeur and manifest destiny, but they could still represent a serious threat if backed by an army.

I was awakened from a light doze by a guard whacking his baton against the metal doorframe. I wasn't even shocked awake, as though in a light sleep my mind had already been running over my few options, and my thoughts continued to swirl as we mindlessly shoved the provided lumps of food into our mouths. This morning Malik seemed totally detached, the fire with which he had concluded yesterday extinguished. He avoided my eyes entirely.

I felt disgusting. I no longer had my pack, so I couldn't change my clothes, couldn't wash, couldn't even brush my teeth. There was no indication so far that these prisoners were ever allowed to do those things.

They let us empty our bowels into outhouses, mere pits carved into the former athletic field outside surrounded by wooden fencing, then led us back up to the street to the same work site as yesterday. The day was cloudy but already brutally humid. There were more guards than there had been the day before, at least ten of them shepherding this stumbling crowd of about a hundred labourers; they were armed to the teeth, by the looks of it, with batons and guns. Obviously, this motley bunch represented one of the main sources of employment for the citizens. I wondered what they got to eat. Better food and shelter might surely be at least a couple of the overriding motivations for giving up whatever shreds of empathy you possessed.

And again, they worked us without any regard for rest, proper food, or water. If you needed to defecate or urinate, you had to ask the guard, who might or might not grant your plea, then go down to street level and into an adjacent building, where there were buckets. I never asked whose job it was to clean those out; that must have been reserved for the lowest of the low. Again and again, I raised that hammer and brought it down, removing small pieces of the structure, and others came in and scooped them away. I was covered in sweat and could smell myself as well as the others. While it was cloudy, the humidity had me constantly panting. At several points in the day, I thought I was going to collapse, but any time one of us stopped working, a guard would scream at us, hand on the butt of their gun. One man was struck for taking too long, and when he fell, he didn't get back up. Malik didn't even bother trying to see if I would react — but I was too beaten down already to offer even a weak protest. Other workers picked him up and carried him down the stairs.

No one talked, which probably wasn't allowed anyway. Malik was still like a zombie. By the end of the second day, the walls, which had been waist-high the day before, had been reduced to knee height, and it was becoming dangerous to work close to the edge — but they still made us do it. Mercifully, I'm not scared of heights, so I was able to keep my balance well. I feared for the others, though.

The view over the trees that had taken over the city toward the tower and the lake that had so thrilled me had already lost its appeal. But even though my body was already giving in to the situation, my mind wasn't. It was clear they planned to work me like this until I capitulated and joined them in whatever plan they might have for me, or they'd be happy to leave me here until I died.

When the afternoon sun would have been low on the western horizon, judging by the sunlight trying unsuccessfully to pierce the thick grey clouds, they called an end to our day and we were marched back to our rooms. I wasn't even sure if I'd make it that far without collapsing. But the body can endure almost endless torments, and there's no end to human resilience. So, I made it, but when we got there, I fell onto the cot and didn't move until the next day.

I continued to chew on my predicament as we neared the same structure we'd been chipping away at for two days. At this rate, it might take months to tear down one building. That was probably the point — a small amount of productivity while eliminating troublemakers. Malik stumbled along beside me, his shoulders slumped, never lifting his gaze from the pavement. The spirited man I'd met two days ago seemed to have departed his frame. He'd barely spoken to me since that first evening, emptied out by the telling of his story.

We were separated out into the same work crews as yesterday, picked up the sledgehammers, and trudged up the stairs. Despite my weariness, something new was growing in me that didn't come naturally: anger. Blind, white-hot anger. I couldn't go through this again.

We got to the fifth floor, and our part of the crew, six or seven people, shuffled over to their different corners to start their chipping and bashing. Malik did the same, though his motions were very slow.

I hefted the hammer in my hands. Then I just stood there, gazing out at that jagged needle in the distance, a broken symbol of our stupid human arrogance. This morning, it didn't amaze me; I hated it and everything it stood for. I knew what I had to do, no matter the consequences.

"Hey, over there. Skinny kid. Get to work!" barked one of the two guards on this floor.

I didn't move. I just continued to stare.

"I said, get to work."

As he came toward me, I finally turned my head to meet his gaze, feeling my posture straightening. I put down the sledgehammer with the flat metal head on the concrete and the handle pointing straight up, and then released it. "No."

He got very close, and I could see the patches in the stubble on his pale skin and smell his breath and body odour. "Everyone works. You'll work. *Now!*"

"No."

I stepped back slightly.

Everyone had stopped and turned to watch dully, including Malik, whose arms had dropped loosely to his sides. I saw something stirring slightly on his face, the first expression he'd shown all morning. No one else moved.

"Last chance. Work or you're gonna get it. You aren't gonna like the punishment — if you survive it," the guard sneered. "I said *now*."

The other guard had stepped closer too, hand on the butt of a pistol at her belt.

"No."

I just kept my arms at my sides and my eyes on him. I had never been more frightened — or felt more in control.

Suddenly, he lunged forward, his hand snapped out, and I felt a blow to my solar plexus. I doubled over and toppled, unable to breathe at the sheer pain. As I rolled onto my side, I saw his arm rise again above my head, and I looked at the clouds, waiting for the next strike as time seemed to stop.

Then I saw a tall figure looming over the guard. Something swung toward him, and his back suddenly buckled. He fell on top of me, shrieking.

I shoved the guard off me and rolled to the side, then to my knees, still gasping. Everyone else stood around, agape, but there in middle of the floor was Malik, radiating energy, his sledgehammer's shaft held with both hands. The guard who had attacked me was writhing beside me and the other guard was fumbling with her gun.

Malik gazed at me, eyes blazing, his face twisted with fury. "Warn them, kid. Warn them!" he yelled.

That was the last thing I heard from him, because we were both jumped by several guards who had raced up the stairs upon hearing their colleague's cries, and he disappeared beneath a flailing pile of bodies. I screamed his name as I was pulled away and backward down the staircase, past the dull-eyed workers standing there, my feet trailing and scrabbling. What had I done to him?

Outside, I was dumped onto the sandy pavement, and two guards rained blows down on my back, arms, and legs until I lay prone. It was frightening how they could apply violence with such precision that I hadn't felt any bones break or sinews snap. How did you learn such skills? Maybe through trial and error.

• • •

I suppose the person running this work detail had been made aware that I was a different, more valued sort of prisoner, because instead of beating me to death or taking me for whatever punishments they dealt out to those who wouldn't work, I was hustled toward a vehicle and shoved into the back. The guard beside me this time had his weapon drawn and resting on his lap. I wouldn't have been able to fight him anyway; every limb hurt, and I could feel blood trickling down my right cheek.

As the car whipped down Bloor Street, I could see it was darkening outside. The wind was picking up and moving through the branches, and the air appeared a bit hazier than it had this morning. Maybe a smoke fog was coming on.

The guards must have thought so too, because they all put masks over their faces before exiting the car. They didn't offer me one.

I saw we were at the city hall building yet again, not the jail. Now what?

They didn't even walk me in; I was grabbed from each side and dragged roughly across the giant plaza, through the glass doors, into the council chamber, and then dumped on the floor.

I held back a groan, slowly gathered myself, and hauled myself up to stand. Whatever was coming, I would face it with as much dignity as possible.

Today, there were only five of the six; the oldest man who had chastised Norbay's philosophies was missing.

Khalil spoke first, as always, preceded by a sigh. "Well, Jay, I have to say we're disappointed. We have a full slate of important decisions to make today, and here we are dealing with you again. Justine?"

The older woman spoke next, and today there was no kindness in her tone. "We've shown you mercy and given you the opportunity to join us. When you refused, we gave you the opportunity to work and take time to consider the error in your decisions. Yet you refuse. We will *not* be made fools of."

I couldn't suppress a bitter laugh. "Opportunity? You're working people as slaves. Working them to *death*."

Justine scoffed. "At any time, those people can renounce their crimes and receive better treatment. The fact that they won't is their responsibility, not ours."

"I don't believe you. They're broken. I'm sure they'd say anything to get off those work details."

Craig Kelly put in, "Did you think that building a brand-new society was going to be for *soft* people unworthy of survival? Don't bother answering that… I can guess."

Doubt crept in. If what Justine said was correct, I should have a new respect for those people on the work detail. Perhaps they weren't defeated and broken — maybe they were refusing to break and obey and become enslaved in mind as well, not just in body.

"This isn't a *society*," I spat. "This is cruelty. You're not human."

Now the middle-aged woman spoke. "Jay, Jay … enough. We're doing what's necessary. You can't understand that. Fine. Frankly, it's not worth our time to debate with you. But now you're a problem for us. And we can't have that. Look at you. You're a mess. You have no standing here. You have no role or purpose."

I could feel the blood congealing and drying on my face but didn't wipe at that or at the sweat on my neck and brow. I knew I was a damaged mess.

Khalil raised a hand. "Actually, concerning finding a use for this boy, I've been thinking over this possibility from the start, right from when this fool wandered into Great Toronto, thinking he could spy out our secrets. I've been thinking, friends, that it's some time since we've had a rally. And now we have something to show them to raise morale and stoke the flames."

Kelly said, "Ah. An enemy." He acquired a hungry look.

Khalil nodded. "Exactly. An enemy. We're going to show you to the people. A spy caught in our midst from a rival city, an enemy of progress. An enemy of human betterment. A threat to our future. Because that's what you are. And then they'll see what's at stake."

"A good idea," the middle-aged woman said. "Not too pleasant for you, Jay, but you've had your chances."

"And what do we do with him after that?" Justine asked. All gentleness was gone from her tone.

Khalil leaned back, shaking his head sadly. "After that … I'm just not sure what use he will have. We can't afford to let him go. He won't work."

"Time's up, Just Jay," Craig said triumphantly, his voice ringing through the dusty confines of this old bastion of democracy. It was dreary and dark, almost like twilight, even with the electric lights; a fog was very likely coming in.

"Jay, Jay," said Justine, clearly trying to soften her tone again. "Listen. This rally will happen soon. If you have a change of heart in the interim, I'll speak up for you."

"Like hell you will!" Craig barked.

Justine shot daggers at him. "Enough, Craig. I've got a headache already." She turned back to me. "I'll speak up for you, if you're sincere. Take some time to consider this. It's your last chance. Your last chance to live and to be a part of the renewal of history, taking us out of the new dark ages, not some sort of utopian sideshow."

The soft-faced woman nodded beside her and spoke gently as well. "Yes, Jay. Think about it."

"The rally will take place in the square in two days. Attendance by all citizens will be mandatory. Guards will be detailed to go door to door to inform them. This ungrateful little spy will be shown to the populace, and this will usher in the next stage of Great Toronto's revival: expansion of our influence." Khalil gestured at me. "Take him back to a cell."

I said nothing and refused to walk, making them drag me again, though they didn't hit me this time.

I was correct about the weather. Outside, the wind had picked up some more, and smoke was pouring in from the northeast. There had been a few days without smoke, but when heat domes relented and weather patterns changed, the pall often returned, at least until the colder rainy season would begin to tamp it down and soak the forest.

The atmosphere was already so dense that it was hard to make out the outlines of the waiting vehicle on the other side of the square, which was itself deserted. This once vibrant meeting place, a symbol of democracy, was now off-limits to citizens.

They packed me inside the car and drove to the police station once more. As I looked out the side window, the haze was deepening into an almost impenetrable toxic fog. The city that had so impressed me was hidden by that deathly white veil.

XXIV.

THE RESCUE

BIRCH

I'd assumed I wouldn't be able to sleep deeply in such a precarious position, so near the enemy and wracked with worry for Jay, but I did, and when I woke it was already light: a weak, grey trickle as though it was very cloudy. Of course, Elm was up and peering out the door. There was plenty of birdsong but no nearby sounds of human activity, even though we were at the western perimeter of a functioning city. I thought I could detect some sort of faint rumbling in the distance, but I decided it must be my imagination.

"Good morning," Elm said as I got up and stretched out the kinks; I thought I'd be used to sleeping on hard surfaces by now, but it wasn't getting much easier on my back. "I think our plan is still the same. It's hard to figure out what's what by night. We'll take a look down the big street, Bathurst, and then figure out the best way to appear to be average citizens and do some scouting. I'd suggest wearing your cleanest and least threadbare clothes."

If this was Elm's least threadbare outfit, you'd never know it. She looked just as ragged as always in some ripped pants and a big, baggy thing somewhere between a tunic and a poncho. I had a T-shirt that was in decent shape in my pack, and that would have to do.

"I'm going to play the helpless old lady, which is easy, and you can act like you're my support. Wish I had a cane, but we'll have to do without. Just hang on to me like I need you to hold me up. One thing never changes in any time: the aged are invisible and can pretty much go anywhere."

The remark surprised me, considering that all Elders were venerated back home, seen as sources of wisdom, guidance, and experience. Maybe she'd forgotten that.

After eating, we tentatively stuck our heads out the door, leaving the bikes and packs behind. We'd have to return for them if we were successful in locating and retrieving Jay.

There was nothing around, not a stir of life, not even any birds, just a line of crumbling front porches choked by vines and blankly staring, mostly glassless front windows. But the air was somewhat breezy, and there was a faint white haze clinging to the facades of the houses and the upper tree branches.

"Smoke fog coming," Elm said. "Let's hope it's a bad one. That'll help us a lot."

With that slightly cryptic remark, we went out to the corner of the side street and Bathurst. Nothing. We looked left. There, a few blocks down, we did see some activity. There was a small vehicle parked beside a giant dump truck, the source of the low noise I'd heard — which made me do a double-take — and people wearing what appeared to be uniforms. By the way they held their arms, I figured they were holding weapons. We moved stealthily a block closer until we neared the ruins of what was probably a transit station — a big, long, very rusty red and white thing that must have been a streetcar sat on tracks behind it — and took cover behind the ever-present shrubbery.

Now only about a block and half away, we could see more people approaching the intersection on foot. They walked slowly, like they were half asleep.

The people in uniform barked orders, and the shambling figures headed for what was left of a tall building.

"Forced labour," Elm hissed. "This is even worse than I thought."

I didn't know what she meant. We watched for a few minutes more, but the people had all disappeared into the building, and the guards stood lazily around the intersection, chatting.

After a short while, though, there was shouting and screaming from far above. Several guards raced into the entrance of the half-dismantled building and came out a couple of minutes later dragging an unresisting person. They crowded around the person, raining down blows. It was shocking.

"What the hell, Elm?" I could feel my eyes were popping out of my head as I turned to her. "What are they doing here?"

"Bastards," Elm murmured. Her hands were trembling and her breathing was shallow. I could only assume she was flashing back to her time in the camp. I grabbed one of her hands and squeezed it.

Then the guards threw the prostrate figure into a vehicle, which sped off, and they laconically went back to their posts.

"I've seen enough," Elm whispered, shaking her head like a wet dog to bring herself back to the moment. "Let's head backward … carefully. We need to find a less guarded spot to enter the town. I'm not sure what's going on here, but it's clearly not safe."

"Elm, do you think Jay could be there?"

She glanced at me. "Why would he be? We have no idea what they've done with him. I don't know what earned those poor people that punishment, but it proves everything I feared about this place. Forced labour is a sure sign of a sick society. There's nothing good here. C'mon. Things are officially very serious now. Bigger than you, me, and even Jay."

We retreated up a few streets to one that ran east-west, paralleling Bloor.

"Okay, we have to be very aware of our surroundings. I have no idea if they patrol up here, and we don't need to be asked questions about being in the wrong place."

I adjusted the gun that I'd shoved into the waistband of my jeans before pulling my T-shirt down. But Elm had seen it.

"Birch—" she started.

"Sorry, Elm, but after seeing that, don't you think we may have to be tough and mean too to get this done?" I interrupted. "These guys are heavily armed. I can protect us both."

There was a pause as she stood frowning. Then she shook her head gently and blew out slowly through her nose. "Fine. I guess you may be right. There's still a time and a place for might makes right — unfortunately. All right, let's go."

• • •

After a few blocks on a street called Lowther and very carefully crossing another large street called Spadina, we went down a smaller one leading down to Bloor. It was risky to be seen coming that way, but we had to enter the downtown somewhere. Fortunately, the smoke fog was now rolling in rapidly and it was already hard to see well beyond a block or two. We slipped on masks. Elm was right; this would be a huge help in going unnoticed.

No guards were patrolling, but there were a few citizens, all now masked, hurrying about their business on foot. I saw some cyclists as well. I didn't even have time to marvel at these few signs of normal life as we shuffled along with our heads down, me pretending to support Elm with an arm around hers. We passed a few uniformed people, but they didn't give us a second glance. I guessed older people really were invisible.

There seemed to be some shops open, and I wished I could go in and see what they sold and how this place functioned commercially, but the urgency of our mission wouldn't allow it. When we got to another wide intersection, Elm said, muffled, "Turn right."

We were now on a grand boulevard with a leviathan, impressively ancient grey building looming on the right. It seemed to be in surprisingly good condition, though a strange glass addition stuck to the side that looked like a crystal growth was shattered and gaping open.

As if in answer to my internal question, Elm said, "Museum."

What I would have given to visit a place like that in its heyday, to see its treasures from all around the world. There was so much to learn about. I wondered if it still held them or if it had been ransacked by pillagers (and even Seekers) long ago.

We went around an important-looking park that had been cleared of undergrowth, passing many more masked people. There were even people sitting around and relaxing on benches in the park. It all seemed so safe and tranquil.

As we got to the south end of the park that split the roadway, I asked, "Where are we going, anyway?"

"Where the bosses probably are," Elm said. "I never spent much time here — but I have a vague idea of where the important things are. Were. We don't have any info to go on. I'm hoping they realized the significance of a prisoner from Norbay and are keeping him close but safe. They'd probably think he's a spy, and Jay has no guile. He'll have told them too much, I'm sure. I have no way of knowing any of that for sure, or what they did with him at all. This is my best guess."

"But what do you think they ... did with him?" Something occurred to me that I hadn't let myself ponder up to now, but having witnessed the vicious beating of that poor forced worker, I realized for the first time that it was possible Jay wasn't even alive.

"I don't know. Like I said, hoping he's too valuable to get rid of. Shhh." Two people approached and passed us in the ever-thickening smoke and didn't even give us a second glance.

I could now barely make out buildings only about twenty metres away. This was a bad one, as far as smoke fogs go. Despite the mask, I had a strong urge to cough, and my eyes were pricking. It smelled like a bonfire, as it always does. I'd never thought that the smoke could get this far south, but it made sense that it would.

Eventually, after passing several more giant buildings that Elm said were hospitals — one of which seemed to be in use, judging by the people entering and exiting — we arrived at another, bigger street. There was no road sign at the intersection. It wouldn't have been easy to see it anyway... The smoke was getting so thick, the tops of the buildings were lost.

"This was Dundas Street," Elm said. "They were supposed to change the name of it at one point, a long time ago, but maybe they never did. Anyway, if we keep going down there, we'll hit the city hall. That's where the people who run this place probably are. I hope."

I looked at her curiously and with a little horror. "You're not actually planning to try to talk to them, are you?"

She waited until a couple walked by. I was amazed at how clean and well-groomed everyone looked. I mean, we obviously kept ourselves clean in Norbay — most had an impeccable sense of hygiene — but these people were so coiffed, they might have walked out of the early twenty-first century.

We looked like vagabonds in comparison. If I hadn't seen that worker taking a beating by heavily armed guards, my attitude toward Great Toronto would have been very positive by this point.

"No, Birch, I'm not going to talk to them. I'm not a fool. Like I said, we're scouting. Hello, what's that over there?"

She peered at a building near the southwest corner that had more vehicles parked outside than even the hospital.

"Let's check this out. Looks official."

We moved slowly along the north side of Dundas, as though I was taking my poor frail grandma out for some exercise.

She slowed even more when we were directly across the street.

"Ah, a police station."

"Police?" The concept was almost alien to me, though I knew what it meant.

"Yeah. And they're using it. Must be their guard headquarters. Maybe... Well, we should take a closer look. Let's sit down for a moment."

We sat on some concrete steps outside the yawning entrance of a former office building. There was some activity: vehicles and people in uniform coming and going, and two guards were stationed outside the front entrance, their outlines hazy in the fog.

"We need to find out what or who is in there. It would have had cells. Whether they keep people there. We need a pretext to talk to one of those guys."

"Talk to them?" I scoffed. "You think they're just going to want to chat with us and reveal their plans to us?"

Elm's eyes blazed with irritation over the top of the mask. "Listen, I'm doing my best here. You want your promised back? Or do you want him to rot here forever? Because that's what it's starting to look like. We need info, and this is the best way to do it I can think of right now."

I raised both hands. "Sorry, sorry. Go on."

The creases on her forehead relaxed. "Right. Let's see. I'm an old lady. Helpless, right? You're a nice-looking young girl. Well, you are!" she added, seeing me roll my eyes. "We may look kind of rough, but base instincts are something you can always count on. You need to help me ... do what? Let's see, there's a hospital. We'll ask the way. It's foggy, and we can't find it. And you find a way to ask some questions about what they're doing there."

"Right, find out what they're doing there ... just change the conversation to that somehow. Sure."

It sounded like a pretty thin plan, but what else were we going to do? Camp out here and watch the place for days?

I nodded and took a deep breath. "Okay."

We walked a bit farther and then crossed the road and came back on the south side, heading east.

As we were in front of the police station, I saw we'd had a stroke of luck: there was now only one figure standing by the door, looking relaxed and bored, judging by his slouch.

"Slowly," Elm murmured.

We shuffled mock painfully toward the door. The man straightened up and put a hand on the stock of the rifle that hung from his shoulder, but upon seeing what kind of people we were, he removed it.

I decided that if I had to be a coquette to get this done, I'd give it a try. I pulled my mask down.

"Excuse me," I called sweetly.

"Yeah?" he said. I could see over the top of his mask that he was very young — possibly my age or maybe even younger; there were prominent red blemishes on his forehead.

"I need to take my grandma to the hospital. She's really sick. But I can't find my way there in this smoke. Can you help?" I smiled as winsomely as I could but drew the line at batting my lashes.

Elm coughed loudly and lurched a little for effect. I pretended to hold her up.

The guy looked concerned and pointed back toward the wide avenue. "Just up there. Toronto General. You can't miss it, even in this."

"Thanks," I said, panicking as I tried to think of what to say next. Elm must have noticed, because she suddenly lurched right over, gasping dramatically.

"Grannie!"

The guy stepped up and helped me lower her to the step, where she slumped, still gasping like a landed fish. She was certainly a convincing actor.

"I'm sorry, she's really sick." I tried to make my voice tremble.

"That's okay, she can take her time," he said.

"Um, what place is this, anyway?" I said, plastering on that unconvincing smile again.

He stood up straighter. "Central law and order. We make sure everything runs smoothly and there's no trouble."

I widened my eyes. "Oh, that's impressive. Trouble from who?"

"Criminals. Radicals. That's what they say." He leaned closer, seeming eager to impress me, so I cocked my head. None of this was coming naturally to me.

"In fact, there's some important guy in there right now. They just brought him back from city hall. They say he's from an enemy city, the first real spy they've caught."

I almost shouted and could feel a zing of excitement from Elm. "There's an *enemy* city?" I said, making my voice tremble a bit and biting my lip.

He nodded vigorously. "Yeah, they want to destroy our way of life and take us back to the Ruin, I heard. This guy was a spy they sent. The Six are figuring out what to do with him."

"What will they do?"

He shrugged. "I dunno. They already tried him on a work detail with the other criminals, but it didn't work out. He wouldn't work. Lazy shithead. They'll teach him a lesson. Then they'll figure out what to do about the enemy."

"Oh, yeah?"

"Yeah, the Six always know what to do," he said reverently. "You must know. You're about my age. Before we were born—"

I'd heard enough, and my temper had won out. The gun was in my hand, and within a second it was under his jaw.

He made a noise of surprise but froze.

"Birch!" Elm yelped, jumping up.

Rage had taken over, but it was steely and controlled. I liked the feeling of power in that moment. It was … invigorating.

"Okay, listen. You know that spy?"

He just stared at me.

"Nod," I said. He nodded.

"We want him. And we're taking him now. You're going to help us. We're going in there, and you're going to get him out."

He swallowed noisily. "Are you crazy?"

I smiled. "Yeah. So, let's go in, you say whatever you need to say, and get to wherever he is, and release him. Can you do that?"

He swallowed again. "I don't know."

"You'll find a way. And if you say anything to warn anyone or try anything, I'll shoot you. You ever seen anyone die?"

He shook his head.

"Well, I have. Let's go. Elm, you'd better come too."

Her own eyes were wide with shock, but she was speechless. Our dynamic had changed, and I was now in charge for the time being. For a flicker of a moment this all felt very wrong, but it was too late to turn back.

The guy slowly opened the glass door and walked through. I put the gun in my right hand and pulled my T-shirt a bit over it.

There was a desk on the left with another guard sitting behind it, eating something that looked like bread. She looked surprised to see us.

"Kyle, who is that?" she said but didn't make a move to stand.

I dug the muzzle into his lower back.

He licked his lips. "This is my ... sister and grandma. Came to visit. Was going to ... give them a tour."

She frowned. "A tour? Your sister? I didn't know you have a sister."

"Yeah, yeah, this is..."

"Brittany," I said. "Hi. You're..."

"Nisha." She still looked amazed.

"And this is Grandma Catherine." I gestured with my left hand.

"Hello, dear," Elm said kindly, clearly realizing she had little choice but go along with this gambit.

"Um, hi..." Nisha looked blankly at us for a moment. "Well, I guess it's okay. I mean, why not? Just stay away from priority areas. You'll get in real shit if you go there."

He forced an awkward laugh. "Well, yeah, of course." He turned to me. "C'mon … Britt."

We went down a hallway toward a staircase.

"I hope this is worth it," he said quietly. "You won't make it out of Great Toronto."

"It's worth it," I said. "Shut up and move."

Fortunately, while there were open doors along the hall, no one came out. He led us down the staircase, my gun still jammed into his back, to a lower level with a sign that said *Priority Area: Clearance Required.*

Before we could go through the door, I said, "Elm, take his gun."

"What?" Her eyes were wide again.

"Just take it."

He slowly handed it to her, looking completely bewildered, and she took it gingerly by the long barrel, like it would go off in her hands.

"If we need you to, you might actually have to point it at someone," I said. "So, try to look more comfortable with it."

I don't know if the situation confused her more than my sudden transformation did. I was shocked myself. Maybe some of Ning's confidence and determination had rubbed off onto me. All I knew was that despite the precariousness of the situation, I had never felt more in control of one, and I needed all that control right now. Elm continued to hold the gun a little too delicately, but at least she was gripping it the right way now.

We were in a hall lined with lots of metal doors. Toward the end stood two men in the same sorts of mismatched uniforms all these guards wore. For all I knew, they were wearing mail delivery uniforms from the late twentieth century.

"Faster," I said, and he sped up a touch.

The others watched us, and as we neared, one guard, who sported a thin moustache, said, "Kyle? Who the fuck is this?" But they still didn't move for their weapons. The old lady effect, maybe?

I took my chance and pulled out my weapon. "Elm, point it," I hissed. "Kyle, down on the floor."

He wasted no time flopping onto his stomach with his arms extended and stayed still, wanting no more of this situation.

"What the *fuck*!" the guy who had called out said, reaching for his belt.

"No!" I ordered. "I'll kill you. I promise." His hand moved away. The other one, who looked as young as Kyle, just stood there, stunned.

"Put your guns down."

"What?" the guy spluttered. "No!"

"Put it down, *now*," I growled. I didn't even have to try to sound this aggressive; it just poured out of me.

He slowly complied, placing the weapon about a foot away from him on the floor. The younger one wasn't wearing a holster.

"Which cell is the spy in?"

"What?"

"*The spy!* You know who I mean."

"Uh, well, this one." The guy pointed to the cell he was standing in front of.

"Open it."

"Are you fucking crazy? We're finished if we do that!"

"Do it, or I'll shoot you *then* get the key from your corpse." Kyle stayed prone, and the other guard looked like he was going to wet himself.

"You, down on the floor with Kyle," I said to the young one. He wasted no time throwing himself down on his face.

The first guard slowly put his hand to his shirt pocket and drew out some key cards, selected one, and put it in the door. Something beeped, and it slid to the side.

I stepped closer, gun trained on his chest. "Give me the key." He extended his arm, and I snatched the card from his hand.

Inside the cell, it was dim, except for a lone dim, yellowy bulb in the ceiling. A form was sprawled on a cot.

"Jay!" I called. The figure stirred. "*Jay!*"

He sat up abruptly and gave a slight yelp. "Birch?"

"Yes, it's me."

"How…"

"We don't have time. Get out here."

He moved a little, but not fast enough.

"Jay, *now!*"

The figure slowly lifted itself off the bed and stumbled through the doorway. The sight of him almost made me start shooting. There was dried blood and bruises all over his face and neck. One eye was partially shut. He stumbled out, and I directed him into the hall with one arm, never taking my gun away from the middle of the first guard's chest. Kyle and the other kid weren't moving a muscle.

"Okay, everyone in."

"What?"

"*In!*" The kid jumped up, and guards one and two moved toward the door. They slouched into the cell, turned, and just stared at me.

"Kyle."

He looked up from the floor.

"In."

He slowly stood and walked in.

I slammed the door in their disbelieving faces, then turned to Elm and Jay, who both looked just as amazed.

"Let's hope there's a back door," I said.

XV.

CHOICES

JAY

It was all like a dream. One moment I was in the depths of despair and in pain, knowing full well that not only was I never getting free of these ruthless people, but I was also likely going to lose my life, and the next I was rescued by someone who should have been safely four hundred kilometres away. Someone I had been longing for every single day. I was in a daze already, but now it was like I was floating; all my suffering seemed to lift away.

There *was* a back door, miraculously unguarded, and by the time our absence would have been discovered, we had disappeared into the back streets. Good thing these guards weren't supplied with radios. I wasn't in very good shape but was able to move well enough that my condition wasn't too obvious.

Despite the heart of the city being inhabited, there were still plenty of alleys and backstreets that were deserted and ruined, and once we got into them, we worked our way slowly north. We passed some people, but they had no reason to question who we were, and the thickness of the fog and the mask Elm handed me concealed my injuries.

When we got to the intersection of Bloor and Spadina after about twenty minutes, Elm spied an unattended bicycle leaning up against a building, took it, and we moved along quickly, darting up a side street and away from Bloor, completely undetected. The city was still basically uninhabited north of Bloor Street this far west, which was why it had been so easy for Birch and Elm to slip in.

I had no idea how long it would take for the other guards to realize I was gone, but it would be good to be well away by the time they did. They had plenty more thugs to scour the city if they wanted to.

I couldn't believe what Birch had pulled off. I always knew she was impulsive and brave, but this iron-willed rescuer, casually pointing a gun around, was a side of her entirely new to me.

We got back to Birch and Elm's hiding place where they had left their bikes and gear, surprisingly near the building where I had been beaten.

I was aching to know what had happened to Malik, but I knew in my heart there was nothing I could do for him now. His brave defense of me came from a burst of defiance and hope, and I would honour it and him.

Elm deemed that there was little chance of Great Toronto's leaders having the resources to search every unoccupied house in that vast sea of buildings, so we took shelter there for a while, leaving our masks on. A mix of relief and absolute exhaustion sent me to sleep on the wooden floor within minutes. My last sight was Birch sitting cross-legged beside me, holding my hand and gazing down at me with concern.

I must have been out for many hours because when I awoke it was dark. Looking up groggily, I heard shuffling.

Birch sat up. "Elm?"

"Yes," came her voice from the other side of the room. "Hang on." Something sparked, and then a spot of light. "I still have some long matches here. Not great. Just enough to get our stuff together and move out. Night is the best time. It's nine o'clock. There's still a lot of smoke. Perfect cover."

Birch reached out to me. "Jay, will you be able to ride?"

I was still lying down and tentatively bent my legs. "Yeah, things seem to be working."

Elm chuckled. "Good. Because I don't much like the idea of doubling someone your size on my bike."

It hurt a lot, but I was able to mount the stolen bike and gingerly ride behind them up Bathurst Street. As Elm steered our course, I wanted to ask

Birch how the hell this all came to pass, but I was still tired and knew that we needed to keep quiet. There'd be time to swap stories later.

It was only after we were well away, north of Eglinton, and had been intermittently riding and walking carefully northbound that we were able to catch up on what had transpired over the last number of days.

When Birch told me about her run-in with the gang and seeing them killed in front of her, and her rescue by Ning, I felt nauseous and had to stop riding for a moment. She had come so close to something far worse than anything I could have endured. And yet she came out of it stronger and more determined than ever. Birch truly was the strongest among us.

Elm was sobered by my story of Great Toronto and my treatment at the hands of the Six.

"It's far, far worse than we ever could have thought. I'd hoped they might be reasoned with, even allied with, but what you've described is an authoritarian government set up by power-hungry zealots with insane dreams. I've lived this before. History has taught us how that *always* ends: tragically."

"And it's my fault for getting caught," I said.

I could just detect her shaking her head in front of me. "No, Jay. They would have turned their attention to us eventually. When people are hungry for power, they always want to expand their influence. Always. They're never happy with what they have and always want more. So, what you've actually done is give us fair warning and time to figure out a response. It's invaluable."

I felt better hearing that.

We didn't take a long rest until we were well north of the boundaries of Great Toronto, back in the endless desolate suburbs, where we had our pick of shelter. It must have been the middle of the night by that point.

We were all tired from the extra effort of breathing in poison while riding, though the smoke fog was already clearing somewhat.

Settling on the carpeted floor of the house we had picked, Elm blew out her long wooden match, and we sat in silence for a while, not yet ready to sleep.

"Well, kids, my mission is clear. It's time for me to head home and confer with Cedar and the other Elders about this threat. We don't know how long it'll take the Six to gather their power and look to expand it. It could be years; it could be never. But the sooner we make Norbay aware of it, the better. Will you be heading on to Kingston?"

I considered this for a few long moments. "No, Elm. I'm going with you. I can finish my mission later. This is more important."

She rustled in the dark. "I've been looking after myself for a long time. I'll be okay."

"If it's all right, I'd feel better if we went together." I didn't know why, but I wasn't ready to part ways with Elm just yet.

"Fine. You're decent company. I'll allow it." There was that low, sly chuckle. "Birch?"

I felt Birch's hand on my arm. "I've done a lot of thinking over the last few days..."

I held my breath.

"I wanted freedom. I still do. I'm not sure if I have what it takes to be a Seeker. I don't know if I want to have that kind of discipline. So, I have more thinking to do. But for now, this was enough adventure. And having gone through all that just to find you, Jay... There's no frigging way I'm letting you out of my sight for a while."

We all laughed.

• • •

It wasn't a sound that awakened me — it was a change in temperature. It was cold for the first time since March. I had a thin blanket in my pack but hadn't needed it till now.

I sat up, shivering, and rubbed my arms. The other two lay on their sides, flanking me. I got up and went quietly up the stairs to the front door.

It was raining, and a cold breeze was blowing. The smoke had been tamped down, and the air smelled almost fresh.

I felt a hand on my shoulder.

"The chilly season is here. Time for our beginning — together," she said.

I turned around and took Birch in my arms.

XVI.

NOW

(A POSTSCRIPT)

JAY

So that's our story.

BIRCH

And it's all true!

JAY

Why wouldn't they believe it's true? I wouldn't take three days to fill them up with a bunch of nonsense. Anyway, that was all a long time ago. Double your lifetimes, in fact. But I went on to a long career as a Knowledge Seeker and am now your (hopefully esteemed) Elder! And Norbay has grown and prospered in that time. And, as I think I mentioned at the start of my story, we've since had contact with other communities like ours, around the world, on radio. Someday, maybe you will visit them.

BIRCH

You all know what happened to Great Toronto and its leaders, so we don't need to recap that now. But I did eventually try joining the Seekers, for a while, and Jay and I undertook many journeys together before he settled down to become a leader and eventually an Elder. I stayed out there a lot longer, but I have to admit, by the end I was more like Elm: a wanderer purely for my own pleasure.

JAY

But she always came home… Yes, Marigold? That's right, Elm stayed here. She went on a few journeys after that, but she mostly stayed here for the last years of her life.

BIRCH

Absolute, pure freedom is a wonderful thing, as Elm and I both learned, but it comes with a price. We need each other. And that's the biggest lesson for you: everything and everybody depends on everything else. Everything is interconnected. What we do affects all life on Earth. We vow always to love and respect the pulse of life around us.

JAY

Go out into this world full of love, because you are the world … and it's you. Thanks for listening. Now, is it time for lunch yet?

"For to adventure is the lust of Youth; and to leave Safety is the natural waywardness of the spirit; and who shall reprove or regret..."

—William Hope Hodgson, *The Night Land*

"Love, by its very nature, is unworldly, and it is for this reason rather than its rarity that it is not only apolitical but antipolitical, perhaps the most powerful of all antipolitical forces."

—Hannah Arendt, *The Human Condition*

ACKNOWLEDGEMENTS

No one creates in total isolation; somewhere along the way, someone has to lift your spirits and give you the resolve to keep going. And if they do, maybe you'll get there.

My journey in writing this book was assisted by many good people.

A million thanks to Heather Campbell from Latitude 46 for deciding this North Bayite's story deserves a chance to be widely read. After spending many years in the artistic wilderness, my gratitude is far greater than you could imagine.

Thanks to Randall Perry for his sensitive editing that did exactly what editing should: greatly improved the text and its elegance.

Thanks to my long-time colleague, Laura Boyle, who is one of the best designers in the publishing industry.

Thanks for encouragement during my lifetime of attempted creativity in various fields: first, to my spouse, Teri, for generously sharing life with me and always uplifting me. Second, to my family, Mum and Samantha, for always caring about the things I do. Third, to good friends for bucking me up: Kerry and Sean Kelly, Greg Janveau, Philippa Dowding, Sylvia McConnell (thanks for the proofread!), and Andy Stimpson from the *Breakfast in the Ruins* podcast.

I'd like to acknowledge the support of some of my fellow musicians over the years. Look up their Bandcamp pages! Particularly Jan of Binaural Space; Matt Borghi; Torontonian Duke Gray of OddsFiche; and Scottish troubadour Ali Murray. Also, the very small but dedicated number of people who have consistently supported my music releases.

Thanks to my boys, Rascal, Harry, and Sampson, for keeping me company during long days of editing and writing.

Lastly, thank you to the world's climate, human rights, Indigenous, animal rights, disability, and 2SLGBTQI+ activists for the example of your bravery during cruel and hostile times.

This book was written under the influence of heavy doses of Hammock (music) and Ursula K. Le Guin (books).